Fall Shook Up

PIPER SHELDON

This book is a work of fiction created from the dregs of this author's brain juice. Any resemblance to real humans of this planet earth and current timeline is highly coincidental and totally unlikely.

No part of this book may be reproduced in any form or by any electronic or mechanical means, including information storage and retrieval systems, without written permission from the author, except for the use of brief quotations in a book review.

Any use of this publication to "train" generative artificial intelligence (AI) technologies to generate text is expressly prohibited.

Copyright © 2024 by Piper Sheldon

Querque Press

Made in the United States of America

1st Edition, August 2024

Cover by Yummy Book Covers

Developmental edits by Emerald Edits

Line edits by Editing4Indies

Proof edits by Proofingstyle, Inc.

All rights reserved.|

Print Edition
ISBN: 979-8-9910755-0-3

To J.R., always
And to all the readers dreaming of sweater weather

Fall Shook Up

CHAPTER 1

Claire

I wished I was one of those people who wore anxiety well. Perhaps a coy blush of the cheeks or a cool indifference. Maybe nobody looked good when anxious. Definitely not this lady. My stomach gurgled, and a splotchy flush crept up my neck as I looked out the front curtain facing the street for the tenth time. Outside, the sun set lower in the wide, bright Colorado sky as the days crept toward fall. In the surrounding Rockies, the tallest peaks already had yellowing leaves splattering through the green pines.

"What is it, kiddo?" Dad asked from the laptop where he chatted a thousand miles away in a small suburb of Chicago.

Fear of forgetting to finish a task or missing crucial information kept me pacing from one side of the townhouse to the other.

The driveway had been empty. "I don't know. It's like that feeling like I left the stove on," I said.

I pressed a hand to my chatty stomach.

"You always get that way when you come out of a research fugue state," Dad said. "Your mother was like that." We shared a quick, soft smile. "I'm sure everything is okay. Maybe still check the stove, though."

"Once a fireman, always a fireman."

I'd been so invested in my work for the past few weeks that returning to the world around me felt like returning to an alternate reality where everything looked the same, but the colors were slightly off, or the dresser was not in the same place.

I went to the kitchen and checked the stove. Again. Still off. All the burners too.

"Is it Kevin?" he asked when I wandered back into the room.

"Maybe," I said. Kevin had been distant lately. Or maybe I had been distant. I was so lost in this article and my research that I wasn't as available. But he knew this about me already. Our relationship had always worked because we were both so career-minded, and moving in together had meant to bring us closer. Six weeks in, and we were as distant as ever. We could work through it, though. As soon as this article was out, I could breathe and take some time to be more present. "I'm just eager to hear how things went today," I finished, instead of sharing my relationship woes with my father.

"What time is it there?" he asked, making the "th" of there more like a "d" and the whole word sounding more like "deer."

There was this old SNL skit where a bunch of Bill Swerski's Super Fans sit around talking about "Da Bears." When Dad and his retired firefighter friends were all together, it was like walking into the skit in real time. In this case, the stereotype was completely accurate. Maybe with slightly better cholesterol. I was always struck sentimental when I heard even the smallest hint of a Midwest accent out here.

I shook my head. "Dad. I've lived in Colorado Springs for five years—"

"Five stupid years."

"I'm always one hour behind you. Take your time. Subtract one. Always."

"I know. I know. But the time change always messes me up."

"That's months away," I mumbled to myself. It was his way of making me feel smart and like he needed me. It was our thing, and I wouldn't complain. "It's September, and it's six o'clock."

"Hey. Don't talk to me in that tone. I taught you how to pull the pin from your first fire extinguisher."

"I'm just saying."

"And I'm not nagging on ya. I was just asking if he was there yet because that was the fifth time you've checked the front window since you started talking to me," he said with a pinch of salt.

I turned and propped my balled fists on my hips. "I don't like the person you become when you win the daily Wordle first."

"Not only did I win, but I beat you by a whole round," he said.

"The power has gone to your head." I took a deep breath in and out and looked around the small townhouse I had moved into officially a little over a month ago. It still looked and felt like Kevin's place, as I hadn't had a chance to get most of my stuff out of storage. This growing sense of insecurity nagged incessantly. My palms itched to pull up my spreadsheets and look through the data I already knew to be true.

"He's actually leaving that place?" Dad asked about Kevin, rapidly changing the subject.

Nerves curled tighter around my stomach, creating an audible gurgle.

See. Not attractive. Hot Girl Anxiety shouldn't sound like the sudden need to use the restroom.

"Of course," I said. "His finance job was always temporary. Why would he choose a soulless corporate job over one where he could help people?" I placed my hand on my stack of folders, overflowing with research, as if to remind myself of its safety.

"And he's fine with the pay cut from the nonprofit?"

"Yes." Except for when I said it out loud, my stomach tightened.

"Well, good. I didn't think he had it in him. Seems very into image," Dad said.

I prickled in defense. "I know that's how he can come off, but there's a good guy underneath." When we met after college, we had the same goals, the same values in life. It wasn't some combustible love affair, but we understood each other and that felt important. Safe. But he also needed to eat, so he took the job with the brokerage firm.

"I know you don't let many people in." I shrugged his accusation away.

We weren't one of those couples who were always together, each enjoying our own space. Moving in with him had been a huge decision that required multiple spreadsheets and pros and cons lists. I had seven teeth-falling-out dreams trying to decide whether I should give up the lease on my place. Ultimately, I made the big move.

In time, it would feel like home.

"You're very hard on him," I mumbled.

"I just want to make sure he sees what a treasure you are."

I bit my tongue. Kevin and I had mutual respect and the same values. That was enough. Having a long-term partner required those two things more than fleeting and fanciful attraction.

"I just want to know how this is all going to work out." I blew out a breath, went to the window, and peeked through the curtain again.

"Change is always scary. But he's doing the right thing, Claire Bear. You both are."

I spun to meet my dad's eyes on the screen. "Thanks, Dad. I'll feel better once the article is out, and we can put all this behind us. Maybe we could take a trip. I heard this little nearby town has this great bed-and-breakfast. I know we joke about a future where our brains can directly connect to some sort of ever-updating infinite resource of knowledge, but I would be the first person to sign up."

"I never thought you were joking about that," he said.

"Imagine being able to instantly know anything you wanted to know, fact-checked and credited." The fine hairs on my arm stood on end, and I pointed at them. "Look. I have chills."

He chuckled. "You're so your mother's daughter."

I smiled at the compliment. Dad found my insatiable search for knowledge to be a quality and not an annoyance like most people. Aside from sharing my mother's wide "toothy smile"—as many have felt the need to point out—her shining chestnut hair and deep-set dimples, I also inherited her unquenchable thirst to understand all things. There was nothing I hated more than missing something important because I didn't have all the information.

"Anywho." I heard him shift and jingle his keys. "I'm off to meet the guys down on Cicero."

"The car show?"

"There's rumor of a 1963 Chevrolet Corvette Sting Ray."

"Split window?"

"You betcha," he said.

"Fancy. Eat a dog for me."

"You know I will. Extra relish, no ketchup."

"Obviously. Ketchup on a hot dog. Imagine," I said.

We both shuddered at our long-standing snobbery.

"Maybe this weekend you can go meet up with some of your friends?" he asked in that tone, which was more of a suggestion than a question.

"Dad. I'm almost thirty. Why are you so worried that I don't have friends? I have loads of friends."

"Do you? Are they corporeal? Are they in the room with you now?" I flicked a look at my laptop again. Technically, they were online only, but that didn't matter. They were more real than anything I'd yet to find. Except Kevin, of course. It was too hard to meet people in this city. I kept waiting for it to happen organically, but the city was too big. And I wasn't exactly the smoothest in social situations.

"Even just since we started talking, I have several unread messages," I insisted.

"Sure. You're just so pretty—"

"What does—"

"And studies show the importance of meeting up with people and having that human connection."

"I'll need you to cite your sources."

He waved a hand.

"Social media is not news," I said. "It's a curated algorithm that reinforces what you already believe."

"I'm aware—"

"I'm just not a social butterfly like you. You know this. Your intense social life is not for me."

"Maybe if you gave it a shot," he said.

Keys rattled in the door, and my middle protested.

"I hear Kev. I gotta go."

"Talk to you later, sweetie. Love you."

"Love you."

I closed the laptop and made my way to greet Kevin.

I was practically bouncing on the balls of my feet as he stepped into the house. "Well? How'd it go? Are you okay? Want a drink?"

He tugged off a cashmere scarf and shrugged out of his coat.

It was still in the high sixties in the afternoon here, but he took seasonal fashion very seriously.

He tossed his arms out to the side and smiled widely. "I got a promotion."

I blinked at him, and my stomach dropped to my toes. My smile was plastered in place, probably less of a smile and more of a grimace, working on being a smile. "Wh-what do you mean?"

He walked farther into his townhouse. I followed him, feeling a numbing sensation traveling to my toes. I must have misunderstood.

"Look. Before you get all ... *Claire* about this. Just hear me out." He went to the fridge and grabbed a kombucha.

"I don't love my name being used in that context." I crossed my arms as if to defend myself from his sharp words but shut my mouth so I could focus on what he had to say.

"I went to quit. Told them about the offer from the nonprofit, like we talked about, but listen." His head sort of bobbed as he spoke, like a chicken looking for pebbles to masticate. I never noticed that before. Had it always done that? "I guess I didn't realize how important I was around there."

I slumped back onto the edge of the couch, causing it to slide on the hardwood floor. "Okay." He glared at the flooring and bent to rub where there was no scratch.

"So yeah." He took a long drink and burped a sour smell. "I told them I was leaving, and this was my two weeks' notice."

"Right." That was the plan. The plan I had made a slideshow for. The plan that was written down in multiple places.

"And then they offered me a promotion with an insane raise. A fat one. I'm talking big money. Money that you and I have only ever dreamed of."

"A promotion," I repeated. A million different thoughts crossed my mind all at once.

I liked that Kevin had been raised a blue-collar Midwesterner like me when I met him out here in Colorado. We talked about childhoods playing until the fireflies came out, being latchkey kids, and block parties in the alleys. We both had an incredible work ethic and time management skills. These things made us great partners. I understood his fear of not having money drove him, but I never thought it was the *most* important thing.

"What about the nonprofit? That's what your master's is in," I said. My tone was calm and cool. Emotions gathered in my gut, knotting together so that detangling them would take time.

His shoulders slumped. "Claire. I know. Maybe with this promotion, I'll have more resources to help people differently."

"Okay. Wow. Okay, I'm processing," I said.

"There's more, the best part—" He paused for dramatic effect here. I blinked slowly at him. "A move to New York!"

"Wait, what? New York City?"

"Manhattan." He grinned thinly. "A gorgeous apartment in a fantastic area." He cleared his throat. "They want me there next week."

"Next week? But you just found out today?"

"Well, it was official today. They mentioned the position, but I didn't want to get my hopes up."

"But we talked about you leaving. We never talked about staying and a promotion." I was missing something and felt like I was living in a different world than he was. This wasn't the sort of promotion that came out of the blue. He had to have known.

"I tried to talk to you, but you know how you get. If you even leave your office long enough to talk." He scratched at his neck, avoiding my gaze.

I slumped forward, arms wrapping around my middle.

"I can't go to New York. My article is due to the editor in three weeks. It's supposed to publish before the end of the year. I can't even think about packing or moving."

He took another long drink as I spoke, and his eyes hardened as he listened. When he set down the glass bottle with a smack of his lips, he sighed and said, "I kind of thought when I told you the big news that you could maybe *not* finish the article. We won't need the money. I mean, technically, you haven't even written it."

My insides flipped around inside my body, like a raw egg being spun, and then stopped suddenly.

"Because I've spent the past year getting insider information. I was collecting interviews in secret. So much data combing and collection," I explained as the dull throb between my temples grew more demanding.

"But you haven't *written* it."

"I gave an outline to my editor. It's already mapped out. We're well past the point of no return."

"You don't think it's going to look bad if they find out my girlfriend is trying to bring down someone in the same industry?" he asked, arms crossed.

"You aren't even supposed to be in this industry, helping the rich get richer." I scoffed.

"I knew you'd be like this," he said with an eye roll.

He wore the same face as when we were at those awful work parties, and I talked too long about the environmental impacts of oil fracking or microplastics. Like I was an embarrassment. We used to be on the same page.

I placed my hand on my chest to try to stop my gooey insides from spinning out. "I thought you wanted to make a difference?" I asked. "To help people."

"This would help people. It would help *us*." An angry flush spread up his neck. "You're being hyper-self-indulgent about this. This is life-changing money. This is a great opportunity. I hoped you might be more supportive."

"It's not what we planned. Where is this coming from? How am I supposed to choose this?"

"It shouldn't even be a choice," he snapped. "This is our life. Why are others' lives more important? I can give you a future we only dreamed about. Never worrying if our kids will be able to take trips or sign up for sports because they're too expensive. Never wondering if there will be gifts from Santa or getting made fun of for wearing knock-off brands. Don't you want that?"

My throat tightened. Too many thoughts rammed each other inside my head so that nothing got out.

"That's not fair," I pointed out.

"You're not thinking this through."

I scoffed loudly. All my brain did was think things through. It never quieted or stopped until I got lost in research until it had a purpose.

"I know that your career is important. I have always supported you," he said.

"Until it negatively impacts you."

"Now you're not being fair," he said.

"You're asking me not to publish a story that will save lives."

"I'm asking you to put us first," he said flatly.

"This is bigger than us. This is about changing and challenging the way things are done."

"You're making me sound like an asshole," he said.

I bit back the words on my tongue. *No. I think you're doing that just fine on your own.*

"How can you be so heartless?" he asked, and his hurt shone through.

Heartless?

Was that how he saw me? How could I be expected to choose between the objectively right thing to do and a relationship that took years to cultivate? I didn't have a gut instinct to guide me. I'd never felt in touch with my intuition. Facts and knowledge drove me.

Save dozens of families from financial ruin or ruin my relationship? I imagined the life he offered in NYC, living in a fabulous apartment and never having to worry about money. It was impossible to even imagine what a life like that would be like. Would it mean happiness?

Not to mention the luxury of *time* that came with financial security. I could, in theory, help people that way too. I could hole up for days and track down sources; New York was the center of the world.

But then.

I remembered the single mother who invested her entire life savings in the exploitive money scheme my article would expose. The tiny ceramic beads she handcrafted lovingly every night after working all day and sold online just to have some money to invest. The hope in her eyes as she spoke of those same freedoms and opportunities for her children.

Who was I to decide to trade many people's lives for the safety of my own? How would I ever be able to live with myself? My hands were clammy, and my stomach continued to churn, but underneath it all, a relentless resolve fueled me.

I didn't need to take time alone to process this decision like I might normally.

I stood and pulled from a reserve I wasn't sure I had. "If you are even asking me to do this, then you don't know me at all."

He sucked in a breath, his eyes narrowing. "I knew you well enough to know you would pick your career over me."

I stepped back, feeling hollow sadness and hot anger battle in my chest.

"I want you out," he said.

My knees felt like they were going to give out. "What are you talking about? I live here."

"Not anymore. I'm leaving for New York. I don't want you

here. It's not a good idea. If you continue with the article, you're risking my job."

"I have to finish the story. You know that," I said, even though my throat was almost too tight to talk.

"Of course I do. That's all you care about. It's all you talk about. When was the last time we even had a conversation that wasn't about your job?"

"I—"

"You don't even remember to feed yourself. You don't talk to anybody. It's like you're not even here anyway."

"You know how I am when I'm working. You said you understood, and that wasn't an issue."

"I thought it would get better when we moved in with each other. I thought you might put someone else first. But you only care about your current fixation. Maybe it's better this way. This clearly isn't working. I need a partner who is going to support my needs too."

"You mean you want somebody who won't make you feel guilty for shitty decisions?" I said.

"You don't live in the real world, Claire. People like us have no control over people at the top. That article is a waste of time, and we both know it. If it even gets published. But you need to hold on so desperately to prove something to yourself, over our relationship."

"I refuse to believe that nothing matters." I glared at Kevin. I held his gaze, though it was like looking into the eyes of a stranger. "You'll see when you finally have all that money that you think will make you happy just how wrong you are."

"Don't be so idealistic. You're getting too old for that," he said, almost bored.

"Wow, double blow," I said numbly.

These weren't the emotions I'd seen in breakups on TV and in movies. My eyes didn't burn with unshed tears. I didn't feel anything. Our words were sharp and nasty, but no emotion was behind them. I couldn't feel anything besides the anxiety twisting its way through my gut. Like the smell of sour milk, I sensed the wrongness brewing around me in this place I called home, but I was still taken by surprise.

All I felt was an unrelenting desire to get away and this man I no longer knew.

I needed a plan to get out of here.

"We aren't the same people who met in grad school," he went on, determined to have the final words. "I thought we could help the world. But I know better now. You, of all people, should see how the world really works. One person can't change these giant broken systems this country runs on."

"So we give up?" I asked, genuinely curious.

"We get our piece and then help when we have the money. The money is the power."

"I refuse to believe that." I shook my head, fists balled, and a numbness spread through my appendages. "If I help one person, then it matters."

I thought of ceramic beads and the tiny apartment housing four people.

He was wrong.

We used to be on the same page. I used to know Kevin, but this person was a cruel stranger. That was what happened when I locked myself away. People changed. The world changed. I promised myself I wouldn't miss the signs of a breaking foundation last time, yet somehow, my life was crumbling around me, and I'd missed it all happening again. I didn't have all the information, and now, I suffered the consequences. But I couldn't think about that right now.

I didn't have a home. I didn't have the partner I thought I did, but I wasn't giving up. I wouldn't let this stranger in front of me be proven right.

I packed my bags and left that night.

First step—find a place to finish my article and show Kevin just how wrong he was.

CHAPTER 2

Levi

I wiped the sweat from my brow before it could sting my eyes. Despite the late September day this high up in the Rockies, I already had to shed my flannel and strip down to a white undershirt. That first smell of fall came with a strong wind, cooling the sweat that covered my body. The sun began its descent behind the tall pines and aspens. That feeling of shifting seasons was all around, and the farmer's almanac predicted a hard winter. Another long, lonely winter.

I grabbed the next piece of wood and set it up to split before I was taken over by a wave of grief, pointedly not looking at the guesthouse.

One of the many perks of living this far up the mountain was that I only had to worry about provisions for myself. An ache clenched my chest like a muscle being pulled, thinking of the last winter I had someone to care for. I swung the axe in a hard arch over my head, letting the physical work of my body push the thoughts away.

The nearest town was Cozy Creek, which was still a good twenty minutes away by winding road. That meant I could chop wood naked if I wanted to. Not that I would risk the family name in that way, but I could. Those left who worried about me never experienced the true freedom that came with solitude.

No nosy neighbors in your business. Nobody guilting you into doing things you didn't want to.

The sound of a truck on the gravel driveway came between the whacks of my axe splitting wood.

So much for solitude.

I didn't stop as I heard the slam of the door and heavy booted footfalls heading my way.

"I come with a six-pack and news from town," Pace said by way of greeting.

"I would like fifty percent of that offer," I said and steadied the next log on the stump. Some of the tension melted from my shoulders.

The only person who regularly visited from Cozy Creek, Pace held a hand to the brim of his baseball cap to block the slanting rays of the setting sun.

"Where's Ripley?" Pace glanced around as he set down the paper bag and perched on the steps of the porch that led to my cabin.

"She doesn't like the cold. She'll be napping in her spot by the stove."

"Such a ferocious beast."

I glanced over when I heard the pop and sizzle of a can opening, not the crack of a cap off a beer bottle.

He took a swig from a tall, thin white can labeled sparkling flavored water. *Peppy Pineapple.* The handle of my axe propped me up as I caught my breath, squinting at him.

"What?" he asked.

"Not what I had in mind when you said six-pack. Now I want zero percent of what you're offering."

"Don't knock it until you try it. Also, I'm cutting back on the drinking," he explained.

"Fair enough." I shrugged and reached out to grab the proffered can. I popped the tab and took a deep drink. "Goddamn, that's refreshing," I said.

"I'm saying. Betsy started selling them at the general store. You should swing by and get one."

I nodded, mildly impressed. Seemed like there were a lot of upgrades happening in Cozy Creek. None of them I was interested in. I drank my drink and kept my thoughts to myself.

Pace held up his hands and made a rectangle with his thumbs and pointer fingers, boxing me in his imaginary frame.

"You could be an advertisement," he said, lowering his arms. "You know, if you recorded yourself chopping this wood and uploaded it, you could probably make thousands of dollars in a side hustle. Or at least sell a ton of this bougie water to the tourists."

"What makes you think I don't already?" I said before swinging through the next chop, pieces flying. My break was over.

"You're right. You just scream social media influencer. The reclusive cabin in the woods really sells that. Do you even have a social media account?"

I blinked at him.

"Didn't think so."

"Social media is the downfall of humanity," I said through huffs of breath. "We pay fake tribute to pretend lives that nobody has and then bully ourselves for not living up to those expectations."

Pace sighed and tugged off his cap to scrub at his dark, reddish-blond waves. "You're awfully sure for somebody who isn't online. Don't forget the cat videos and hours of disassociation. There is some fun to be had."

I split the next log.

"Speaking of. How goes the Real-E-Space advert?" he asked.

"Stop trying to distract me. What is the news from town?" I asked.

"Ruth said that old Billy Mackenzie was finally retiring and looking to sell his space to a local before any 'outsiders' could snatch it up."

"I can't afford one of those Main Street storefronts." Cozy Creek had managed to stay a hidden treasure for now, but the cost of the tourist trap shops still drove rent up on Main Street every year.

"He's willing to take a hit before selling it to anybody who might make it a chain. Also, you could afford much more if you rented out the guesthouse," he said.

"Who says I even want a shop?" I rolled my shoulders. "Regular hours. Interacting with the tourists. Sounds like a nightmare." *Locals talking to me about things I didn't want to talk about ...*

"I see we are still avoiding my question about the listing. And the shop would be worth it. You know your stuff would sell like hotcakes."

I raised an eyebrow at him. "Hotcakes, huh?"

He shrugged sheepishly.

After swinging the axe to lodge it in the stump and stacking the last pieces in the pile, I sat next to Pace. We tinked our cans. "Thanks, man. I just don't want the constraints that come with a brick-and-mortar storefront. Betsy sells plenty of my stuff at her shop."

"Just think about it. A video of you working on your art and you could go viral," he said with a sigh.

"I'm starting to feel objectified."

"I'm just saying, if I had a fraction of your talent and looks, I would be a millionaire," he said.

"Definitely objectified." I took another sip, then had to burp the intense carbonation. "Excuse me. And don't be so modest, Mr. Fireman. You're not exactly an eyesore as you're busy saving kittens and dousing fires for all the Cozy Creek ladies."

He sat up straighter and drank his soda water before belching loudly to beat mine. "I am hot, aren't I?"

I chuckled with a shake of my head. While I had a couple of

inches on Pace, there was no doubt he had me beat in the muscle department. Being a firefighter came with the additional superpower of automatically being perceived as attractive. I carefully curated my loner, woodsman reputation and wasn't planning on changing that anytime soon.

"I've inflated your Thanksgiving float-sized ego even more," I said.

"There's always room for growth." He set down his empty can and dusted his hands. "Now that we've sufficiently stroked each other's egos, are you going to tell me if you've advertised the guesthouse for rent yet?"

I made an annoyed exhalation.

"Levi, my man. You said you were going to do it last month. You're bleeding money. Cozy Creek Inn and the Lodge are always booked now, even in the off-season."

"I don't care—"

"I know. Money doesn't matter to you and your artistic soul. Unfortunately, even you are constrained by the realities of our capitalist society."

"But—" I smacked my mouth, blinking slowly at his sarcasm, annoyed at being mocked. "I did post it. Last month, like I said I would," I finished.

He widened his eyes and looked over the twenty yards to the one-bedroom guest home, as though expecting it to be occupied. "Good man. Any bites?"

"Not yet," I said. I didn't follow his gaze to the house.

"What?" He pulled out his phone from his coat pocket and unlocked it in one smooth motion. "That's crazy. Every other rental around here is booked out as far as they open their calendars." He typed on his screen. "Where are you? I don't see your listing."

I sighed. I reached back and grabbed my phone from the rocking chair. "Here."

After pulling up the site, I handed it to him. As he read, his hopeful, good-natured smile melted off his face.

When he handed me back my phone, he took off his hat again to mess with his hair. "You don't want to rent this place, do you?" he asked.

"What are you talking about?" I squinted at the ground, feeling defensive.

"I get your whole vibe is grumpy mountain man, and I'm not trying to strip you of that finely tuned aesthetic, but maybe, and just hear me out, this ad is slightly off-putting."

"The price is more than reasonable," I defended.

"Sure," he dragged out the word. "But it's the mildly threatening undertone that has me concerned." He looked back at the phone resting on the step between us. "Wait, no. Not mildly. There's an actual threat in there." He ran a hand over his chin.

"I can't have some thin-skinned city dweller coming up here thinking this is going to be a cute pic-to-gram moment or whatever. Hashtag mountains." I crossed my arms as heat burned up my neck.

His head dropped to his hands. "Oh my God," he mumbled in his palms.

You are a grumpy ass.

Unthinkingly, I glanced at the guesthouse shrouded in cold darkness as a shiver of guilt ran through me. I pushed her voice away and instead dug some dirt from under my nail.

Composing himself, Pace asked, "How many inquiries have you had?"

I grumbled.

"I'm going to take that as none."

"Not my fault people can't handle Colorado conditions."

"Okay. Here's what we'll do. I'm gonna make a few changes. Things like instead of the hostile tone, say something like 'cozy one-bedroom home located in the dense and wild Rockies and precautions should be taken to avoid danger.'"

I grumbled, not even bothering to hide my annoyance anymore. Why should I have to sugarcoat it?

But on and on Pace went until he'd completely rewritten the listing. All that remained the same was the asking price.

"Okay. There. I'm going to submit this," he said, tilting the phone so I could review it one last time.

I tugged at my bottom lip, leg bouncing. A growing sense of urgency I couldn't explain made me want to get up and chop more wood.

"Ready?" he asked. Pace's thumb hovered over the "accept changes" button.

"Wait." I shot up off the step and paced in front of him.

He carefully set the phone down, like he was in a bomb squad.

There was an inexplicable tightness in my chest. It must have been that stupid fizzy water. I probably just needed another good belch.

"What's wrong?" Pace's gaze flicked to where I rubbed my sternum.

"I see that these changes will help," I said.

"Good," he said skeptically.

"My concern is that they *will* help."

"And that's bad? You don't want to rent the house." It wasn't a question. He looked at the ground, the brim of his hat hiding his features. "If you aren't ready, that's okay. I'm sorry if I was pressuring you."

Ah, shit. Now I felt bad. He had that wounded puppy look that Ripley gave me when I told her she had to wear her booties to go outside.

I cleared my throat. "It's not that. It's more ..." I squinted back at the house that was now totally in the dark as the last of the sun was below the tree line. Goose bumps broke out down my arms, and I pulled my flannel back on. "It's more that I only want to rent it to the exact type of person who will fit within these terms."

Pace sat back and nodded, chewing his lip for a minute before he spoke. "I see. Now—and try not to take this the wrong way—but what sort of sociopath is going to check all these boxes?"

I opened my mouth to respond but was interrupted by the ping of my phone. I almost didn't recognize the sound; it was so rarely heard. It was my email inbox.

Pace's light brown eyebrows shot up. "Is that—?"

"Well, well, well," I said, unable to hide my smugness. "It

seems there's at least one other person like me."

"God help us," he mumbled.

I opened the email so that we both could see.

Inside the email was one simple line.

"I'll take it."

I waited for the feeling of relief to come. Instead, it was a tumult of disbelief, but I had protested too much already.

Pace shook his head. "I was wrong."

"Another way of saying that is, 'You were right, Levi,'" I said, trying to keep my tone light.

Pace opened his mouth, but another uncommon ping trilled through the air. "Wait, there's a follow-up," he said.

I frowned. Same emailer. CLW@journalCS.net.

Another single line.

"See notes below."

I opened the email and quickly scanned it. My scowl grew more fierce with every word.

"This is too great." Pace had trouble speaking through his laughter. "I wish I could take a picture of your face right now. Oh, wait. I can."

I still stared at the screen. Staring, seething. They have notes, do they? How dare they? Take it or leave it. I couldn't care less.

They responded to the demands.

They implied partial ownership of Ripley. Absolutely not.

To the left came the sound of a camera shutter clicking as he asked, "Did you just growl?"

I glared at Pace.

He grinned down at his phone. "This might be this year's Christmas card."

"I'm not sure I want to rent to them now." I locked my phone.

"Why not? They agreed to all the rules. I don't think you can find anybody better than this."

"C.L. Wells. Sounds fake," I said. "Probably not even a real person, just some robot. Isn't that a thing on the internet—"

"A C.L. Wells lives in Colorado Springs," Pace interrupted, reading from his phone. My eyes narrowed distrustfully at how quickly he found that information. "A journalist. That vibes with their comments. Seems legit. No picture, though," he finished.

I bit my tongue to prevent any more skepticism from escaping.

"Don't make that grumbly sound. Ask, and ye shall receive. This is perfect. Better let them know. They seem in a hurry," he said.

Pace looked at me hopefully. It was the same look he'd been giving me for months, confident this was the moment things would start to turn around. I couldn't crush that hope. The only thing worse than interacting with people was disappointing my best friend after how he's stuck by my side when I'd been a total shit. I could at least try for his sake. When it failed, I would go back to the way things were.

Peace and quiet.

I responded to the email. "*It will be available tomorrow.*"

"Good job. I'm proud of you," Pace said gently, causing my throat to tighten. Was this how low the bar was for me now? "This will be good. You'll see." He looked so damn hopeful I couldn't help but sigh a nod. "Plus, they seem…" Pace hesitated.

"Intense? Nosy? All around too much?" I asked dryly.

"They seem perfect for you," he settled on. He shook my shoulder, an all too entertained look on his face.

My phone pinged with their immediate response.

An all-caps explosion of punctuation and yelling greeted me.

"OMG!! Thank you so much!!! You are a lifesaver!!"

I winced.

"This is gonna be great." Pace didn't bother hiding his glee as he read over my shoulder.

I stared at the screen and wondered if I'd just made a horrible mistake.

It didn't matter. They were paying up front. I wouldn't even interact with them. Nothing had to change.

I glanced at the guesthouse one last time.

About damn time.

CHAPTER 3

The Listing

> Single-bedroom guest home available in the Colorado Rockies. Ten miles north of downtown Cozy Creek, Colorado. **(My replies below in bold—C.W.)**

> Serious inquiries only. **(I'm very serious.)**

> This is my land. If you can't follow these rules, don't bother applying. **(I cannot tell you how much I love lists and rules. Look at that! We already have something in common.)**

> This guesthouse is on my property, but it is completely private and separate from my home. There should be no need to interact. **(Fantastic. Perfect. I'm very much in a place of not talking.)**

> One tenant only. This home has one full-size bed. One kitchen

area. One bathroom. **(Lucky for us, I'm a single occupant all the time. As of yesterday.)**

› The water heater is old and takes several minutes to warm. We share the well. No flushing of anything but toilet paper. **(I hear ice baths are trending because of supposed health benefits. Also, I grew up on a well. I know the drill.)**

› No heat or AC. That will not change. If you are cold, you can build a fire in the wood-burning stove. **(Pretty sure I can start a fire. We will find out! Just kidding. Mostly.)**

› No guests at any time, unless I have given explicit permission. **(Definitely will NOT be an issue. No people in my foreseeable future if I can help it.)**

› No internet in the guesthouse. No plans to add any. **(This is rough - does the nearby town, Cozy Creek, have Wi-Fi? I imagine so since it's not the 1600s.)**

› Amenities include stove, refrigerator, coffee maker, microwave, washer/dryer. Must provide your own food and drinks. A general store in Cozy Creek has everything you could need. I recommend stopping before making the trip up the mountain. **(What else could a person need!? I'll hit Ye Olde General Store on the way up. This town is so cute. I love it! Is it true there are several fall-themed events?)**

› Has not been occupied in a while. Sheets will be changed, but I will not clean up after you. This is not a hotel. **(I would prefer if you didn't go through my stuff. And as long as there aren't other animals/insects in the house, that shouldn't be an issue. It's not** disgusting, though, right? The pictures made it seem tidy. I don't know that you can legally rent a home that's infested with little critters. I'm sure it's fine.)

- No loud music. No loud sounds. No warnings given. **(Like I mentioned above, I will always be working. Chances are you won't even notice me.)**

- If a door is locked, that means it's not for you. **(I'm a journalist, naturally nosy and contrary by nature. You should know that telling me not to do something only makes me want to do it even more. Probably shouldn't have even mentioned it. But now that's all I'll be thinking about. Is it bodies? Is it a secret laboratory? Is it a collection of 1990s Beanie Babies that was supposed to make you wildly rich one day?)**

- This is high altitude. You will get sick if you aren't used to it. That's on you. **(I'm from The Springs. I'll be fine.)**

- This is wild land. There are wild animals and unpredictable weather. Don't be stupid. **(I know how to hike smart. I'm basically a local.)**

- It will get cold. That's also on you. **(To avoid being sued for copyright infringement, picture a beloved Disney princess with white hair. I'm not bothered by the cold, anywho.)**

- It will snow, and the plow doesn't come up this far. I will maintain the driveway, but you must have a 4WD vehicle. **(You know what I'm gonna say at this point, right? Not my first rodeo. My compact SUV handles the snow like a pro.)**

- There is no cell phone service of any kind. I have a phone for emergencies only. **(Okey dokey!)**

- I have a dog who wanders my property unleashed. She is allowed to go to the guesthouse as she pleases. **(This is the only exception to my no critters rule. I love dogs. I've never had one before! Can't wait to meet her.)**

- I can evict you at any moment for any reason. **(I don't think so. Not if I sign a contract, but I'm not really worried. You won't even notice me.)**

- Must be at least 25 years of age. **(The legal age to rent a car, I presume? Or because that's when the frontal cortex is fully developed? Either way, I respect the decision. I am creeping ever closer toward thirty. I shake my fists at the young'uns of today.)**

- I own the house, but do not expect me to talk to you unless there is an emergency with the house. For all other emergencies, call 911. The Cozy Creek Fire Brigade is sufficient. **(Is that really the name of the local firefighters? My dad is a retired firefighter, and I CANNOT wait to tell him this! But don't worry about a conversation with me. I am not a small-talk person, despite the verbosity of this response. I'm a big-talk person. I would rather walk on nails. No offense, but something tells me that you aren't going to be offended.)**

- Must book for at *least* two months. No shorter stays. No negotiation. **(This literally could not be more perfect. I have an extremely important deadline, and lack of home, as of yesterday - mentioned above. I am fine.)**

> Must pay the first month in advance. **(I'll pay everything up front in cash, to guarantee I have a place for at least the next two months.)**

I assume since I'm cool with all these rules and regulations, I can have it? Please let me know ASAP. I'm in a bit of a bind.

Thanks,

C.L. Wells

CHAPTER 4

Claire

The half-and-half would be my downfall.

I stood staring at the cold section, debating between the eight-ounce half-and-half and the full quart. My brain was stuck in a loop because I wasn't sure how big the refrigerator was. Small one. Big one. Just pick one. How often would I be able to get to town? How easy would it be for me to get back into Cozy Creek once I got up to my new home?

My new home.

A wave of nausea curdled my empty stomach.

The landlord of the guesthouse, L Carmichael, hadn't specified in his oh, so informative listing. What if it was a college dorm size? The pictures of the listing were scant, to say the least. There was almost no information at all. If this were a scary movie, I would be calling myself an idiot for even considering going there. But this was the real world, and I was in a hell of a pickle. If I got bad vibes when I got there, I'd get the heck out of Dodge. Also, I wasn't a total nimrod and had bear spray and a big ol' knife that I was very comfortable using.

Everything had happened so fast. My fight with Kevin turned ugly *so* fast. Kevin had changed into a stranger when I hadn't been paying attention. I'd been in flight since then, as in fight-or-flight. Kevin didn't speak to me as I packed up and left. Nothing even felt real yet. I was on a delay. I would never tell my father, but I spent the night in my storage unit on my old couch. Thankfully, it wasn't too cold yet. I searched high and low for a listing and managed to find one that would take me with cash only and on this short notice. My stomach gurgled with nerves, and I pressed my hand on the cold glass to steady myself.

I pushed away the worries and focused on my dad asking questions in my ear. The car was already loaded up with my important belongings and cold-weather clothes. The rest of my stuff would have to be moved from storage when I got back. Again. Something I just wasn't thinking about yet.

One crisis at a time. And that thing was getting food, getting to my new home for the next two months, and finishing that article.

A flash of guilt as Kev's hurt face came to my mind.

Was I really a heartless career woman sabotaging my own chance at happiness for others? How had I missed the signs of a crumbling relationship?

La la la, not thinking about that right now.

I had to block these thoughts, or I wouldn't be able to write the article. My brain, God love her, was incredible when on track and focused but utterly useless when derailed. Right now, my brain was that GIF of Homer Simpson spinning on the ground, getting nowhere.

"I don't love that you haven't shown me the listing of this place. How many reviews did it have?" my dad asked in my headphones.

I was glad it was not a video call because I hadn't hidden my wince well.

"All the reviews were great," I said, abandoning the cream to debate how many cups of yogurt to get.

It wasn't exactly a lie. All the reviews were great. They were all also terrible. Because there were no reviews. It was the Schrödinger's cat of reviews.

"I want you to video call me as you arrive. I want to see the place," he said.

"About that." I closed the door to the refrigerator section and set my empty basket on a display of stacked cases of beer. "There is no internet and definitely no phone service."

I waited a beat and then another.

"Nope. Nuh-uh. Just come back here," my dad said, and my shoulders sagged.

"Dad. It's fine." I hadn't lived with him in ten years. I was just shy of thirty, but if I mentioned any of those things, he'd give the same line about how I would always be his child and his main cause of stress. "It would take me almost three days to get to Chicago. Do you really want me driving solo across the country? I'm already here. People do stuff like this all the time. I'm not worried. You'll see. Plus, I'll be coming into town for email and stuff all the time, so I'll check in often."

He made a sound of sucking his teeth—a familiar gesture of concern. "I don't like this."

I didn't like it either. Last week, I was making plans for the rest of the year that looked totally different. Now, I stood in the dairy section of Ye Olde General Store in the middle of nowhere, wondering how I would feed myself in a place I didn't know anything about. What if I was walking into the den of a serial killer? What if the advertisement was a money scam, and I was the idiot who fell for it? Honestly, being an idiot sucker almost felt worse. Almost.

My throat tightened, and the backs of my eyes burned. All at once, I felt like a little kid who wanted so badly to just give up everything, fly to my dad's house, and curl up in my childhood bed and cry.

Maybe my dad felt the shift in my energy even through the phone. "I'm sorry. I know you're capable of handling things. I know you aren't going to do something blatantly dangerous, but in the script of life, my lines will always be to worry about you."

I bit down on the inside of my lip, eyes searching the ceiling until this surge of emotion passed. "I know," I choked out.

"I'm furious at Kevin. I hope he's forever stubbing his toe on the bed frame and catching his pockets on door handles," he said in his soft, cajoling tone.

I sniffled a laugh.

"But you are Claire *freaking* Wells. You are journalist extraordinaire, and you can handle this and anything else life throws at you with grace and aplomb."

I took a deep breath in and out and nodded. "Yes." I sniffed. "Or at least faux aplomb."

He sighed again, and I could hear the smile in his voice when he spoke. "And I'm so incredibly proud of you," he said. "And you know your mother would be too. I love you, kiddo. Just a worried old man."

I smiled as another threat of tears hit. "Okay. Okay. Stop trying to make me cry in front of strangers."

"God. Imagine having feelings and people seeing them," he said with mock horror.

I glanced up when I sensed someone waiting nearby. An older woman dressed in a brightly colored caftan hovered cautiously, probably needing access to the eggs I had blocked. I sent her a tight-lipped, apologetic smile and shuffled out of the way to collect myself.

He was right. I was stronger than this. I was fierce. I had a purpose.

I struggled to remember it at this moment.

We ended the call, and though I could tell Dad felt better, I felt worse. It wasn't a great plan. It was a CliffsNotes plan. I found a place to live. Now I just had to finish the article.

After that? I couldn't think about it yet.

I returned to the dairy section when it was free of people again. *Just choose the cream you want for coffee.* The next choice. I'd been making choices my whole life. I could figure out what size cream to get.

As my hand reached for the fridge handle, it didn't look quite right. It didn't look like mine. I froze in place, studying this stranger's hand. The knuckles were white as they gripped the handle, fingers trembling. The lights around me faded, and my eyes seemed to vibrate. It started with a ringing in my ears, a strange, disconnected feeling from my body as a cold stung the back of my neck. A sudden and very intense feeling of dread crept over me. The first telltale signs that something wrong was barreling toward me.

I looked around to see if maybe something had caused it.

The small grocer appeared normal.

My insides were far from it.

An employee came out from a side door leading to the back of the store with a blast of cold air that must have been from the refrigerator section. His jeans and flannel were covered in a long leather apron, reaching almost to his well-worn work boots. His unruly beard covered most of his face, and worn and clouded protective glasses covered his eyes.

"Excuse me?" I stepped in front of him.

He stopped, shoulders tensed as if I'd pulled my knife on him. He stood a good five inches or so taller than me with a broad frame and smelled lightly of a campfire and hand soap.

"Is there a restroom here?" I asked with a surprising wobble to my voice. My ears felt like they needed to pop, and the burning on the back of my neck grew worse.

This *dread*, something was wrong.

He shook his head. "I don't—"

"I know. I saw the sign that there isn't a public restroom, but this is an emergency. I'm having a-a—I just need the restroom."

He grunted; his head moved subtly, giving the impression that I was being scrutinized.

I suddenly felt silly for stopping him at all. I was fine. I was just having a moment. It would pass.

"Maybe I'm okay. I don't know what I'm doing." I pressed my cold fingertips to my cheeks and was shocked to find they were wet. "How humiliating. My cream crisis sent me into a full-on spiral. There is a chance that I'm in a state of delayed shock." My words came out choppy and tight as I struggled to take a full breath. "This happens sometimes."

That had to be what this was. The rushing panic and complete upending of my life was just now hitting me. I didn't have a plan. I couldn't catch my breath. Was I dying? The blood rushing through my ears blocked out all other sounds, emphasizing just how hard my heart was pounding. I pressed a hand to my chest to make sure I was breathing. To make sure there wasn't an elephant sitting on it.

"Cream crisis?" he asked with obvious and understandable confusion.

"I'm sorry. This was totally—I'm not normally—" I stumbled backward and into the corner of a shelf, wincing when it stabbed into my side.

You're dying. You're dying.

His arms shot out to balance me before he stopped just short of grabbing me. His palms were raised, and his eyebrows shot up behind the grimy glasses, as though waiting to see if I would topple over. I wished I could see him better, then I'd be able to read his features. I wasn't great at reading people, but when I couldn't see their eyes, it felt that much harder. He could have been glaring at me or staring disinterestedly over my shoulder. He could be rolling them like Kevin did when I had an opinion that varied from his own.

But sometimes, I wondered if it wasn't my lack of reading social cues that helped me get to the meat of a good story. I made people uncomfortable, and uncomfortable people talked. So, this curse was also a blessing.

One thing was sure—this man was uncomfortable.

My stomach gurgled.

"I-I think I'm-I don't know." I flushed and shook my head. I pulled at the collar of my jacket to let more air in. It did not help.

I should have been more embarrassed, more in disbelief of my irrational behavior, but all I could feel was that sense of growing panic.

The employee looked around the store and came to some sort of decision.

"Come this way," he said and spun on his heels.

"Okay," I said, but my feet didn't move. This same sense of dread kept me locked in place.

Seeming to notice I hadn't followed, he turned back. "Can you walk?"

I sputtered as though the question was absurd. "Of course."

We both looked at where my feet stayed put.

"Normally, they listen to me." I tried to joke, but even as I chuckled, it sort of melted into a panicked sob.

"I'm going to help you, okay?" He said it in such a gentle way; asking permission but also still supplying a level of confident assurance I needed.

I nodded, sucking in my lips so that I wouldn't make any more embarrassing sounds.

He tucked his arm through mine, gently guiding me into motion, and led me back through the door he'd initially come out of. Sure enough, it was behind the refrigerator section, and a toolbox sat next to an open panel exposing wiring. He tugged over a short wooden stool and led me to it. He helped me settle on to it before carefully releasing me to straighten. I took a cool and slow breath. The cold air and change of scenery helped. I didn't feel as much like the world was ending or like I was dying.

He stood, legs spread, one hand scratching his beard as he seemed to contemplate me. "Just take a few deep breaths," he instructed.

I wasn't usually one for being told what to do, but at this moment, having someone command the situation was exactly what I needed.

I took a deep breath in and out. He nodded with approval.

"Anybody I can call for you?" he asked.

"No. I'm all alone," I said, and my voice squeaked.

"Are you okay?" he asked, and I felt like he actually meant it. Not in the way a stranger should mean it, like he was concerned for me.

It was too much. His gentle question pushed me over the edge. He didn't want to be here, but he still asked. I shook my head. "I mean that I just got to town. I've had an interesting few days. I'm not okay. I'm a mess. I slept in my storage unit last night because my boyfriend just kicked me out. Just like that. No warning." His forehead crinkled, and I would likely be embarrassed about that overshare later. I flopped my hands out. "Delayed reactions. Sometimes that happens. It takes me a while to feel what I feel, and then suddenly, five days later, I'm sobbing. In the sixth grade, my dog had to be put down. It was literally days later, watching some TV show, when I just started sobbing uncontrollably. It was wild."

He frowned and dropped his hands to tuck them both in the pockets of his jeans.

"Normally, choosing what sort of creamer I want doesn't send me into a spiral, believe it or not."

He nodded again, but his body language remained that of a man who would rather be anywhere else on the planet. Even I could see that.

"Do you still need the facilities?" His voice was rich and deep and matter-of-fact; his tone soothing despite the humiliating question.

I dropped my face into my hands. The skin was burning hot.

"No, I'm okay. My insides just riot when I'm having any emotions. I typically try not to have them." I laughed again but it was manic sounding still.

"Try not to have emotions?" he asked.

I shrugged.

"That works?"

"Yes." I nodded but it wobbled into a head shake. "No. I am so sorry. This is not normal behavior for me. I probably need a friend to talk to, but besides my father, I don't really have anyone besides Kevin." I sucked in a breath. "And now he's gone too. I can't talk to my online friends about this; it's not something you can gently toss between hilarious memes. 'Hey, my boyfriend left me because he's only driven by money and lost all the ethics he once had. But also, by the way, I'm fundamentally broken, so it's probably my fault.' Oh my God." My hands flew to my mouth and covered them to stem any more words that might try to escape. "I have to stop talking."

Truly, though, this stranger had already seen it all. Unmasked and unfiltered. More than anybody else in my life that I actually knew. Even at this moment of shock, there was a wild freedom in this confession. I could tell him anything. Get it all off my chest so I could move on.

I looked up at him, eyes still hidden behind cloudy plastic. I let the truth rip out of me.

"I-I think there's just something wrong with me. Aside from all this." I tossed up my arms to gesture wildly around my head. "I have this thing, it's like this secret compartment I keep tucked away that makes me operate differently. From stories, I've heard that my mother was similar. I just never know when to quit. There's a little voice that says, okay, stop now, but I ignore it and keep going. Like right now, for example."

I broke to suck in a breath; the words came out so fast I forgot to breathe. I thought he'd have run by now, thought he would have called the fire brigade. He hadn't moved. If anything, he seemed to be listening.

"I struggle to get close to people. I know this is a *thing* with me. But I had let Kevin in. I trusted him enough to put my guard down. To be myself." I was talking to myself at this point, processing these feelings in real time. "And it's like I came to find out that he was not the person I thought at all. It makes me feel stupid for not seeing the truth. I cannot express to you how much I hate feeling stupid. You wouldn't think that with everything that happened in the past five minutes," I teased.

There was the slightest twitch at the side of his mouth.

I let out a long sigh and met his would-be gaze.

"It's like I feel simultaneously too soft and too hard for this world. I can't let people in but somehow still manage to feel hurt by them all the time," I said.

His lightly parted mouth shut with a smack. He swallowed as his large Adam's apple moved up and down the column of his throat. After another moment, he slowly opened his mouth again to say something, but I held up a hand. "You don't have to say anything. I know this is so far past normal and appropriate. There is nothing you *can* say. It's just what it is. I guess I didn't realize I needed to verbally process with someone who had no skin in the game." I shook my head and stood. The earth spun a little at the sudden movement. His hands shot out to steady my shoulders when I lilted to the left. It felt like safety, and I yearned to lean into his protection. I searched to find his gaze but was only met with stormy lenses and a beard. This man was a stranger, and I was pathetic. "I'm sorry you were caught in the crossfire of my battling emotions."

I patted one of his hands awkwardly, so he released me. He cautiously pulled his hands back, his mouth in a grim, flat line.

"Anyway. I think the only healthy and rational thing to do now is allow me to flee with any scrap of dignity intact. Sorry again to interrupt your workday, and sorry for the possible psychological trauma I have inflicted on you." I tucked my hair behind my shoulder. "Thank you for being a kind stranger and not abandoning me with what I now realize was the beginnings of a panic attack."

I puffed out my cheeks and blew out a sharp breath. I would have to save groceries for another day. For now, I needed to get the heck out of dodge. I couldn't stand to be in this place a second more.

Once again, I cut him off before he could talk by turning on my feet and running out of there. Not my finest moment, but nothing else to be done.

I had shared everything with this man. Once this numb state of shock wore off, I was going to be mortified. One hour in town and I was already scaring the locals. A new record, no doubt.

Good thing I was going up to the safety of my temporary cabin and would never need to interact with this man again.

CHAPTER 5

Levi

I was going to murder Pace.

Or at least really shake up his fizzy water the next time I saw him.

I stared at the forgotten grocery basket of the woman who'd just run off and cursed my best friend's name.

Recent breakup. Existential crisis in the dairy section. Verbal vomit for the *second* time.

There was no doubt that this twirling dervish of a woman was my newest tenant. I could hear her in the response she mailed back to me as she was speaking. Would she have unloaded if she knew I was the owner of the house she was about to move into for two months? She seemed to think that I worked here.

Had I mentioned I would be murdering Pace? At the very least, he'd be the victim of several very long, uncomfortable scowls.

It was his fault that I was here in town to begin with. He volunteered me to come look at Betsy's ancient refrigerator and then I had been all but *attacked* by that woman.

It's like I'm simultaneously too soft and too hard for this world.

Was that some sort of prank? Had somebody gone into my head and plucked out my exact thoughts and found her to verbalize them? Her wide, unguarded brown eyes left no emotion hidden. Every single thought came out of those full lips twisted in distress, and she walked herself completely through her crisis.

As I, as always, stood silently by offering absolutely no help.

This was exactly why I never left the cabin. It was hard enough to interact with people; I never could have planned the alluring but weird little stranger having a panic attack in the dairy section.

I bent and grabbed her basket, then came out of the back room. I hesitated in front of the dairy section, glaring at the creamers as if they had something to do with it.

"Well, she's an odd duck, isn't she?" Ruth said as she appeared at my side.

I raised an eyebrow at the owner of the local bed-and-breakfast, dressed as always as though she were stepping onto Fifth Avenue and not Main Street, Cozy Creek. If she had any room available, this wouldn't have happened. It was everybody else in this town's fault that I had just been through this.

"Fair enough. Pot and kettle and all that." She waved her hand through the air around her. "Was she okay?" she asked, gesturing to where she'd probably seen the woman escaping the scene.

I grunted.

"I heard that she was renting your place?" She leaned forward, her eyes heavily made up under thick, designer glasses.

I grunted again. My shoulders rolled forward as if I could block the questions.

"Good. It's about time. Lily wouldn't like her space being abandoned like that. You know she wanted everything full of life and vitality," Ruth carried on, oblivious to her words cutting me like daggers.

The shock of hearing her name, so unexpected, when I was already on edge, slashed through me. I ground my jaw. Even though what Ruth was saying was true, it didn't mean I wanted to hear any of it.

"Sounds like she's running away from something. I heard her talking to her father a little. She's in pain. Even if she shows it a little funny. You know better than most that the weird ones need handling with kid gloves." She sniffed as she pointedly looked me up and down, pulling a fur wrap further up her shoulders.

"Thanks for that, Ruth," I said quietly. She clicked her tongue as though annoyed at me for finding offense in her comment.

"I know you'll take care of her and not let your big grumpy facade scare her off."

I turned my head slowly to blink at her.

"Good man." She patted my cheek. "Also, don't forget, Pace said you'd come look at the light switch in the Aubergine Room."

"Of course he did."

"You can be a grumpy recluse all you want, but this town is still gonna worry and care about you all the same. You're kin as far as I'm concerned. And you know it's what she would have wanted."

I ground my jaw. "I have to go."

That was exactly the problem: feeling the need to be in the safety of my home, clawing up my spine.

As I was walking away, she added, "Maybe trim up that beard and hair? You're too handsome to be buried under all that fuzz."

I ran a self-conscious hand over the beard that had, albeit, grown a little wild in this last year. Shaving was low on the priority list when my heart was so broken.

The exit of the store was in sight. The freedom and safety of my cabin called to me. Tension locked my shoulder near my ears. I was steps from walking out the door when I noticed the empty basket still gripped in my hand.

That woman would be going up to an empty house and it wasn't easy to come back into town. She'd left so quickly she never did go back for her cream or anything. What if she didn't have any food to sustain her? The last thing I could handle was her being hangry on top of everything else. Her poor planning didn't necessitate an emergency on my end.

I would just grab a few things. I didn't actually care.

Then I recalled how many people brought me casseroles, crockpot chicken dinners, and other miscellaneous meals when I was too sad to function. I would help out this woman in crisis, just once, and then I could go back to ignoring the world.

I growled loud enough that a passing woman pulled her kid to another aisle. It wasn't much as far as supplies went: the catastrophic half-and-half, a few protein bars, some trail mix, fresh ground coffee, a couple of cases of water, extra toilet paper and paper towels, and some fresh fruit jam from Sutton Farms. And vegetables. And a couple of extra blankets for when the temps dropped this week, as predicted. Maybe a fresh loaf of bread from Cozy Creek Confectionery and some sharp cheese to pair with the jam. Hopefully, she wasn't gluten-free. I would not be getting her special bread.

At the register, Betsy let out a low whistle as she scanned the last-minute purchases. Betsy was everybody's grandma and took care to always have a soothing presence, but she was also downright nosy like the rest of the lot.

I braced myself for the next round of small-town inquisitiveness.

"Did you finally rent your house?" she asked sweetly. As if she didn't know.

I blinked up at her.

She lifted her palms up to me. "Sorry. You're just such a sweetie. I hate to think of you all alone up there."

The tips of my ears flushed red as I furiously tugged cash out of my wallet.

"We all knew Lily's passing would take its toll, but—"

"Thanks." I threw down more money than necessary—worth it to get out of there—scooped up all my purchases and left without another look back.

Not very polite.

With laden arms and a bristling heart, I stomped to my truck, ignoring her voice in my head. This wasn't my fault. I shouldn't even be here. I was going to set the expectations very explicitly when I got back to the house. Crisis or not, this C.L. Wells needed to have clear boundaries. Not even a day in town, and look what was happening? It wasn't Pace. It wasn't Ruth or Betsy; it was this newcomer's fault. She had come to town and brought all her drama with her, and I wouldn't be caught up in it.

I should have known, based on her reply to my listing, that she was going to be trouble and not the quiet working guest she promised to be. But it would be fine. There would be no further need to interact after I delivered the groceries and made it clear the way things worked around here. I should probably stop and fill the extra gas can in case we need to share the generator. But then that was it. I wasn't going to interact with the new woman.

Three emotionally draining conversations with three different women in less time than it took me to let Ripley out for a wee.

I was going home and wasn't leaving the house until the new year.

CHAPTER 6

Claire

No need to think about that freak-out at the grocery store. I was fine now. This was fine.

So what, I unloaded my biggest trauma on the nearest person to walk by? No biggie. That was on him, really. He had been the one with the kind and open body language—well, that wasn't exactly true. He looked like he was desperate to jump out of his skin, but he *had* listened. He could have run away, like most people would have, but he stayed. He let me unload.

"Oh gawd," I groaned loudly to the car. I was going to replay this humiliating interaction for eternity. Every shower I took, every silent car ride, any time my hands weren't occupied with a task, my brain was going to drift to that conversation. What had I even said?

"No. We are done now." Sometimes, saying it out loud helped stop the spiraling thoughts.

The drive up to the Carmichael house was easy, so that couldn't account for this low-lying anxiety stewing in my belly. Luckily, the sharp, consistent cross-backs required so much of my focus that I didn't have the mental capacity to question my sanity in all this.

The delayed shock had passed and my backroom confessional had lightened my load to some extent. Any other unpleasant worries or feelings were to be strictly ignored. Focus on the story. Then figure out the rest. One step at a time.

The decision was made; all I could do now was follow through. No point in playing through the what-ifs.

And anyway, this would all work out. It didn't matter that I knew very little about the man I'd be living next door to for the next two months. I got the impression this L. Carmichael was just a grumpy, lonely mountain man who didn't have the technological prowess in conversation that the younger generations had. Or maybe that was ageist? Maybe he was an old-fashioned blue-collar worker who begrudged any communication that wasn't carrier pigeon or good ol' face-to-face conversation. I'd exchanged a few texts with Levi about finding his place and how to get in. Every interaction was equally as charming as his listing for the house had been.

I wasn't here to make friends, despite my dad's concerns. In fact, I was quite content to cut all physical contact with humans for a while. When we eventually hung up at the general store, my father was a lot more comfortable with the situation, and I'd settled on once-daily phone calls. I would still need to figure out how that would work. He promised to wait to do the daily Wordle, but first things first.

"Here we are," I said as I made the final turn according to the directions, slowing as I drove up a steep gravel driveway.

The concerns about future snow were real. Gravity tugged my head back against the headrest, like shooting off into space. Okay, maybe not that steep, but even as a person who's always lived with snow, I would find this driveway intimidating in a few feet of fresh powder.

I would be gone before the worst of the winter storms arrived.

I brought the car to a stop in front of the tiny cabin and got out. The exterior was exactly as pictured: small, made of logs with a couple of steps up to the simple deck complete with a single handcrafted looking chair. With a deep breath, the cool mountain air filled my lungs and settled my nerves. It was considerably cooler up here, but only because there was just enough cloud coverage that the sun couldn't do its thing. The dry, thin air usually meant that even if it was cold, the sun made it bearable, but with it tucked behind the clouds, I was thankful for my jacket.

I was really here. I was doing this.

Just a few thousand feet higher, and the air held a clean briskness that the city could never match. Palms pressed against my lower back, I stretched to face where the sun would be. I twisted side to side, nonchalantly scoping the main house as I did. It was the big brother version of my temporary home. No truck or car that I could see in the covered car park. No signs of life.

The owner's main house was a modest-sized, two-story log cabin style that was very popular in these parts. It had a tall, deep-slanted roof and plenty of large windows. A full porch wrapped around the front. It was a surprisingly tidy place and well taken care of. That, too, reassured me. I leaned to the side to peek as much as I could behind it, catching the side of a large garage or shed, some sort of work area. I debated going to poke about but, even though I didn't see a car, there was no way of knowing if he would catch me creeping around.

My imagination provided his shouts if he caught me and decided it wasn't worth it. After a few more furtive glances toward the house, I got to work. I would meet him eventually, no need to rush it.

The lockbox holding the key was brand new and opened easily, reminding me once again that nobody had ever rented this place as far as I knew. I'd searched a three-hundred-mile radius from Colorado Springs, and this was the only place with anything close to the availability I needed aside from trying to rent a house, and I couldn't commit to a year. I couldn't think past Halloween at this point.

First, I'd bring in the suitcases and the groceries. Maybe make a tasty little assortment of snacks as Girl Dinner before getting straight to work. My stomach growled in support of that decision. Then I remembered that I'd panicked and fled the store with no food. Looks like I'd be eating the old protein bar at the bottom of my bag and the rest of my road trip Twizzlers for dessert.

The sturdy wooden steps creaked as I made my way to the front door of my new temporary home. Worry and disappointment in myself threatened to taint whatever awaited me on the other side of the door.

No matter what, it was temporary, and I would be okay with that.

I opened the door and was greeted with ... peace. The air was slightly stale but not unpleasant. In fact, there was hardly a scent at all. I hadn't been expecting the sense of rightness that spread over me. It was almost like a feeling of safety and comfort that I had been expecting when I'd moved in with Kevin, but that had never come.

"Huh," I said, spinning slowly to take in the small space. Maybe because it was mine alone, or perhaps because I could finally breathe, but whatever it was, this space felt right. Even the walls seemed to creak with a welcome like it took a big sigh of relief.

A full-size bed was pushed against the right wall, made with a thick comforter and a pine green throw blanket at the end. I bent over to sniff. Smelled fresh. Okay, so that was good. To the left, under a window, was a well-loved but comfortable-looking loveseat with a short bookshelf next to it. It was stocked with a few recognizable thrillers, romances, and cozy mysteries, as well as several coffee table books about photography I would definitely be browsing later. The other side-facing window had the wood-burning stove, a small desk, and a chair, where I would spend most of my time. Past this main room was the kitchen area with a breakfast nook that sat two. Plus, a full-size working fridge and a brand-new coffee maker. *Score.*

There were two closed doors, one that led to a simple bathroom with a shower. The second was a closet with a small stacked washer and drier with cleaning supplies and extra linens. A quick sniff told me those were freshly laundered and critter-free. Tucked away in the back of the small house was another door, this one locked. Though I hadn't even met the man yet, I heard his grumpy voice telling me to stay away from there too.

If a door is locked, that means it's not for you.

"All right, sorry," I grumbled to the imaginary man in my head.

The place was perfect, and it was mine for now. All anxiety melted away as I opened a few windows to circulate some fresh air. It wasn't nearly as bad as Mr. Grumpy Pants made it out to be. Why rent out a place if you didn't actually want anybody to stay there?

I returned to the car to bring in a few more things when movement in my periphery toward the main cabin caught my attention. A jolt of adrenaline had me widening my stance and tensing my shoulders as a grayish-brown blur bolted at me. I had just been reaching for my pocketknife when I realized the blur would not reach higher than my kneecaps and was thin enough to get lost behind a sapling.

It was a *dog* running full speed in my direction. I may have braced for impact in any other situation, but this little thing wouldn't intimidate a house mouse. Its whip-thin tail and high-arched back reminded me of a Greyhound, but one shrank to a fraction of its original size.

This must be the dog I was warned about.

Terrifying.

"Are you the ferocious protector of Château Carmichael?" I knelt to catch her as she approached.

She was not having it. She trotted right past me, barely sparing me a side-eye. She stopped at the front door and scratched, her little frame wracked with shivers. It had to be in the upper fifties, yet she shivered like she'd been left out in the tundra. How did this dog handle these conditions in the coming months? This was *not* an outside dog.

Her whine increased, along with the shivers rattling her bones, and her thin tail tucked under her legs. I couldn't tell if she was malnourished or just built like the child protagonist of a Dickens novel. I made my way to the door and touched the handle.

"You wanna come hang out?" I asked.

She looked up at me quickly with beady little dark eyes as though I would deny her more porridge at any second.

"Hi, I'm Claire. We're going to be friends for the next few months." I spoke calmly and sweetly as I held up a hand and slowly squatted down, studying the tagged black collar. "Can I get your name?" She stared ahead, whining quieter but with no outward signs of aggression. Thankfully, her tag was angled in my direction. "Ripley. Nice to meet you. You're a good girl, Ripley. You don't have a secret dark side that leads to sudden acts of violence, right?" I said in a sweet, high voice reserved for dogs, children, and birds that intimidated me at the park. Not cats.

They hated that voice.

I slowly extended my hand, but she only gave a cursory sniff. I stood back up and opened the door. "Okay. Why don't you give me the full tour? Good idea." She zipped in and out of sight.

"Ripley?" I turned around in the room slowly, looking for the furry blur. The quick whipping motion of a tail caught my attention from where it stuck out under the throw blanket, lying across the heavy down comforter on the bed.

"No. This is good. You make yourself at home. I'll just do my thing, and you do you, boo."

Her tail wagged harder under the blanket before she let out a contented sigh and settled.

"I'm sure your owner is wondering where you are." I looked out the open door up at the house but didn't see any grumpy old men clambering at me. Maybe she snuck out.

I closed the door and set up my computer next. Then I remembered the idea that came to me on the drive up about a sharp hook in the introduction paragraph and I needed to jot it down before I forgot it. As promised, there was no internet and no reception on my phone. No matter, I had plenty of notes and files saved to my external hard drive.

My note turned into a sentence that turned into a paragraph, and the next thing I knew, I reached for my headphones so I wouldn't lose the flow. My phone was filled with downloaded playlists because I'd planned ahead, and I let myself sink into my work.

Working eased more of the tension from me. I was safe here

in this little bubble. This was what I was meant to be doing. If Kevin's hurt features drifted into my mind like a floater in my vision, I just blinked him away and focused on the importance of this work and getting the article written.

Hours must have passed when I finally came back to my body and its physical needs. And possibly Ripley's too. She wiggled restlessly in my lap. I blinked down at her.

"When did you find your way here? Sneaky." She sat in a shivering ball on my thighs with the throw blanket wrapped around both of us. I paused my music and took out my earbuds, stretching my neck.

"Okay, potty break," I said.

She balanced on pointy paws to stretch, as yet another chill wracked her body.

"We gotta get you a sweater or something."

She whined and placed a paw on my desk. Her tiny pointy face aimed at the window with intense focus. She growled, the muscles of her upper body tensed. All at once, the hairs on the back of my neck tingled with the awareness of being watched.

I wasn't alone.

Ripley started to bark a surprisingly deep protective bark for such a wispy thing.

My heart hammered as I reached for the pocketknife in my jeans. Should I pretend I don't notice the dog looking out the window? Pretend I didn't know a person stood just a few feet away from me? And then what? I had a little more sympathy for the victims in scary movies. You always assume you'd know exactly what to do in these situations, but in the span of just a few seconds, a thousand of the dumbest ideas I ever had rotated through my brain.

Where would I even get plastic wrap and Vaseline on such short notice?

I slowly dragged my gaze to the window, feeling every deep punch of my heart against my chest.

There, shrouded in shadow, was a tall figure, hooded and glaring at me through the glass.

I screamed. Ripley barked.

Somewhere, there was muffled cursing.

CHAPTER 7

Levi

"For fuck's sake—" I held up my arms as a feminine startled scream cut off.

Ripley barked as though she'd never seen me before in her life. Acting, quite frankly, much tougher than she had any right to. She was the reason I was in this predicament, to begin with. "It's my house—I'm Levi Carmichael. That's my dog!" I shouted through the window, but the woman showed no signs of hearing me over Ripley's cacophony.

I had knocked. I had shouted through the door. I'd tried every other way to get her attention, to no avail. My dog was missing, and I was panicked.

Ripley, for all the lore of her prestigious *Alien* namesake, was not equipped to be on her own, especially at night, in the dropping temperatures, and in a forest where even owls were potential predators. She resented when I left the house, and I hadn't been able to take her on my errand into town today. She tended to pout by hiding in various places to prove a point. It was because I was so distracted by that strange interaction that it took me a minute to realize that Ripley wasn't tucked into her bed when I got in the house.

I had noticed the tenant's new car as I came up the drive, searching for the spiraling woman I met at the shop. She made no signs of life, and I thought it best to give her some space before I introduced myself officially.

It was meant to be a quick trip to help Betsy, but then everything went downhill from there.

I spent too long going through what I bought for the guest, debating if I should stop being such a weirdo and bring the stuff down there or leave it be because any interaction would go directly against the expectations I set and might imply a friendliness I didn't want to encourage.

No. More. Talking.

Not that I had talked much earlier. It was clear that she just needed someone to talk at. Would she be embarrassed to find out it was me? Would she even remember being in such a state?

Also, how would I explain going to the house but not *in* the house? When Pace graciously offered to change the guesthouse sheets, I accepted with only mild humiliation. I entertained leaving the food on the porch and dashing away like the well-adjusted adult man that I obviously was.

I might not necessarily want guests here, but I didn't want them to starve or freeze to death on my watch either. I kept going to the window to peek through the blinds and see if anything was amiss. So that by the time I realized Ripley was gone, it was well after dark, and I felt like shit for being that distracted.

I raced over to the guesthouse. If I knew Ripley—and clearly, I did—she would try to worm her way in. I tried all the aforementioned attempts to get the attention of someone inside before finally spotting the glowing blue light of the renter's computer and ventured to the side of the house. She was hunched over her keyboard, a blanket covering them both. Ripley noticed me first and wiggled her way out, barking and startling the guest.

This all led me to this moment—the potential trauma of my first, and hopefully only, tenant.

Not much of her was visible behind large, highly reflective glasses and the blanket. But the abject horror on her face was clear. Crystal clear.

And, of course, she was. Even I'd be startled to find a large, fumbling man knocking on my window in the middle of the night.

"Who are you?" she called after pushing her headphones down. I waited to speak in hopes that Ripley would quiet. The woman looked down with a stern expression at Ripley and said something when she finally ceased her barking.

"I'm Levi," I repeated and held up a palm in what I hoped was a universal gesture of *I come in peace to get my dog despite looking like a creep*. "Levi Carmichael. This is my house. And my dog," I added, pointing at Ripley.

The woman, this C.L. Wells, looked at Ripley and mumbled something I couldn't make out. Ripley blinked back at her and shivered. They both turned back to me.

"Prove it," she said.

My jaw dropped. My hackles rose. Not an auspicious start to demand respect and set up clear boundaries. If this—

"Listen. Before you get upset." I stilled. She said, "I can see you're already getting your boxers in a bunch. If you really own this place, then it should be no big deal to prove it. You could understand how a lone woman may not be so quick to trust the large, hairy man standing outside her window. Guard dog aside." *Hairy man?* Was that what Ruth's comments referred to? "I'm not about to risk my literal neck for the sake of being polite." She leaned back, crossed her arms, and pursed her lips to the side.

My own mouth snapped shut. She was right. I scratched my hair under my beanie. Ruth and Pace commented about needing to tidy up for the tenant. My shaggy brown hair was almost to my shoulders now and stuck out all around my hat. My beard was a little past woodsman and venturing into vagabond. I wore Ripley's HuggieHoodie, which normally provided nonthreatening vibes, but she probably couldn't see that with the low lighting and glass.

"Okay. Fair enough," I said and tugged out my wallet.

Her shoulders relaxed the smallest amount, and she lifted her chin in defiant confidence.

The lady had gumption. I wouldn't have believed it was the

same person from earlier if I hadn't heard her firsthand.

I slid out my driver's license and pressed it against the window. She stood, carefully setting Ripley on the chair before pulling off her glasses. The blanket fell to reveal a form-fitting henley and a grip of shining chestnut hair in a high knot on her head. I quickly averted my gaze as she leaned forward over the desk, shining her phone's flashlight on the ID.

I hadn't gotten a good look at her earlier, distracted as I was by her crisis. I only took in her large brown eyes, bloodshot and glistening with tears, the rapid intake of short breaths that warned of an anxiety attack, and the trembling of her full lips on a face so colorless she looked seconds from passing out. This was an entirely different woman, assured and not taking any chances. To her, I was a total stranger.

Too soft and too hard for this world.

It wasn't like I felt the loss of a connection that I didn't even want. I cleared my throat and looked to the side, waiting.

"That's you?" she asked.

Okay, so it wasn't the most recent picture, but in my defense, it had been a long and intense year.

"That's me," I confirmed.

The beam of her light moved to me again. I winced, blinking back, but tried to be still as she looked between me and the ID. Through the bright light, her face was just a few inches from mine, separated by the pane of glass. I swallowed with unexpected trepidation under her intense gaze. Would she recognize me?

"What was the first rule on your listing?" she asked, lowering her phone.

I huffed a small laugh but kept my face neutral lest she think I was laughing at her. I had to admit that even though it was currently keeping me from my dog, I appreciated her thoroughness.

I thought for only a second. "It was the one about this being private property and how there shouldn't be a need to interact." As I spoke, I realized the trap I'd inadvertently stepped in.

She raised one pointed eyebrow and crossed her arms. When I made that rule, I hadn't expected my dog to go rogue and betray me. At least not so fast.

Her arms fell to her sides as, once again, she looked at Ripley for feedback. Seeing whatever she finally needed to see, she tilted her head, nudging it in the direction of the front door. She scooped up the dog, stepped out of the light on her laptop, and melted into the darkness.

I walked to the front side of the house as the flood light flicked to life. Several inside illuminated at the same time.

She was just opening the front door as I came to a stop at the bottom of the steps, not getting any closer. I figured it best to give us both a wide berth for the time being. Also, seeing this new side of her, I realized that she might be more embarrassed by the earlier interaction than I initially thought.

"Hi." She waved. "I'm Claire."

Claire.

My heart thumped once, almost audible, at least to me. The light of the now bright cabin illuminated her from behind and her luscious figure was once again confirmed, even though I was not paying attention to that.

"I'm Levi. That's Ripley." I pointed at the dog, who shivered at *her* legs and did not run directly to me.

"We've gotten well acquainted," she said and smiled down at Ripley. I had a mini-surge of jealousy for *something* but quickly quelled it. When she lifted her face back to me, she was still smiling, and I almost gasped at the magnitude of it. Her deep-set dimples perfectly balanced a wide grin and shining straight white teeth. With a quick gesture, she tugged the pen that had been holding her hair in the ball on her head, and it unfurled in shining waves down her shoulders.

She was stunning. How could I have possibly missed that before?

"Sorry, I accidentally dognapped her. I lost track of time." She thumbed behind her and shook her head.

Maybe it was being this close to the guesthouse, the betrayal of man's supposed best friend, or the fact that I had seen Claire at her most vulnerable and wanted to level the playing field, so to speak, but whatever the reason, I found myself talking.

"It's not your fault. She used to hang out in there a lot." A brief sadness gripped my chest. I was talking too much, saying *too* much. Where were those boundaries I came to set? I needed to get back to the house.

"She did seem very at home." Claire leaned against the doorjamb and nodded. "I didn't even notice we were snuggling until you scared the crapola out of me." The slightest hint of a Midwest accent I noticed earlier was stronger when she had been upset, but I could still hear hints of it in some of her words.

I winced. "Sorry about that. Ripley's a cuddle junkie. If she can't get them from me, she gets them from the streets."

Claire chuckled, her dark eyes gleaming as she looked me up and down for the first time.

We stood in silence for a beat. Her arms wrapped around her as she shivered.

Ripley barked, breaking the tension, which was much appreciated because I had forgotten how to speak, but I wasn't smashing that skill to begin with.

"Have we met?" She leaned forward and squinted her eyes.

I stilled. Every single anti-social cell in my body screamed for me to end this conversation by any means necessary. I could lie, protect her pride, and get myself the hell out of there.

When I looked to the side, just past her, my eyes drifted to the interior of the cabin, so different but so much the same: a glimpse of the bed, the interior of the house. A flash of memory.

Don't you dare lie to that sweet girl.

I glared at the ground. Goddamn this conscience. Life would be so much easier if I never cared about doing the right thing or people's feelings.

"Yes," I said.

She waited for me to elaborate. I didn't.

I sighed at the ground before stepping forward so the porch light would shine on me. In doing so, I revealed my full size. I wasn't wearing the same work smock I had on earlier, but I can't imagine many people looked like me, safety goggles or not.

Sure enough, as I hesitantly lifted my gaze to her face, her eyes moved over me, widening as realization set in. "Oh, God."

The color drained from her face. She barked out a laugh, then a hiccup, covering her mouth as her shoulders shook.

I didn't think I could take any more crying.

But a second later, I was reassured when her laughter broke out.

She collapsed forward, hands on her knees as her laughter rang through the night. "Of course. Of course, it was you. *Levi*," she said.

With every passing second, I grew more uncomfortable.

"I didn't know—" I started, trying to explain.

"How could you?" She was borderline hysterical. "I basically assaulted you."

"I wouldn't—"

"Do you work there?"

"No. I—"

"It doesn't matter." She shook her head and eventually stopped laughing—or whatever that had been—with a deep breath.

She blew out a breath so hard, her full lips blew raspberries. "Can we pretend that didn't happen? Back at the store? I cannot begin to tell you how out of character it was for me to dump all that onto a stranger."

I held her gaze. She met mine for a long beat before the color returned to her cheeks, and she glanced away.

Much to my horror, I wondered if she didn't need to talk more about what happened. Her ex-boyfriend sounded awful and thoughtless. Maybe she wasn't ready to forget it happened? But then I remembered who I was and what I wanted, and the answer to that was alone and quiet.

"If that's what you want," I said.

But I wouldn't forget. I couldn't. Her words had imprinted on me. My fingers twitched with the need to go to the workshop and start on my next piece.

"Come on, Rip." I knelt and started to unzip the sweatshirt that was sewn diagonally across my chest.

I flicked a nervous glance at Claire, who watched with amused confusion as Ripley finally left her side and ran at me full speed. She leaped into the kangaroo pouch and situated herself as she'd done a hundred times before. I zipped her up as I came back to standing.

"Stop. It's too much." Claire pressed a hand to her chest. I couldn't tell if she was laughing at me or with me.

I shrugged sheepishly. "I do what I can to keep her warm. She gets cold easily."

"I would love it too." She flopped her hand and blinked rapidly. "I mean, if I was an almost hairless ten-pound dog."

The image of scooping up Claire and holding her for warmth flashed through my head before I quickly pushed it away.

Ripley rested her head on the lip of her cocoon and sighed, almost already asleep. "She's a hearty fifteen pounds. For the record."

Claire smiled again and stepped closer. I looked away. "I can't believe not five minutes ago, I worried you were a serial killer. No offense." She brought both her hands to her temples, pressing her thumbs and forefingers to the corners of her face, eyes wide and head shaking.

I grumbled. I didn't do easy banter. This wasn't me. Time to set those clear lines.

She rubbed up and down her arms and moved to the side, revealing the cabin's interior. The wood stove sat dark and unburning.

"You'll need to start a fire." My voice sounded angrier than I meant. The shift in my tone was not subtle. I'd never been good at hiding when I was upset. I stepped forward, then stopped when she tensed and straightened.

I had been about to walk into the house. *Her* house. Cold sweat broke out along the back of my neck.

This whole interaction had caught me by surprise. This wasn't who I was. She tricked me. She stole my dog and disarmed me with her soulful eyes and raw vulnerability. Okay, that wasn't entirely fair. Ripley really was a ho for hugs. But I felt off of balance, out kilter. Flip that. Whatever. I needed to get out of here and think. I didn't want someone living here. I didn't want to talk to people. I definitely didn't want to go into that house.

"Like I said, I just lost track of—"

"I have to go," I said suddenly, spinning on my heel to leave. "Make sure you open the flue. There's kindling and matches there too," I said over my shoulder as I retreated like a coward.

"Okay. Thanks." I didn't need to look at her face to feel her confusion.

This was the image I was protecting. The grumpy mountain man. Best to keep things as they were.

No more coming down to the guesthouse.

No more interacting with Claire.

And most importantly, no more making her smile.

Just after I delivered a few essentials to get her through the night.

CHAPTER 8

Claire

I blinked awake to the sun slanting through a single crack in the curtains directly onto my face. At that first moment, I couldn't connect to the unfamiliar room around me. It took several nanoseconds of my poor brain working at full sleep-addled power to remember the past few days' events and how I ended up here in this new space. A weight like regret sat heavy on me as I tugged the comforter over my head and debated staying in bed.

I hid my face in my pillow and groaned loudly.

Levi.

It felt weird to think of him as a person with a name. Obviously, he had a name, but why did it feel so weird to refer to him as that, even in my head? Thinking of an amorphous nonhuman entity that spewed rules and grumbled at joy felt more natural.

That had been fine with me. But to know Levi was the man in the grocery store had been a rough blow. But also karmically sort of perfect. Because if I didn't want one person to know about the tragedy that was my life, it was the man renting me his home. But alas, what was done was done.

I'd have thought that realizing Levi was the man from the store would cause some sort of humiliation, but since I'd hit peak embarrassment, there was really nowhere else to go. He'd seen me at my worst. There was a freedom with him now. He'd seen me unmasked, unfiltered, and he'd helped. I didn't need to pretend to be a normal person around him. And in fact, this almost guaranteed I wouldn't need to interact with him at all. I had all but ensured that.

No wonder he left in such a hurry last night. I had accosted him, then had a maniacal breakdown when I put two and two together. I moaned again.

I froze in place when I heard something thump outside the door. The shuffling sound of something being dragged and dropped on the porch finally got me moving from the bed. I sat straight up, ears pricked in the quiet cabin.

Another loud smack of something heavy, then Ripley barked. Levi's deep rumble in response wasn't discernible but sounded less grumpy than he had last night.

Well, not at first. At first, he had been funny. And *sweet*. Not at all what I expected. Plus, the obvious fact that behind that overgrown hair was a man who was, by any measure, incredibly attractive. I'd been too lost in my suffering to notice during our first meeting. And without the protective glasses, his eyes were piercing and soulful—somewhere between brown and green, hard to tell. He'd been decent about showing his ID, and then, as I studied his picture, a wave of sudden shyness hit me. I had meant to be grilling him, ensuring that he wasn't some weirdo watching me through the window, but I found myself getting flustered as he patiently let me study him.

Thankfully, I'd never been a person moved by conventional attractiveness so that reaction was neither here nor there.

I let out a long breath through pursed lips as I pressed my cold fingertips to my flushed cheeks. The fire had gone out, but the small space wasn't uncomfortably cold yet. It was a good chilly temp while sleeping, but I might need to start another fire if I want to get to work. My stomach growled loudly. I hadn't remembered to eat anything but a protein bar. I had to get to town and get food.

But first things first.

I crept slowly out of bed. The wooden floorboards squeaked, trying to give me away as I went to the window that faced the front porch. The blackout curtains were drawn tight, save the alarm-clock crack on my face, but by standing at the edge, I could just barely get a glimpse of outside without moving the fabric and alerting him to my presence.

Watching from inside my house to the outside wasn't weird. I was sure there was an unwritten rule somewhere that would support that.

Levi was walking back toward his truck, parked a couple of feet from my porch. His jean-clad backside worked it on the steep incline as he bent and reached across the bed of his truck. Ripley trotted alongside him in a neon orange puffy vest. He slid a case of water out, walked it back to the porch, and dropped it next to a pile of other food, which explained all the sounds.

Food. He brought me food and supplies. My stomach celebrated by growling loudly.

"Enough out of you," I said quietly, placing a hand to silence the rumblies in my tumblies. Why did my gut choose to advertise all my needs loudly?

Either I hadn't been as horrifying as I thought, or I was so scary that he brought me food to keep me from accosting him or the other patrons in town.

A win was a win.

It was easier than thinking he did it out of kindness because that didn't line up with the image he was trying to impress upon me. Even still, I couldn't help the smile I had to bite back. When was the last time I was cared for besides by my father?

Levi's head wasn't covered today, and his deep brown hair looked freshly washed and pushed back off his forehead, reaching down to the hood of a sweatshirt—similar to the one he had on last night. What had he called it? A HuggieHoodie?

Freaking adorable.

Levi looked directly at the window where I stood a few feet away, protected by glass and blackout curtains. I stilled, worried I'd been thinking too loud. He couldn't see me. There was no possible way. But my heart picked up its pace nonetheless, and

I slowed my breathing. He stepped forward toward the stairs, a look of stern determination pinching his brows.

I glanced down to where I wore only a sleeping tank and panties and panicked. But just as he came forward, he stopped, spun around, and left again. Mirroring that conflicting behavior from last night. His mood had changed on a dime. It didn't make sense. Neither did this sneaky early morning delivery. This time, I was fairly sure I hadn't done anything weird. Yesterday, for sure. I had done the Classic Claire thing where I shared too much or put my foot in my mouth ...

But no. This man was just confusing. He seemed simultaneously annoyed by my existence but also responsible for my survival.

Well, as a fellow introverted little weirdo, I couldn't say I blamed him. And I was more than a little relieved when he left. I hadn't even had coffee yet. I ended up working until well after midnight and then lay staring in the pitch-black cabin for a long time, unable to shut down my chatty brain despite my exhausted body. It was just so dang quiet out here, and my mind was so loud. No internet to check out with. No traffic to act as white noise.

Thoughts were very insistent when there was no way to block them out.

Caffeine was required before I drove into town to check in with Dad, let alone try to have a strained conversation with a total stranger. I could already feel that this once-a-day call to Dad wasn't realistic. The town might only be ten miles away, but winding roads at a creeping pace meant at least an hour a day, if not more, lost to driving. I would need a better system.

Levi opened his truck door and gingerly lifted Ripley inside like the passenger princess she was. I rolled my eyes, which felt much more natural than acknowledging the little tug on the heartstrings that his gentle ministrations caused. Once they were almost down the driveway, I moved the curtains to the side to get a better view of everything he'd left.

"Cookies, yay!" I said.

I waited to open the front door until the truck traveled down the winding road, peeking through the trees until it was no longer visible. A cool blast of morning air helped wake me up as I went to the pile of stuff.

The scrawled note on top read, "Use as needed."

"Chatty as ever." I began lugging the stuff into the kitchen. "Mmm trail mix." I was a kid at Christmas as I explored his booty. *The* booty. The provisions.

Not thinking about his booty.

He had gone out of his way for a guy who didn't seem to want me here in the first place. His whole listing had been designed to be off-putting, but something in my personality with people like that made me want to poke them like a bear.

The brewing coffee made from the fresh grounds he provided smelled heavenly as I slid on some warm layers. I had no idea what to expect from the weather today. If only I had an ever-present bot listening at all times to ask the temperature. I wandered around the small space to the locked door off the kitchen and wiggled it just for funsies. Still locked. Based on the size of the house, it had to be bigger than a closet. Maybe another bedroom? It was hard to say. The contents of that room called to me.

It might as well have been a bright red button that said, "DO NOT PRESS."

I sighed and stepped away. I was restless and curious, a dangerous combination for me.

I stood in the kitchen, staring up at the main house, sipping my coffee. My mind drifted in a hundred different directions when I noticed the front door of the cabin was slightly ajar. Or at least it looked like it might be.

I perked up.

"Somebody should go close that," I told myself aloud, hoping it might justify whatever I did next.

It did not. I was tugging on my boots before the coffee pot was even cool and stepping out onto the porch.

"If I shouldn't go check on his house, give me a sign?" I said to the air around me.

In the fresh morning, I stood for a minute listening for any sounds of life, but only a few birds cawed, and the creek of the tall pines swayed slightly in the breeze, needles rustling.

Nothing. Okey dokey, that settled it.

I walked/jogged the steep drive to his place, slowing when I approached the front door. It was cracked open just a little. I hesitated only a second before closing it the last inch. I wasn't going to go in. I wasn't that nosy. I knew about laws.

The front porch was sturdy, my boots clomping loudly as I

walked the length of it, peering into the windows as I went. Windows whose curtains were wide open, by the way.

"Wow." It was gorgeous in there. Sleek, clean, and modern, with no signs of anything sketchy.

I jogged down the steps and around the side of the cabin to the big shack that had intrigued me when my phone vibrated against my butt. I didn't even remember putting it in my back pocket, but I must have done it without thinking after years of always having it glued to me.

Still no service but—

"That sonofa—!"

On-screen, a message popped up reading, "Connect to Wi-Fi network *cleverwifiname*?"

"Uh. Heck yes, please."

He did not strike me as a customized Wi-Fi name guy, but alas, the dad jokes get us all in the end. I selected connect, but of course, the password option showed up. I tried the old standby of password and password1234, but neither of them worked. I tried various combinations of Ripley to no avail as well. *Damn.*

"Ugh. There isn't even anybody around. Why would you have a password at all?"

Somewhere in the distance was a loud bang. It could have been anything, but it was enough to freak me out of my explorations and send me back to the house. I'd have to investigate another day. On the walk back to my cabin, I held up the Wi-Fi settings, waiting until the exact moment his internet name went away. It was maybe ten feet from the house.

"Stingy!"

There was nothing else to it. At this rate, it would be lunch before I returned from town, and I still needed to get work done. I didn't even need food, and thinking of the drive made my motions sluggish.

"Blah." I got back in the car, my sore backside remembering all the hours spent in the car yesterday, and began to make my way into town. Twenty minutes into the drive, I already decided that I would have to negotiate Dad down to once or twice a week tops, but even thinking about it caused my heart to clench with unexpected loneliness. I could hear his deep accent saying, *but whadabout the daily Wordle?*

As if with magic, my phone lit up on the dash, displaying the map that went out here about this part yesterday.

"Aha!" I checked the rearview mirror and pulled over to the side of the road. Two bars of service barely flickered with life. I pulled up the Wordle app, and slowly but surely, it loaded.

"There she is!" my dad said by way of greeting when I dialed him through the Bluetooth.

"Hey, Dad. Can you hear me okay?" I sat back against the seat and closed my eyes, surprised by the ache in my chest.

"It's a little tinny, but I hear ya. Tell me all the details. Are you liking the place?"

"Yeah, it's great. Not as—" I had been about to say, "not as bad as I was worried it would be," but thought I better keep that one as an inside thought. "—close to town as I thought, though. We might have to cut back on the calls. I'm sorry. Just until I turn in the story."

"Aw, but whadabout the daily Wordle?"

I smiled to myself.

"We will still do it. Or at least you should." I was going to lose my streak. It was over five hundred days at this point. Crap. This was more upsetting than I thought. "But this drive is just too far."

"I understand. You gotta do what's best for you. Nothing lasts forever," he said gently.

"Sorry," I said. "Let's do the Wordle before I have to go back."

I beat him by seconds with "rupee," but the strain of searching for reception already had my power down in the red. Also, I forgot to charge it last night.

"Ah, you win," he said. "Those double vowels always get me."

"Yeah," I said softly.

The call was ending so fast. I knew I had made a big deal about the inconvenience of driving out here, but the thought of returning to that quiet all by myself threatened me with that same heavy feeling from this morning, wanting to keep me in place.

"Hey, what's wrong?" he asked, sensing a shift in my tone.

I shook my head, eyes still closed, knowing he couldn't see me. "I don't know. Just emotional. I don't know why."

My dad waited a beat. "You'd think you'd had some sort of traumatic event happen or somethin'."

I sniffled and pinched the area between my eyebrows, trying to stop an unwanted tear, to no avail. Dad's gentle worry pushed me over the edge, and I quickly dashed away a tear. "Yeah. How about that."

"You miss him?" my dad asked softly.

I thought for a minute; the truth blaring in my head. "A little." But honestly, I think I missed having a plan. Maybe even more than him, but I wouldn't ever admit that out loud. I felt unmoored and silly. I felt like a kid who was playing an adult. Shouldn't someone almost thirty with a thriving career and purpose feel more certain about their wants? More established in their body? I needed a place to live. A plan for after this story. A quick look at homes in Colorado Springs made me realize I had no desire to return to that city. Nothing tied me to it since I worked my job remotely and traveled anyway. I never felt connected to it.

"You should give yourself time," he said. "Get some ice cream and watch that movie that always makes you cry. Or maybe punch something."

I chuckled. "Maybe." I didn't feel sad or angry—or maybe a little bit of both but mostly listless. Determined to finish that article and make my choices seem worth it.

"Why don't you come home? When you finish the story."

I opened my mouth to fight but found I didn't want to. It sounded nice.

"Not forever," he added. "You've always been so independent, but you know you always have a place here."

"Yeah. Okay, that sounds good."

"Yeah? Great, kiddo! I'll clear out the old room. Just stay until you get back on your feet."

I let out a sigh as he chatted on happily. It wasn't an ideal plan, but it was a plan, and when I got there, I could think about where I wanted to live next. I couldn't even imagine that right now. It felt like too much.

My eyes were still closed, and I was so focused on my dad's voice that I didn't hear anybody approaching until it was too late.

There was a knock on my window, and I screamed.

CHAPTER 9

Levi

This was beginning to feel like a pattern.

I stepped back from the window, constantly checking for traffic on the winding dirt road.

"Levi?" Claire asked in disbelief, hand to her chest as the other lowered the window.

"Who's Levi? What's going on?" a man's thickly accented voice called through her dashboard.

"It's okay, Dad. It's just the landlord. The rentee?" She shook her head and settled on, "The guy who owns the cabin."

"You shouldn't be here," I said. This part of the road had a sharp turn with very little visibility. Those who were used to driving on it often come whipping around these bends without slowing. "It's not safe," I said.

"Where are you?" her dad asked worriedly.

At the same time, she said, "It's fine."

"It's not fine," I said to her. Louder, I said, "I'm Levi Carmichael."

"Ralph, Claire's dad, former firefighter, and still have many friends on the police force down in your neck of the woods," the man explained.

I bit back a smile. So that was where she got her gumption from. Claire dropped her face into her hands and mumbled, "For crying out loud."

"She's on the side of the road," I explained to Ralph. He's a man who would understand the risks. "It's a one-lane mountain pass with poor visibility."

Ralph clicked his tongue. "Claire Bear, I taught you better than that. If you heard all the stories..." Her father went on, and she glared at me.

I shrugged off her malice. "It's not a designated pullover," I said.

I had thought something was wrong when I spotted Claire's small SUV on the side of the road. I assumed the worst and rushed to park without thinking. Now, we were both taking up so much space a single car would barely fit by. I shot a worried look back to Ripley. She stood on her hind legs, barking with her paws on the window and adding to the tension in my neck. I glanced up the road again. We needed to hurry this along, and though I knew I was being gruff, we didn't have time for coddling.

Now that Claire wasn't glaring so hard, I took a moment to really look at her, something I had been avoiding. This close to Claire, my first time really seeing her in the light of day, she was too pretty to look directly at. My gaze flicked to take her in pieces; her cheeks were splotchy, and her eyes red-rimmed and glassy, her dimples nowhere to be seen. Not as bad as she'd been in the store, but upset, nonetheless.

"What's wrong?" I asked before I could remember that I wasn't supposed to care.

"Why's he asking what's wrong?" Ralph asked.

"Nothing," she said.

"She's crying," I said at the same time, leaning forward so her father could hear me over her protestations.

"Okay, can you two stop ganging up on me?" She turned toward me, causing our faces to be closer than I intended. Her warm scent, like coffee and sweetly floral shampoo, filled the tight space. Her gaze moved from my eyes to my beard and lips. A little furrow formed between her brows. She swallowed and leaned back slightly. I was too close. I clenched my jaw and pulled my upper body out of her space.

"I'm fine. Dad, I'll call you back tomorrow. Love you," she said.

I stepped back and examined the road, pretending I couldn't hear the exchange.

"And you're okay?" he asked.

"Yes. But he's right. I better get out of here now to appease you both," she said tightly. I flicked a glance her way to find her shoulders at her ears and fists balled against the steering wheel, staring straight ahead and avoiding my gaze too.

"Love you. Don't worry about the calls, sweetie. Whenever

you're able will be fine," the older man said. "Bye, Levi. Make sure my girl gets home okay."

With hands tucked in my jeans, I studied the trees and loudly said, "Yes, sir. Nice to meet you, Ralph."

She closed the window as I glanced nervously up and down the road, listening for any cars. "Get in your truck if it's dangerous," she yelled through the glass.

"I'm making sure you go," I said, arms crossed.

"I swear—" The rest of her mumblings were cut off by the start of her engine. She maneuvered a three-point turn and headed back in the direction of the house. My palms didn't stop sweating until she was safely out of sight. I got in my truck just as a larger one came racing past, speeding twice the limit. He swerved into the dirt where Claire had just been, kicking up a cloud of gravel and dust.

He had his middle finger out his window and yelled, "Get off the road, fuckwit!"

"Good idea," I said with a sigh, even though he was long gone.

I caught up with Claire soon enough, following at a safe distance until she turned off into my drive. She parked in front of the guest cabin but moved quickly to stop me before I could go the rest of the way up.

She knocked on the window, foot tapping impatiently. I put the truck in park and rolled down the window, a reverse of the scene just a few minutes ago.

Ripley jumped across the cab, pointy paws jabbing into my goods. "Oof," I said, wincing.

"Hello, darling." Claire scratched Ripley behind the ear, causing her back leg to thump repeatedly against my junk. Some of the anger melted from Claire's features as Ripley's sharp tail whipped my face.

I had planned to head straight back to the house and hide for the rest of the day. My socializing quota for this week had been surpassed. Yet I wasn't agitated by the growing silence between us. If anything, I found myself hoping that Ripley would cause more distractions, extending this unexpected interlude. Claire debated with something internally before finally letting out a sigh.

"Thank you for the food. And the water. And the various supplies and sundries. And the coffee was so good. Really, you saved us both with that one." She chuckled but pressed on when I didn't do anything but scratch the back of Ripley's neck. Our fingers accidentally brushed, but I didn't pull back. "I was a disaster yesterday and completely abandoned my hopes for provisions, so I really appreciate it. Tell me how much I owe you."

I growled and narrowed my eyes, putting an end to that. "It's part of the rental." I stared at the dashboard.

She hesitated a beat. I felt her studying me, though I refused to look at her. "In that case, you have some explaining to do," she said to me. Ripley had calmed down and settled back into the passenger seat.

I lifted my gaze to find her watching me with narrowed eyes, hiding a dimpled smile, as she tapped her foot impatiently. I preferred this to gratitude.

"You were the one trying to get rear-ended. Or worse," I said.

The clouds broke long enough to shine on Claire, highlighting the bits of darker brown flecks in her eyes, reminiscent of Leopardwood. Her wide, full lips weren't grinning as they had been last night, flashing those deep dimples. Which was exactly what I had promised myself I didn't want to see.

"Not about that." She cut a hand through the air. "That was me being too lazy to go all the way to town. It might have been a little bit reckless. I won't do it again."

I couldn't hide the surprise on my face at her culpability. "Then what do I need to explain? How the flue works in the stove?"

"I—no."

"Are you sure? Because temps are supposed to drop tonight, and there's no fire going." I looked pointedly to where no smoke came out of the chimney pipe.

"Okay, I'll start a fire when I go to work. Good grief, you're worse than my father. Why did you lie and say you didn't have internet?" she blurted before I could say anything else.

I ran my hand over the dash, dusting it. "I said the guesthouse doesn't."

Her mouth dropped open. "You have Wi-Fi." She tilted her head when I didn't say anything. "You really aren't going to share the Wi-Fi password?"

"It won't do you any good down here." I shrugged.

She sucked in her lips and scrunched her nose in a way I would not find charming.

"Why were you calling your dad on the side of the road? What were you doing?" I asked.

"Wordle," she said, or at least something that sounded like it. "Oh, don't make that face," she said. "You've really never heard of the word game that took the world by storm a few years back? We still play against each other every day. Or at least we did. I'm going to lose my streak, but it's whatever—" She cut herself off abruptly.

"You pulled over to play a game?" I asked skeptically, wondering if she was lying.

"It's more about the tradition. I know we're weirdly close. But we're all we've got. Or at least he's all I've got. Now. Besides my career. I'm going to stop talking. I promised I wouldn't do all that again."

Shit.

The exact thing that I didn't want happening was happening. Feelings. Understanding. I felt the guesthouse glaring at me. Tangible judgment poured out of it.

Keeping a young woman from her father. Really, Levi?

"I know most people don't understand my father and I being so close. Oh, good, I'm still talking. It's because you're being stoically nonverbal. It's very triggering to me."

I felt the words bubbling up in my throat. A voice in my head screamed at me to shove my fist in my mouth to keep from speaking. The other voice, suspiciously sounding like Pace, cheered me on. I made the mistake of looking at her again, noting her big, sad brown eyes hiding a self-deprecating grimace. She looked so … alone. Or maybe I was projecting. I gripped the steering wheel until it creaked.

"You can use my phone," I blurted so quickly she startled. My heart was racing like I was chopping wood, palms sweating like racing around the curve of an overpass.

"What?" She wrapped her arms around her middle cautiously, stepping back.

"I have a landline. I never use it. You can use it for your daily weirdle calls."

One of her dimples popped. I glared just to the left of her head. "Wordle. But no." She shook her head as my offer settled in. "You have all the rules. And listen, I wasn't kidding when I said I appreciate a good list of rules. I'm not great at subtext. I like knowing exactly where I stand."

"Especially when it's on the side of the road?"

"Look at you with all the jokes," she deadpanned.

Ripley lifted her head and sniffed. Probably realizing we were close to home, she started doing the potty prance next to me. I had to hurry this along. Especially as because every second that passed, I regretted this offer even more.

"It's not a big deal." I turned the truck back on. "I'm gone most of the day anyway. You can use the phone when I leave."

"I can't go into your house. I don't have a key. It feels intrusive or something." She didn't meet my gaze as she spoke.

"I don't lock it."

A look passed over her features I couldn't identify. "Hmm. Trusting."

I shrugged. "There's nobody out here."

"But that Wi-Fi, now that's too precious." Her voice was thick with sarcasm.

"You're really bothered by that." It was my turn to watch her until she looked away, flustered. "They set it up that way," I explained. "The password is a long string of numbers and letters I don't have memorized. If you absolutely insist, you can have that too. It's not going to do anything for you down here, but it's not some state secret." Heat burned the back of my neck.

"You really don't care if I go into your house and use your phone? What if I rob you?" She looked as confused as I felt.

This wasn't the plan. This wasn't what I even meant to say. Something about her had me speaking without thinking. I wished this was a new quality in me, but it wasn't. The only difference was that with everyone else, it was much easier to stay away and avoid the whole situation to begin with.

Yet here I was, still talking, still sharing the same air. Still instinctually wanting to make her life a little easier.

"I know where you live," I said. Ripley whined next to me. I put the truck back in drive.

"What if I snoop?" she asked.

"Haven't you already?" I asked, remembering how the cameras had caught her near the shed.

Her cheeks flushed, and it was too much to look at. "I—Your door was open. I was closing it."

"It's fine. Nothing exciting to see." I turned to check the side mirror, but really, it was to hide the half smile caused by her embarrassed blush. "It's up to you. If the truck is gone, feel free to go on in."

"Okay. Wow. That's really helpful, actually. Thank you. Ralph and I appreciate you."

"Yep. No biggie." I took my foot off the brake and began to drift slowly away.

"You're not—" Thinking better of whatever she'd been about to say, she said, "Thank you." She called out, "And sorry about the snooping."

"No, you're not. Password is taped to the router in my office," I shouted over my shoulder.

In the rearview mirror, I caught her biting that bottom lip, both dimples on full display with a smile.

So far, my plan to stay away from Claire was going exceptionally well.

"You're an idiot," I mumbled as I pulled under the carport.

CHAPTER 10

Claire

The next week, my curiosity finally got the better of me.

I waited roughly five minutes after Levi and Ripley left before I got dressed at record speed. To be fair, I'd made good progress on the story in the couple of days I'd been here. It turned out that not having internet was great for focus. The one time I went into town to send off what I had to my editor, Melanie, I ended up chatting with Ruth, who owns the local B&B, and she told me about the history of the popular local tourist destination. It was interesting enough that I was inspired to start up the old online journal I did for a class project in college. The story needed to be documented. Eventually, I might go back and add more details and pictures. But for now, the main focus was my exposé.

After one quick look at Levi's house.

Another bizarre interaction with the supposed grumpy recluse, and I'd been left as confused as ever. His offer to let me use his phone was amazing, but it didn't jibe with the man who wrote the listing or who I'd interacted with. Every conversation was more confusing than the one before. To be fair, I wasn't exactly the consistent overthinker I usually came off as. I'd cried more in front of Levi in barely three days than I had with Kevin in three years.

It all made me want to investigate him even more. Who was this enigma of a man? What did he do to afford this land and property? He didn't work at the grocery store, but he'd been there doing some sort of repairs, it seemed.

I scurried up the drive to Big Cabin. (I had very creatively dubbed his house Big Cabin and my place Little Cabin.) Sure enough, it was unlocked. I hadn't even thought to try entering in my snooping, or at least not for very long. Because that would be weird. Weirder than being invited to use his landline. Weirder yet than the fact that he even had a landline.

"Whoa." I walked into the main open front room. Large windows made up the north and east walls, giving the impression of opening right out to the forest. It was breathtaking. The highest tips of the Rockies were already powdered with snow, and the lower elevations were just starting to change from green to yellows and oranges. It smelled fresh, like pine and lemon cleaner. The counters of the modern kitchen were bare except for a few appliances. It was tidy, with a hint of artistic inspiration in the wall art that decorated the areas that weren't all windows. Lovely wood and metal pieces complemented the modern design and simplicity.

My feet pulled me down the hall, where I found a few personal photos of people I obviously didn't recognize. Again, surprising. There were several with him, including an older woman who must have been his mom or a woman who gave him the same intense hazel eyes. In every picture, they both shared identical bright smiles. I hadn't seen Levi smile so openly like that since I'd met him, and I felt a pang of loss at not getting to meet that side of him. Before whatever happened that changed him so permanently.

There didn't seem to be a partner in any of the photos. Not that I was looking.

The first door led to his bedroom, which was just as clean as the rest of the home. There was a large bed and dresser, but ultimately, it was simple, with another massive window. I didn't let myself linger and closed the door quickly because I did have some integrity.

The small office was easily spotted (as well as the intricate Wi-Fi password taped to the router as promised). My phone buzzed to life as soon as I connected. I quickly caught up on important messages and checked in with a few friends who were mildly panicked at my sudden absence. I explained the situation vaguely, mentioning a story that had me out of reach—and replied to a few work emails—including a check-in with Melanie, who was eager for the rest of the story.

"This is really going to be something, Wells," she said. "If you can pull this off, this might change the whole broken system."

I was more determined than ever as I worked through more emails. I worried less about the future or my breakup and was determined to finish that story. I even added a few more details to the post about Ruth and her B&B. A few people had found my online journal and asked for more information about Cozy Creek.

Surprisingly, after being back on my phone for a good twenty minutes, I was ready to turn it off again. It had been nice to be unreachable.

Wrapping up the call with my dad didn't fill me with such dread this time, knowing that we would be chatting again the next day.

In fact, we did chat the next day, and the one after that. The new system was working.

After five days, I had almost finished the first draft of my story while managing to keep my Wordle game streak alive. Each morning, I'd make a cup of coffee and walk over to spin in Levi's office chair while I solved the puzzle with Dad.

On today's call, Dad beat me with the Wordle "squat," and I was fine losing to such an unattractive word.

"When these two months end, I'll fly out and meet you at your storage unit," he explained this morning. "We'll load it up, and I'll drive with you back here. Truck reservation is already taken care of."

"Thank you for doing that, Dad. I haven't even been able to think."

"I know how it is right now. Not much longer, and you'll be home."

"Yeah. Thanks."

I sighed and focused on the relief of having a plan instead of the fear deep in the back of my mind that I was going backward in life.

My eyes drifted to the lone piece of art on the wall. It was a chunk of twisted and angled driftwood but with more intent and feeling. It had been sanded and covered in a shine that gave it emotion somehow. Every time I looked at it, I found a new secret detail I hadn't seen before.

Dad and I talked a little longer before I ended it under the ruse of working. Truthfully, I was restless and curious again.

I still had no idea where Levi wandered off during the days. He was gone anywhere from three to eight hours, and when he came home, he often went into the garage behind his house, where the hums and buzzing of power tools would drift out for hours. A couple of nights, we were both up until almost midnight working. Notes of sad indie rock would drift down the driveway, and I'd open the window despite the chill and for the comfort of the noise. I liked hearing him nearby.

But what did he *do*? He always brought Ripley, so it couldn't have been any standard corporate job. But I could have guessed within minutes of meeting him that he wasn't cut from that cloth. Maybe he was a hunter? But wouldn't he bring *them* home? *Bleck*, I hoped not. Maybe he had a shop in town? But I had a hard time picturing him in any customer-facing role. He clearly wasn't hurting financially. The cabin itself was beautiful and well-maintained. He even mentioned a cleaner who came every other Thursday.

The man was a mystery, and with every passing day, that itch in my brain to get some answers grew more insistent on being scratched.

I was stepping out of his house to the front porch when I heard his truck coming up the drive. I waved hello brightly with a burst of adrenaline at having company. He lifted his chin in a sort of acknowledgment before awkwardly looking away.

We were basically besties.

He pulled forward to park in his spot near the garage/shed thing I had yet to explore. On the passenger side, Ripley was losing her mind to get to me, so I met her and reached in to lift her out. She convulsed with happy, shuddering dramatics.

"I've missed you too." I laughed, pulling my head back to avoid some of the wet kisses slathering up my neck and chin. I felt Levi's gaze on me but couldn't meet his eyes. When I set her down, she ran straight toward the mystery building through a small doggy door I hadn't noticed before. I probably could have fit my head through there ...

I was wiping my chin on my shoulder when Levi's boots came into view.

"How are you—whoa," I said.

When I finally met Levi's gaze, he was almost unrecognizable. His hair was still long enough to go past the nape of his neck but had been neatly trimmed and freshly washed. Head tilting, he tucked some loose strands behind his ear. He'd shaved back his beard so that it was a little more than a five o'clock shadow, emphasizing a *very* square jawline that'd been hiding and a mouth that was forming words. Words that my brain wasn't absorbing because it was too busy noticing two perfectly shaped lips moving as he pursed his mouth slightly, eyes squinting as confusion pinched his fine brows.

I stepped forward, hand raised. Levi stilled, his nostrils flared. His eyes narrowed on my movement, and his hands clenched at his sides. Only then did I realize I'd been about to reach up and touch his face, so enthralled by him that I was.

That wouldn't have been weird or crossing any boundaries at all.

I dropped my hand and stepped back to give him some space. His shoulders relaxed.

"You shaved," I said, using all my genius investigative skills as a journalist to break the tension.

"Oh. Yeah." He ran a hand over his chin. "It's been known to happen."

He tucked his head, cheeks flushing, and stepped to open the bed of the truck.

I followed him, even though he hadn't asked me to stay. He probably wanted me to head back to Little Cabin to keep the unspoken space between us. Where did this fit in his list of rules? He didn't explicitly say I couldn't be nosy. Well, he had, but I was choosing to ignore that.

I wouldn't be me if I wasn't a little curious about the massive shape hidden under a bright blue tarp.

"What's that?" I asked.

He jumped to find me standing right behind him, peering on tiptoes over his shoulder. He also expected me to go back to my place.

He turned to face me, and I smiled widely. Sometimes, it helped disarm people. He scowled.

Well, damn.

"Work stuff," he said, briefly meeting my gaze before glaring back at his truck.

In the sun, his hazel eyes looked lighter than the last time we talked. There was a sparkle of excitement in them as he glanced back to the mystery tarp.

"What work stuff?" I asked. "What do you do?"

He stiffened, shoulders tense. "Aren't you on a deadline?"

"Always. What is that?" I asked again.

He sighed and rightfully decided that I was like Ripley when she was in search of a cozy spot—not to be distracted from what I wanted. Eventually, he said, "Hopefully, it's my next piece. There's a little bit of root rot, but I'm cautiously optimistic."

I came to stand by his side, taking it as an invitation. "Piece?"

His elbow brushed my arm, and he shuffled a step away. "Yeah. I do woodwork. Make sculptures." He flipped the corner of the tarp up to reveal the gnarled and dirt-covered root system of a massive wooden stump. He dropped it back and shot me a look. "Excuse me."

"Oops, sorry." I backed up, a little stunned and very much in the way. He was an *artist*? A sculptor, more specifically. A million more questions split off in all directions to take root in my mind—pun intended.

As if it were nothing more than a package of warehouse paper towels, Levi wrapped his arms around the whole massive lump and lifted it. Muscles in his forearms, biceps, and shoulders all engaged, flexing with the momentum as he leveraged it out of the truck with a masculine grunt. A sound that I would not be forgetting any time soon.

Today, I learned that forearms with popping veins are a breathtaking sight to see in real life.

"So this is where you go all day? You're hunting for wood?" I asked, proud of myself for not making a juvenile joke. "A wood hunter," I said with no extra emphasis at all.

He looked at me a second too long, eyes narrowed in skepticism like he, too, was waiting for a joke.

"Some days." He walked, legs wide, leaning slightly back as he struggled toward the garage door. That had to weigh as much as two of me. I mean, he really could just throw me over his shoulder without even breaking a sweat. You know, just for measurement of strength's sake. Not that I was thinking about that.

"Do you often hunt for wood?" I asked innocently.

I really tried to keep it together.

He didn't respond, but the silence was telling.

"I, myself, appreciate a good piece of wood," I said.

He stopped as we reached the garage and gave me a blank stare.

"Not every day does life deliver a fine piece of girthy, hard—"

"Are you done?" he asked, the tendons in his neck straining.

"It's impossible to say." I covered my growing smile with both hands. "I never really meant to start, but the jokes write themselves."

"At least you tried," he said, shifting the load in his hands with a grunt.

"Do you need me to get the door?" I asked as he attempted to heft the mass to one hip.

"If you aren't too busy amusing yourself."

I snorted.

"The key is on my hip," he said.

I had to bend awkwardly to avoid brushing his arms and toppling the load as I maneuvered the carabiner holding the keys from a belt loop on the front of his jeans. I would not risk an accidental junk brush. Not with all the wood jokes hanging in the air.

"This door you lock?" I asked with cheek, because why not poke the bear instead of thinking about where my hands were?

"There are a lot of very expensive tools in here," he said, winded. "I trust my neighbors, but I'm not an idiot."

"Fair enough."

"Any chance you could hurry it along?" he asked through gritted teeth.

"Yep. Sorry. Almost got it. Okay, there we go." I unlocked the sliding door and bent down to pull it up. I jumped on my tiptoes to push it all the way open.

"Thanks," he grunted.

There was a large space in the middle of the floor where he had to carefully squat—that stupid word again—to set the piece down with a groan. His thighs stretched the seams of his jeans to capacity. When he stood, he stretched his back and cracked his neck.

A light flickered to life, and I spotted Ripley under a pile of blankets on a large doggy bed in the corner. The whole space was filled with large saws and power tools, as well as pieces of wood in various states of completion. The air smelled like sawdust and something sharper, maybe varnish? I thought back to some of the pieces I'd seen in his house.

"Whoa," I said again. "You are an artist."

He mumbled something and busied himself, dusting his hands on his jeans.

"I'm not sure what I expected when you said woodwork. Like maybe those bears made of tree trunks you always see for sale on the side of the road. Or maybe tables or something. But not this." Along the back wall were several pieces I wanted to explore but was afraid I was already pushing it.

He went to the wall and flicked a switch that caused a couple of space heaters to hum to life.

He came to stand by my side. I remained standing in the middle of the workspace, my shocked eyes never settling in one place, desperate to learn everything I could about this fascinating discovery. I was all but bouncing on my feet to go look closer at the various sculptures. "I've never met a bona fide working artist, especially not a sculptor."

He cleared his throat. "You, uh, want to see—"

"Yes, please," I responded before he even finished the question.

He chuckled lightly and scratched at the back of his neck. "Okay. But remember, most of these aren't done."

"Tell me everything." That familiar tingle of a new fixation gave me a boost of adrenaline.

He looked down at me, and a hesitant, almost worried look furrowed his brow. "You don't have to pretend."

"I'm not. I want to know everything." I could picture my eyes sparkling like a cartoon with sincerity as I looked up at him, hands clasped hopefully under my chin.

His gaze moved between them, then moved to my mouth briefly before moving on. I licked my lips without meaning to, but he quickly looked elsewhere. I ignored the fluttering in my chest.

His shoulders relaxed as he stepped toward one corner and began to explain his whole process, from looking for a good wood—heh—to the tools he used and how he worked with the natural flow of material. His hands were deep in his pockets as he spoke slowly, with quiet, bridled passion at first. As he grew more comfortable, he'd get lost in a tangent, speed up, and start using his hands expressively, but as soon as he caught himself, he pulled back to that cool demeanor. It was like there was this excited little nut trying to break free but who had been censured before and learned to keep some things at bay.

I looked up at him, soaking in every detail. Nodding and asking questions, I tried to understand as much as I could in a short time. Nothing was cooler to me than a person who was deeply good at something, no matter the subject. Humans were so cool when they found their happy niches to learn everything about. I could never settle on one thing. I wanted to know something about everything. People who had enough patience to become experts were fascinating.

"But how do you know what it will be when you start?" I asked, running my hands down my arms to smooth the frisson of titillation from new knowledge.

His gaze moved as he thought. "I never really do. It's that old cliché. Eventually, the piece will tell me."

"So cool." I thumbed in the direction of the new hunk of wood on the floor. "Any idea what that's going to be?"

He held my gaze a fraction too long. "No idea." He shrugged, but the tips of his ears had gone red.

"But it called to you? The wood?" I asked.

He narrowed his eyes again. "I can feel you trying so hard not to make a joke."

"So *hard*." I squeaked. "No. No. I'm good. I got it all out of my system." I held up my palms in seriousness.

He gave me one more skeptical look before checking the mass he just brought in. "Yes. I have a good feeling about it." He lifted an arm to point at a specific part of the root system. "See that knot there?"

"Um?"

"Here, look." He put his head next to mine to see from my

height. "See there." He grabbed my fingers, loosening my pointer with his calloused hand to gesture to the specific spot.

All at once, the rest of the world went on mute. No hum of the space heater, no soft snoring from Ripley, only the sound of the heavy pulse beating throughout my body. It wasn't an overtly sexual gesture or even remotely flirtatious, but the air must have shifted around me. I was aware of his masculinity. His scent. The hairs on his muscular arms where his shirt was pushed up to his elbows.

I tried so hard to remember that I was supposed to be looking for something, but I was so in my body that it was like my mind went offline. Even when I'd been attracted to somebody on a mental level, it never felt like this. I never felt it so deeply in my body like electrical pulses. Was this what normal people felt? A physical presence that seemed to weigh me down while simultaneously making me float.

The hierarchy of my being was always brain first, then maybe gut instinct and heart, and somewhere way down on the list was libido. I never led with libido. I was not a person who felt visceral reactions to people. Give me incredible wit or intense specified knowledge of one area of study, a skill set nobody else has, and I'm gone. Competence kink suited me. It had taken months of getting to know Kevin before I felt any sort of lust stir.

Simply put, I was a cerebral girly, and this physical reaction was intense.

It was much better when I hardly thought of him at all.

CHAPTER 11

Levi

She went quiet. I didn't know much about Claire Wells, but she certainly wasn't shy about making her thoughts known.

I'd overshared her into silence. She had seemed so genuinely interested in my work, but I had a habit of always going just a little too far and not realizing it until the person was already gone.

Then again, her silence could be because she was currently caged in by my arms. What was I thinking? I wasn't. As was beginning to be the pattern around her. I was so caught up in the moment that I touched her without thinking. Now she stood in my embrace like a lover, her sweet floral scent rattling my peanut-sized brain. She was soft and warm and pliant.

All I'd touched for so long was unforgiving, weathered pieces of wood—she'd have a field day with that one. When was the last time I'd even touched a woman, let alone one who seemed to infiltrate my brain with her nosy questioning, deep dimples, and wide smile that made my brain blank out? Had I remembered to breathe? My lungs ached. If I inhaled her now, the memory of her would be latched to this exact moment, and I'd be cursed to relive this yearning every time I smelled anything close to this combination of sweet florals, wood shavings, and whatever made her scent hers.

It wasn't only my obvious physical attraction to her. Loathe as I was to admit it, I missed conversation. Was it a conversation? Or had I verbally bombarded her? I quickly replayed the past hour, and it had been rich and fulfilling conversation. Her questions were specific and genuine. There was no reason to fake caring about any of this when she got nothing in return but information. Aside from brief interactions in town and Pace's check-ins, I was more isolated than I thought.

Wasn't that what I wanted?

"Anyway, that's what drew me to this old stump." I dropped her arm and stepped back.

"It's incredible," she said, color high in her cheeks, eyes glancing around and not at me.

Was she trying to be polite to protect my feelings? Did it matter if she hated it? I was by all accounts successful enough to sell every piece every year, so what did her approval matter... yet.

"You sell them in town? That's how you make your money?" She stopped, and her brows pinched. "Sorry, that might be an incredibly invasive question. Sometimes, I forget to filter thoughts before they leave my mouth. As you have most likely noticed." The blush grew darker.

I swallowed, knowing exactly how that felt.

"It's fine." I grabbed a chisel. I wasn't even sure which one I grabbed, but I needed something that wasn't her body to occupy my hands. Maybe if I looked like I was going to get to work, she'd leave me to my solitude. That was what I wanted.

"I do okay in tourist season. Usually, it's enough to last me through the year. Sometimes, I help with odd jobs around town. My friend Pace knows everybody and is constantly offering my help."

"I see. Well, I'm not surprised. These are fantastic." She turned around the space slowly again, eyes tracking everywhere. My gaze roamed over her body, lingering on the way her hips and legs filled out her soft pants and how the slope of her neck smoothed gently into her shoulder. I wondered how easy it would be to replicate that shape, how it would feel to run my hand over it, like testing the final sanding of any imperfections. She had none that I could see.

"Thanks," I grumbled, accepting the compliment that eventually sank in even though it made my skin itchy.

I never felt like I deserved praise for something that worked through me, like thanking a keyboard for an author's work.

We stood facing each other. Her top two teeth nibbled on that damn bottom lip again. I wished she wouldn't do that.

I'd been about to not so subtly shoo her away when her gaze flicked over my shoulder. "What's this one?" She moved quickly toward it.

I knew without looking that she found the one unfinished piece covered in a sheet. And it probably never would be completed. "Not that one. It's not—"

She gasped as she pulled the sheet away. "Wow." She sucked in a breath.

"That one was hidden for a reason," I snapped, and she winced. I wanted to cover it back up, but if I snatched the sheet from her fingers now, I would scare her. Growing unease coiled my muscles, tightening my shoulders and neck. This was too close to the thing we didn't talk or think about.

"Sorry. I can be a little bit—"

"Nosy."

"Inquisitive." She sniffed. "It's one of my many charms."

"That right? Who told you that?" My fists balled to keep from reaching for the sheet.

She made a soft sound of *never mind*. "Why is this covered?"

I took a sharp inhale in and out, anger growing. I shouldn't have let her in here. I kept my back to them both. I didn't need to see the work to remember the pain that it represented. I closed my eyes. I saw her in my mind's eyes, the agony, the sadness, the disbelief of a life ending too soon.

"It didn't come out right. It's trash," I lied.

"It's breathtaking," she said quietly. "It's so different from the other ones."

I ground my jaw. She needed to leave. This was too much.

Her feet shuffled on the dirty floor as she presumably took it in at different angles. "It's making me feel ... lonely." She made a soft noise of thinking. I fought to keep from watching her watching my art. "But in a sort of universal, connected way. This is the sadness that we all feel. Like how the same patterns repeat in nature. Like the swirl of the inside of a shell will sometimes mirror the swirl of an entire solar system. We are all creatures that grieve and hurt. Nothing is special about our pain, but also in that sadness, we're all connected and made of the same things."

My heart hammered against my chest. She was poetic for a journalist. It was what I could never convey in trying to explain my work. This stranger understood things about myself that I was still not close to processing.

"It's a universal loss but still feels so personal," she finished reverently. "This is exactly what I want to do in my articles, but it never—" She stepped closer, but whatever she'd been about to say, she stopped herself.

I clenched my jaw. Having her here was a mistake. I wasn't thinking clearly. I needed her to leave, but I was the numbnuts who had invited her.

"You could absolutely sell this," she said. "God, if I were loaded, I would buy it, but I couldn't afford what this is worth. It's worth a lot is what I'm saying."

"It's not for sale," I said sharply, ending the discussion.

"I know you said you don't think it's done, but I think that's what makes it so honest—"

"Can you just drop it, Claire?" My words slashed through the air, cutting any connection we'd been sharing.

The beat of silence that followed rang like a gong in my head.

"Hey," she said, placing a hand on my shoulder. I flinched, and she lowered it. "I'm sorry. I had no right. I do this ... I go too far ..." Her shoes shuffled on the dusty floor.

"You didn't know."

"I never seem to," she mumbled. "I'm going to go." She lightened her tone, and if I wasn't still glaring at the pile of sawdust on the floor, I would probably find her wide smile locked in place. "I appreciate you showing me around."

I grunted something of a goodbye and flicked the air compressor to life so I could blow off the dirt. The machine was loud enough that I couldn't hear her leave.

Now that I was alone, I was too pissed off to wallow like I wanted to. I was pissed off at myself for getting mad at her. I was mad that she had to be so damn ... so incredible. With those eyes and those lips. When she looked at me. And her curiosity was just so ...

That young lady was showing interest, and that's how you act? You make art but get so mad when people like it ...

"Stop making me feel bad!" I kicked the stump with my work boot, and it hardly moved. The steel tips protected me from breaking a toe.

But what did I expect? Whatever bullshit was happening inside was just that. Bullshit. Nothing to get all worked up about. These feelings would pass. Maybe I did need to get out more. The first woman to show any interest in my art and I lose my shit.

"Get your act together, man," I said, shoulders at my ears as I gripped the side of my workbench to flex my throbbing foot.

After several minutes of breathing and collecting myself, I decided to apologize to Claire. Like the grown man I was under all the aforementioned bullshit. I had been all over the place since I met her, and it had to be getting annoying. After I apologized, that would be it. No more finding excuses to linger in her presence. No more thinking about her at all. I could compartmentalize and shut things down. That was a strength of mine.

I got three feet outside the shed and almost smacked into her.

"Hey." Her brows shot up.

"Hi." I relaxed my "resting jerk face," as Pace referred to it.

She'd changed her clothes, now sporting a thin windbreaker and a small bag strapped to her side. Her long cargo pants and hiking boots made my next question moot.

"Where are you going?" I asked.

"For a walk." She smoothed her thick hair, now pulled back into a ponytail. "I just wanted to let you know. Not that you would worry, but you know, they always say to tell at least one person when you go hiking solo. And as you are the only person, that makes you the winner." She wiggled her fingers like jazz hands. "Huzzah." Then she dropped them to twist behind her back, schooling her features.

I made a sound of acknowledgment, and she fiddled with her sleeves. I was supposed to apologize, but this weird sensation of trepidation or exhilaration made my adrenaline go haywire. It happened when we were inside the workshop, too. Maybe I was getting sick.

"Also, I just wanted to apologize again for pushing my way into your workshop. And then asking all the questions." She winced. "And then pushing about selling that one piece," she said.

I was the one who meant to apologize. I was the one acting like a grumpy ass because some things were still too painful for me to process. Her gaze moved over my clenched jaw and balled fists, and her frown grew.

"You were very clear when you made the listing for Little Cabin that you didn't want to have any sort of interactions," she said, pressing her fingertips to her chest. "And I love rules and lists and clear expectations. I should have respected that. I promise I will print and laminate the list of rules and pin them above the bed so I see them when I first wake up." She chuckled anxiously as she ran her fingers through her ponytail. "I will leave you be. I'm almost done with my work, so I need to focus on that anyway. I will probably go to town for the internet. So I won't bother you, is what I'm saying."

My intentions to apologize got lodged in my throat. She was right. This was what I wanted. I continued to blur the lines of the boundaries. "Okay." I was furious with myself but respected both of our lives by sticking to the plan. "Thank you," I added.

She started to step backward, pursing her mouth to the side with a series of quick nods. "Okay, then. I'll just be—" She thumbed to the road.

"Where are you going?" I asked. "I should know. For safety."

"Just up to the Cozy Creek Short trailhead," she said.

That was a beginner-level trail that was family friendly. Other people were likely to be hiking there at this time of day as well. She made it clear she was used to hikes, so I had to trust that she knew what she was doing.

"There is supposed to be a storm tonight," I said.

Well, I tried.

"Don't worry. I'll be gone an hour, tops. Remember, this ain't my first rodeo." She slid on a corny country accent.

"Do you have your phone?" I focused on the questions. Her nervous weirdness made her exceptionally adorable, and I was not equipped to handle that.

"I do, but you know." She pointed at the little bag with a shrug. Unless she hiked pretty high up, she wouldn't be in sightline of any towers.

I couldn't think of anything else to say. I didn't want her to leave. This was exactly the problem. Maybe I needed a laminated copy of the rules too.

Instead, I cleared my throat as the awkwardness settled between us.

"Okay. See ya," she said, waving as she spun on her heels and walked away.

I opened my mouth, hand reaching for her and then pulling back. I shut my mouth tight.

And it was fine. Who cared if I wasn't friendly? This wasn't summer camp, and we weren't weaving baskets together.

I stomped back into the shed, refusing to look back at the guesthouse—what had she called it? Little Cabin? Ridiculous ... but feeling the judgment rolling off it, nonetheless.

I got back to work and lost myself in prepping the tree stump. I enjoyed the physicality of woodworking and loved how it shut my brain down and helped me get through hours of the days that sometimes felt endless. When I looked up again, two hours had passed. There. Two hours and I'd hardly even thought about her.

I went to the window to make sure she was back at Little Cabin. The desk lamp was not on, and the curtains were still open. No signs of life. I let out a long sigh.

"Ripley," I said loudly. She jumped up out of her covers to stretch, her tiny butt arching into the air. "Oh, you need to go out? Whatever you do, don't go down to the guesthouse."

Her tail started to wag, and she sprinted down toward the guesthouse. I followed right behind, assuring myself Claire had come back and I'd missed her. A whipping wind cut through the trees, and dark clouds to the east raced this way at a noticeable clip.

Without having an excuse ready, I jogged up the steps to knock on the door. My heart beat out of control despite my best efforts to calm it. The house looked even more lifeless and cold this close-up. I stepped back and off the porch. Waiting.

Nothing.

She was smart. She had lived here in Colorado for a while, so she knew how fast the storms moved in.

She wouldn't appreciate some stranger chasing her down like some nutjob.

"Goddammit. I'm going to regret this."

I got Ripley in the truck and went to find her.

CHAPTER 12

Claire

How had I never *seen* trees before?

As I hiked, I took in all the different varieties: the ones with spiking pine needles I remember from elementary school to be coniferous, even though they were wildly more varied. And the leafy ones I never cared to register. The tall, thin ones with an almost white bark with black scratches were definitely aspens. Their leaves sparkled when I looked up through the canopy; their changing yellow leaves danced like sequins as the bright Colorado sun shone through them. The clear blue of the sky contrasted against the sharp yellows and oranges just starting to speckle through the verdant swatches of forest.

How far did Levi travel each day to look for the right wood? The roots of the newest one were so massive they didn't look like they belonged to anything around here. Did he travel to barter for tree parts? Was it legal to take fallen trees from the forest? A thousand more questions I wish I asked whorled through my brain as my legs pumped up the dirt trail.

Before he caught me leaving, I had my phone open, stealing his Wi-Fi to look him up in terms of the art world. I had searched for him before I came but never associated the man from that posting with the few articles about a local artist. One person was reselling an earlier piece of his, supposedly bought about five years ago. I was shocked at what they were asking for it. No wonder he could take his time and refuse to sell some of the pieces. He could probably ask for a lot more, and some super bougie-rich tourists would pay whatever.

Like that piece of art that he left covered that I couldn't stop thinking about.

At first glance, it was a woman's face, turned away, unfinished yet so realistic that I had to stop myself from reaching out to run my finger down her cheek to check the texture. She was carved from a log that still had its bark on the bottom half, and it spread up to cover her mouth. Her visible features were twisted in pain, and a natural split of the wood cracked from where her shoulder met her neck, splitting down through where her heart would be. Silenced. Broken. Desolate.

I had already suspected that Levi was grieving based on his tetchy behavior. Was he mourning a lost love? Was that the reason for the massive mood swings, or had I brought out the worst in him?

I regretted pushing him. It wasn't something I consciously did to people. I was so curious about everything, and I never seemed to register those subtle social cues of going too far that came so naturally to others. I had noticed his clenched jaw and angry brows when I pushed him about selling that last sculpture. I groaned at the tangible wince it caused when I thought of his frustration.

Kevin always gave me that flat look or sighed loudly, so I knew when to stop.

But then, when Levi shared his work and processes, his warm passion overflowed to me, and I felt like I was lit up for the first time in a while. It was so rare to have a genuine conversation with someone. Then he wrapped his arms around me. The short-circuiting of my brain. The unexpected attraction. The desire that blurred my rational mind.

"Nope," I said loudly, startling a nearby bird from its perch.

I wouldn't be thinking about that.

I stopped to take a drink from my water bottle, frowning when I discovered it was almost empty. I panted, wondering just how long I'd been walking, lost in thoughts of strong hands and competent workmanship as I was. A chill blew against my sweat-covered neck as a dark cloud moved over the sun. My watch said I'd walked almost two hours out. But that couldn't be right. The trail I chose was only a two-mile loop. I should have circled back to the trailhead by now.

I took a deep breath in and out. The worst thing I could do was panic. I must have accidentally cut over to Cozy Creek Long at some point where they intersected. I concentrated on pulling up the mental map in my mind. Cozy Creek Long was a ten-mile loop. Based on my pace and how long I'd been going, I had to be halfway through, at least.

The only way out was through.

I was pretty sure this trail led to an overlook that might have a better range of the cell towers. I tried my phone map, but when I zoomed out to find the dot that was me, I lost all reception, and it wouldn't load.

"It's fine. You are *fine*. You have had plenty of water. You have a protein bar, and the temperatures are still mild. You are on the marked trail and have at least three hours until sunset. You are safe." Saying it out loud managed to buoy my determination.

I shifted my pack and carried on. After another half mile or so, I was relieved to find the trees clearing and the terrain growing flat with large gray rocks—the sure sign of the overlook was coming up.

"See. You're fine." I reached the cliff's edge and took in the glorious valley below.

The trees below had started to pop off this high up, and the red, oranges, and yellows exploded in bursts throughout the tall green pines like fireworks.

The last sip of water would be saved as a victory chug when I got to the main road, so I would also need to wait on the chewy chocolate protein bar that would only activate my thirst. I stretched my arms over my head, resting for a moment. I turned to head back, feeling better and confident that I had only made a minor misstep. But I was young and healthy and would look back at this and laugh one day.

That was when I noticed the storm front.

A mass of dark gray clouds loomed over the eastern horizon. Streams of water and possibly snow poured from the quickly moving front like a massive eraser dragging over the earth's surface to remove all color.

"Okay. You're okay. Just need to head back with more speed." I pulled out my phone, and with the towers in sight, I had a couple of bars of service.

"Hallelujah," I mumbled.

I texted my dad and then decided to text Levi, sharing my exact location. The map wouldn't load with the little bit of reception, so I continued to trust my mental math and keep a cool head.

I would be fine. It was far more downhill on the return. I could make good time.

Without any further discussion with myself, I began to walk/jog back the last half of the trail. I couldn't think about how much I had left. I would be okay.

"Please don't end up on the news," I grumbled to myself.

No matter how I planned and thought things through, life had a way of throwing unexpected curveballs at me when I was distracted. I wasn't a fan. I couldn't blame anybody else for this either. It was my own stupid mistake. I'd been lost in thought and not focusing, and this was what happened. *A consequence of my own actions*, I could almost hear Kevin's judgmental voice explain.

I wasn't stupid. I was going to be okay.

As if to warn me, the wind kicked up, slicing right through my ironically named windbreaker.

"You had one job," I said to the useless jacket. The wind brought the smell of moisture and colder temperatures with it.

Sure enough, the temperature dropped with every passing minute. The gathering clouds blocked out any light breaking through the canopy. It was light enough to see my feet scrambling over rocks and dirt, but just barely. The adrenaline kept me numb to the cold for now. I focused only on my feet, going as fast as possible while remaining safe. I recognized a few spots on the trail and felt reassurance of my plan.

I had this.

I was okay. I was kicking myself for walking to the trailhead instead of driving up from the cabin. It was less than a mile, and I thought it would only add to my short, pleasant walk. Now, when I got there, it would be almost another mile walk down the scary main road, possibly in the pouring rain at that point. Nope. Not thinking about that right now. One thing at a time.

Then the first drops of fat, freezing rain hit my face and blurred my vision.

"You're okay. Stay calm."

Maybe it was the adrenaline or the stacking fears or the rain falling heavier and soaking through my thin layers, but shivers began to wrack through me, causing my teeth to chatter. One foot in front of the other. One foot in front of the other. Just like my whole life. You do the next step. One choice and the next.

When my foot slipped, and I fell, the last remaining calm began to shatter. I yelped out more in surprise than anything, but it was lost in the rain hammering the leaves. I pulled myself up and refused to look at my leg but felt cold, wet air hitting exposed, burning skin.

I wasn't a stupid person. I knew better than this, and now I would be a cliché. I was going to die with everybody thinking I was an idiot.

"They're just pants. You can still walk. You're fine." Even as I said it, I felt my eyes burning hot from tears and not the snow-rain combo.

I was limping heavily now, body frozen and soaked.

Just keep going.

One more step.

People have made it through way worse.

But the reality was I was alone. Alone in a life of my own making.

I stopped and sagged against a tree that provided a decent amount of shelter. I had one person I could tell about this hike who would actually care if I never made it back. My online friends would be sad, but we never met in real life. It would be so much easier to compartmentalize the loss in the constant bombardment of terrible news shared online every day. Kevin might be sad but maybe also a little smug in thinking that I would have been safe if I had just chosen him.

My poor father. To lose us both. He would be okay. He had his friends.

I wiped a hand over my face, unsure what was tears from my imagined death or the weather.

The absurdity hit me all at once.

I cackled loudly in the now-pounding weather. I was really sitting here planning out my own funeral?

"You. Are. Fine." I gritted my teeth. I pushed myself off the tree even though my leg was smarting now. The break gave my adrenaline a chance to settle down, and the pain in my extremities sank in.

"You have an article to finish and an ex-boyfriend to prove wrong."

I quickened my pace. As I rounded a tight bend, a flash of light caught my attention. Up ahead, a tall, dark figure, hooded under a heavy poncho, shone a flashlight in the clouded-over afternoon.

A shout was muffled as it carried on the wind.

Was that for me? I stumbled ever closer, warning myself not to be too hopeful or let my guard down.

"Claire!"

"Levi?" I gasped out.

It was him. The closer I got to him, the more clearly his sharp features, long hair, and tall figure focused.

I was close enough to see his worry as he yelled.

"Here!" I shouted with my whole being.

His gaze shot straight to mine. Several yards and swirling snow, and he found me instantly.

Levi had come for me. The relief was so all-consuming and instant that my knees almost gave out.

I couldn't help myself. I started bawling.

I totally would have been okay on my own, but now, I didn't have to be.

The same relief coursing through my body just moments ago was written all over him as he ran my way. I wanted to shout to him to go slow and be careful, but all I could do was stumble in his direction, arms reaching like an unsteady toddler.

My teeth chattered, my body shivering so hard I almost couldn't talk. "H-hi," I said and threw myself against him.

He made an *oomph* of surprise as he absorbed my impact.

I held on like I had any right to. I wrapped myself up in him, his body heat infusing my bones with warmth I thought I'd never feel again. His scent, like home, overtook the wet, earthy smell of the world around us, a balm to my panic. I sank into his strength, protecting and comforting. His arms banded tight around me; my ear pressed against his chest, listening to the solid and erratic beat of his heart. His large hand cradled my head, pressing me into him like he was also seeking comfort in the knowledge that I was okay and safe. His fingers stroked my soaked hair, soothing even as they snagged.

And it all felt so right.

CHAPTER 13

Levi

Every single ounce of fear gripping me melted away as her arms squeezed me tight around my core. Her arms shook as she held me with all her might.

Every possible worst-case scenario that had played rapid-fire through my brain for the past hour—poof. Gone.

When her text sharing her location came through, my blood went icy. There was no way she'd be back before the storm, and my response went undelivered.

As I sprinted up that trail, a ferocious fear propelled my feet. Nothing could happen to her. Protect her at all costs.

The moment I heard her pathetic shout in the distance and saw her blurry form up the trail, it was like I returned to my body all at once. I slammed into myself so hard I thought I might stumble. I had been all action, and now she was here. All the driving panic fell out of my body, leaving me floaty with adrenaline.

She limped pathetically toward me, and I saw a flash of red running down her shin. "Stop moving," I shouted toward her, but she must not have heard because she kept coming at me.

I braced myself just as she ran into me. A tremendous force for such a little thing. As her soaking arms wrapped around me, she sobbed out an anguished relief that had my chest almost collapsing. Her entire body shivered so hard, her lips blue and cheeks alarmingly pale. Her light hiking gear had done nothing against this early winter storm, pelting us mercilessly.

She was safe and in my arms, and my lungs took in air for the first time in hours. My sanity returned to me, and I held her back. Nothing else mattered. The previous boundaries were lost in the quickly falling snow.

"H-hi." She looked up at me like I was the key to her salvation, and I cursed myself that she had even had to go this far without me.

I smoothed a hand over her freezing cheeks, pushing back rain-soaked hair. I shrugged out of my heavy wool-lined coat and wrapped her tight into it. She'd need to get out of these soaking clothes as soon as possible, but for now, this would at least help her from getting any colder.

Her eyes rolled back as she sank into the oversized coat, and she sighed loudly in pleasure.

I flared my nostrils and looped my arm around her waist to carry some of the load.

"Come on. My truck isn't far."

"Th-that's great news," she stuttered. "I wasn't s-sure how much more—" She cut herself off when her voice got high and tight.

"You're okay." I ground my jaw and kept her steady.

The rain lessened, but only because it was transforming into heavy, fat flakes of snow. The sounds around us shifted from a cacophony to an almost eerie quiet. We were going too slow. She was favoring her leg too much.

She shivered so hard and kept mumbling over and over. "I'm not stupid. It was just bad luck. I swear I'm not stupid."

I couldn't take it for another second. I stopped abruptly and turned to face her. She lifted her chin to meet my gaze. Fat flakes fell on her face; her eyes were red and full of tears. "I feel so stupid," she admitted, and her face crumpled. "I hate this feeling."

I wanted to hold her, to comfort her. She was worrying about the wrong thing. We didn't have time for this.

I cupped her chin, using my thumb to brush away a fresh snowflake. I met her gaze with my own, unwavering with determination. "Never, not even for a second, did I think you were stupid. Mother Nature gives no shits, is all. You did everything right."

Her bottom lip trembled, and she nodded. After another beat, she said, "Th-thank you."

"Can I carry you?" I asked.

"I don't think—Okay, then." I lifted her in the fireman carry I learned when Pace made me take that local Search and Rescue course. I could kiss the guy for pushing me to do it as I cataloged all the things I would do to help Claire. Not that I wouldn't still be a grumpy shit about it.

Snow blasted her face, and I used my hand to gently tuck her head toward the heat of my neck. I hissed when her icy nose sat on my pulse point. Once in my arms, I felt a release of her tension.

We moved much quicker now, and I hardly noticed her. Except the tremors. I must have been mumbling assurances because she shifted her arms tighter around my neck at one point and whispered against my skin, "I'm okay, really. Just so glad you're here."

My feet flew.

Ripley assaulted Claire the moment I set her in the cab of the truck. "Get back, girl. Give the lady some room. She doesn't need you taking any of her body heat." Ripley was too busy twirling and shivering to listen. I'd left her in there with the heat going and was so glad that it was noticeably warm.

"She's o-okay." Claire sighed again, moving her hands to the vents.

"No. Keep the coat closed and your hands tucked. We need to keep your core and head warm." I blocked most of the snow from blowing in on her. It clung to my back, soaking through my extra flannel.

"Levi, it's not hypothermia. I just g-got a little wet."

I reached across her, and she leaned back with a soft gasp when I glared, face closer to hers.

"Okay, a little s-soaking." She chuckled nervously.

I came back forward with two more blankets; one, I wrapped tightly around her lower half and the other around her soaking head to create a hood. "We'll be home soon, but this is a good start."

"So fussy," she said and leaned her head back, eyes closing. Ripley burrowed her way into the mass on her lap and disappeared. I slammed the door and ran around to my side. My hands shook so hard that I missed the handle the first time and had to try again.

I took a steadying breath before I got in.

We drove in silence, an occasional tremor in my periphery making me speed up.

"How did you come to own a designer dog?" she asked out of nowhere.

I had a white-knuckle grip on the steering wheel, focusing on the road, so it took me a second for her words to sink in. I raised an eyebrow at Ripley, who was nothing but vibrations under the blankets. "I wouldn't say she's built for much," I said.

"That's where you're wrong. Italian greyhounds are worth a pretty penny. Bred for speed. Why do you have her all the way up here?"

Again, I looked at Ripley skeptically.

"A little less than a year ago, I found her near a dumpster behind Ruth's B and B. She was in a fight with a raccoon and holding herself against the snarling little jerk. Reminded me of the movie *Alien*."

She clicked her tongue. "Poor thing. Someone abandoned

her?" Claire said with the same shock I'd first shared.

"Yeah," I grunted.

I remembered the anger when I found Ripley. It was the first emotion to pierce through the haze of my depression. She was dirty and terrified. Nobody claimed her. Nobody posted about losing her. Nobody had even chipped her. Knowing some rich prick paid all that money just to tire of her when they were done brought all that rage back up.

I reached my hand under the blanket to scratch Ripley's head. Just thinking about her hurting or hungry made me need to pet her. I accidentally grazed Claire's thigh and quickly pulled my hand back like I had ... well, like I'd groped the thigh of my tenant.

"Sorry, I was—"

"No. I know. It's okay," she insisted.

She cleared her throat. I focused on the road.

We sat in awkward silence for the rest of the drive.

The snow was already sticking to the gravel road back to the house. This storm was just ramping up. We were back in front of the cabin in no time. I pulled open her door and carried both the ladies out.

"I'm going to get used to this," she teased.

I almost said, "Good, you should," but kept my mouth clamped tight. "Door locked?" I asked as we climbed the short steps.

"I don't think so."

I kicked the door open without meaning to and brought her straight to the wood-burning stove. Thankfully, plenty of hot embers were still glowing. I set her down and grabbed wood to stack until the flames caught. Ripley jumped free to wiggle her way into her favorite spot at the end of the bed.

With my back to her, focused on my task, I said, "Take off those clothes, quick."

She cleared her throat, but I heard the soft fall of the blankets and the louder thump of my coat hitting the floor. I clenched my jaw and went to the small bureau beside the bed.

"I'm just grabbing some warm clothes," I explained.

"Not that—"

I quickly shut the drawer filled with bras and panties, ignoring the sweet, clean scent that drifted up. I scored big on the next one, grabbing long, fuzzy socks, a pair of heavy cotton sweats, and a buttery-soft but warm-looking sweater. I was sure she'd want undergarments, but this would have to be good enough for now.

She sucked in a sharp, pained breath behind me, and I spun without meaning to at the sound of her distress. She was in the process of bending at the waist to roll down her hiking pants. Her skin was alabaster white and pebbled with goose bumps. My eyes swept over her, cataloging for injuries, keeping my gaze cool and perfunctory, never landing on one place for too long. She was still in her panties, and no matter how hard I tried to detach from the scene before me, I wouldn't be able to forget the sight of those bare thighs and the perfectly round curve of her ass anytime soon.

"Do you need—" I stepped toward her, and she stilled, eyes

wide as she noticed I'd turned back. I averted my gaze and pointed at her leg. "You're bleeding."

"I slipped and cut my knee. Nothing bad, just need to clean it." She straightened and watched me approach. A drenched undershirt clung to her soaking skin, revealing a black sports bra. Her nipples were hard, but all I could focus on was how pale she looked. How her lips were still not the right shade of pink. She needed to warm up. She needed to get these clothes off.

"I'm just shivering so much I'm struggling…" Her hands fumbled as she tried again to take off her pants.

I closed the remaining distance. "I'm just going to help you. I'm—I won't look," I explained, focused pointedly on the wall behind her.

She stiffened in my periphery.

"Is that okay?" I asked.

"Yeah—" She hesitated, then added another, "Yeah. Thanks."

With jaw clenched and focus narrowed in on her bleeding knee, I knelt before her. I carefully tugged her pants the rest of the way off her hurt leg.

"Whoa." She steadied herself with a hand on my shoulder as she switched feet to help me help her. I was kneeling between her legs, and it took all my focus not to look up and see what her face was doing at that moment. I especially wouldn't pay attention to the shape of her calf, her creamy thighs, or the cute arch of her foot as it balanced on me. Kneeling before her like this, caring for her, it was clouding my mind.

I made the mistake of looking up to find her studying me,

cheeks slightly pink, breathing shallow, and her brown eyes locked on me in this position of supplication.

I clenched my jaw, promising to punch myself if I got the slightest bit aroused right now.

But the room had grown stiflingly warm. Her skin under mine was soft despite the cold.

She reached down and pushed back a lock of soaked hair that was in my eyes. "You're all wet too," she whispered.

Her words seared down my spine, and I stilled my hands. I forced a hard swallow. After a beat, she let out an awkward huff of a laugh. "That sounded—"

I looked up at her and forced myself to hold her gaze. "Is this going to be another 'wood' situation?" I asked lightly despite the heat burning in me, desperate to break the tension.

She bit her bottom lip and shook her head innocently. The dark look in her eyes, though—

She stepped out of the other side, and I grabbed the pants and the soaking socks, tossing them with a loud splat in the direction of the dryer.

Head tucked, I stood and went behind her. "Arms up." My voice rolled out deep and demanding.

She did as I instructed.

Slowly and carefully, in case she was hurt anywhere else, I lifted the hem of her shirt over her body. Chilled skin brushed against my knuckles. More goose bumps spread over her neck and shoulders. If I wrapped her in my arms, my hot skin would burn against her cold by contrast. I would warm her up so fast.

I wasn't sure why I was naked in that fake scenario that flashed through my brain.

I added the shirt to the pile.

"Can you get your, uh—"

"I can get my bra—"

We both spoke at the same time, and she laughed awkwardly. Thank God for small miracles.

Her arms wrapped behind her to undo the heavy snaps, and I spun to look away. I stacked the fresh set of clothes near the fire. I grabbed the wet pile and carried them to the laundry closet, taking my time and focusing on the task of starting the washer. Still without looking in her direction, I made my way to the kitchenette and turned on the electric kettle.

"I'm coming back," I announced as I made my way to the bedroom/living room area with her hot cup of tea a few minutes later.

"'Kay. I'm dressed."

Her hair was down, and she'd been running her fingers through it, leaning toward the fire as I stepped into the space. She snapped up, disappearing under her long sleeves.

"Feeling warmer?" I asked.

"Much. Thanks for, uh, helping me get out of those. And for *finding* me," she said, seemingly exacerbated with herself for remembering everything.

The sweater I chose for her was too large, and the elegant slope of her shoulder was on display as she reached for the tea. I wanted to pull it up and insist she move to sit directly in front of the fire. But the color was high on her cheeks, and she smiled softly at me, just a little dimple showing. I averted my gaze so as not to be drawn in by those dimples when I noticed her breasts were easily defined through the soft fabric of the sweater I chose.

There was nowhere safe to look at her. She was too beautiful. Even the slightest glimpse and I risked a deadly amount of exposure to her beauty.

"Can I look at your leg?" I asked.

When she nodded, I rolled over the desk chair to make sure she'd still be in the direct warmth of the stove and gestured for her to sit. She set the tea down at her side after taking a satisfied sip. "Mmm, thank you."

She perched her foot on my lap, and I knelt before her for the second time in a few minutes. She bent to pull up the pant leg of her sweatpants. My willpower to keep my gaze focused was a sand dune pulverized by crashing waves.

I held her calf in my hands, comforted to find the skin as warm as my own. My forefinger brushed the back of her knee, and she sucked in a breath.

"Sorry. Ticklish." Her color had really returned now.

Heat rushed through me at her reactive sensitivity. I longed to run my hand farther up her thigh and see what happened.

I growled at myself to focus.

The gash on her knee was dirty but shallow. It was still bleeding slightly as her body warmed.

"Did you just growl?"

"I don't like that you're hurt," I said smoothly.

"Ah. Well, me neither. But like I said, it's not so bad. Mostly, I just feel—"

I narrowed my eyes at her in a warning. I wasn't going to hear any more of this talk about stupidity, and she took my warning for what it was. She sucked in her lips and reached again for her tea.

I cleared my throat. "I have a first-aid kit around here. Let me see."

I stood quickly, and my head went fuzzy for a second as I spun in a circle, looking for it. It wasn't in any of the usual places. I dug out my keys and went to the locked room, determined to finish helping her and get the hell out of there before I did anything stupid. Anything else.

I found the kit in the locked room and was halfway out when I realized what I had done. What was happening. Where I *was*.

I'd come in the house. Not only that, but I'd also been so focused on helping Claire that I went into the locked room before it even registered.

The truth of it rocked into me and took away my breath.

Claire

What the hell was happening?

My damp hair felt suffocating as I hauled it up off my neck and tugged this sweater away from my body to let some air in. The room was too hot. Ten minutes ago, I never thought I would know warmth again, but with Levi kneeling before me, those intensely handsome features twisted with focus the heat, it grew. And grew and grew.

As Levi left to explore for the first-aid kit, I slumped back, covering my face with mortification. Was it written all over my features what his touch was doing to me? It was just the brush of death that made my hormones or adrenaline or whatever take over.

I bit my lip, finding it swollen from the action, and looked at the ceiling when I remembered how my insides melted when he brushed the back of my knee. I didn't even know I was sensitive in that spot. Kevin certainly never spent any time gently caressing my legs with focused tenderness to find out. Yet one graze of Levi's finger and I gasped out, my insides clenching. Hopefully, he bought the ticklish excuse.

God, what was wrong with me? A man saves my life, and suddenly, his touches make my brain misfire. If my brain was even involved at this point.

Maybe he should just leave. Perhaps he was just too much for the small space, *my* space. This house ain't big enough for us both.

Should I kick him out?

But then ... I was enjoying this pampering, this being taken care of. I hadn't even realized I was missing it until I experienced it. To be the focus of someone's attention and worry that wasn't related to me by blood was nice. It felt like security.

All at once, a cold dread filled me.

This wasn't security. I didn't know what this was and didn't want to look at it too closely. I had just promised him I would stick to the rules, and I went and broke one on the same day.

I had to get him out of here and get back to work.

But when he returned from the extra room, I could already tell that my rushing him out wouldn't be necessary. His face had done that thing. He went slack and pale like the first night. I knew it as sure as anything he was about to leave. His focus was somewhere else. At least I was fairly certain his shift in mood wasn't about me anymore. Hopefully.

It was this place. It was why he tried so hard not to rent it out. How he hated being inside.

He set down the first-aid kit.

"I'm going to go," he said, not meeting my gaze.

I bit my cheek to keep from asking what was wrong, to stop from prying.

Whatever was going on with him wasn't my business. This wasn't my life or world. I was passing through, and I'd already done enough damage.

"Okay," I said softly.

He stood, the color still gone from his face. He wasn't looking at me but seemed careful not to look around.

"Thank you," I said again.

"You would have been fine," he said, almost to the door.

"Probably," I admitted. "But I appreciate you all the same."

He nodded.

As his hand was on the door, he stopped moving, his back to me.

"I'm glad I could help," he said. His stance had a set intensity like he battled to say more.

"Are you okay?" I meant, in general, from the rain and cold and the adrenaline rush of saving someone.

He didn't take it that way. He thought I meant the shift in his mood. He shook his head. "It's—It's hard for me to be here. In this house."

"Oh." I was taken aback by his sudden honesty. "I'm sorry."

"My mother lived here. This was her place. She was very ill at the end, and—" He shook his head, back still facing me. "It's hard for me to be here," he repeated.

His *mother*. He was grieving his mother. The missing piece explaining his mercurial temperaments slid into place. My heart stuttered in sympathy. I lost my mother over ten years ago, and I still ached for her every day.

"I just wanted you to know. This house, there's a lot of memories here." It was like he wanted to say more and make me understand something. His sadness was a heavy storm that blocked out whatever light had been trying to break through. How long had he been grieving? How was he handling his loss?

"That's understandable," I said.

"I'm sorry. I have to go."

"Okay," I repeated.

I clenched my fists to keep from getting up and reaching for him.

Instead, I focused on cleaning my wound and putting on the bandage. He snuck out so quietly that only the blast of cold air signaled his leaving.

It was silent after he was gone, except for the sloshing water of the washer and the crackle of the fire.

After several minutes of silence and processing what happened, I noticed the door to the mystery room was ajar. The room he'd normally left locked and explicitly told me to leave alone.

I could be bigger than my curiosity to learn more about this enigma of a man. I could wait for him to reveal more parts of himself to me. I wished I wasn't so drawn to him. I wished that I could leave him be and respect his need for privacy without wanting to peel back his layers.

I had to respect his rules.

Right?

CHAPTER 14

Claire

I was a terrible, terrible person.

I hesitated at the entrance to the room that had once been locked. The room that had piqued my interest since first arriving. It was still dark inside, but enough light from the kitchen cast into the space to reveal several stacked boxes, folded-up medical equipment, and what could have been a sink in the far corner. There were no windows in this room. It was too small to be a bedroom but too big for a little house's closet.

The air held a musty smell of disuse, with a lingering smell of disinfectant and a hint of something softer, like fabric softener or perfume.

My thumb brushed absentmindedly along my lips as I stared into the room. I warred with myself, my insides twisting with guilt but also with drive. What was this thing that pushed me so hard for truths and answers? Why couldn't I let things lie? This curse afflicted me even worse if the truths were held from me. There was this primeval need in me to get to the bottom of everything and know everything, no matter the cost to those around me.

This had to stop.

I pictured Levi's face when he talked about his art. I saw his features twisted with concern as he found me on the trail. I remembered the gentleness of his fingers as he removed my clothing and tended to my leg.

He was a *good* man. He was suffering. He was alone.

And I knew a little bit about loneliness.

"Poor man," I whispered, my head dropping to the doorframe.

I couldn't do it. As much as I was desperate to explore the hidden stories of his past, to learn more about the woman who used to live here, I couldn't. The hurt was too raw in his features. Anything I could learn needed to come from him in his own time.

I pulled the door shut. It was locked again when I turned the handle to check.

"This is for the best," I told myself in the same tone a mother might tell her child as she moved the cookies to a higher shelf.

I paced the room, testing my leg, and it felt fine. The heavy clouds outside blocked out much of the light, and when I went to the window, enough snow had fallen to blanket the surrounding area. It was beautiful but wild and intimidating.

"Shoot!" I remembered too late that my dad was waiting to

hear back from me. It had been so many hours he was probably in a state of panic.

I whined and stomped my foot as I watched the falling fat flakes stack outside.

I slid my boots back on and winced when I discovered a blister. Tugging on my heaviest parka and winter hat, I grabbed my phone and took a bracing breath.

As carefully as possible, I made my way up to the main house. I was so not ready to see Levi again.

His footprints had already disappeared from only a few minutes ago in the fast-falling snow. The lights illuminated his cabin like a beacon, but there were no signs of him through any of the windows facing this way. Hopefully, he wouldn't see me creeping up toward his house. Most likely, he was washing away today's adventures.

Not that anybody was thinking about him in the shower.

When I reached the Wi-Fi zone, I sent a series of rapid-fire texts at the same time as several worried ones arrived.

"Dad, I'm back at the cabin. The weather is getting crazy. I might not be able to go to the main house for a couple of days. But I am totally fine. Love you."

We messaged for a few more minutes as the snow came down in fat flakes that blurred my vision and had me wiping the screen continuously. I bounced on my feet to keep warm, and when my exposed fingers started to go numb, I ended the conversation. The snow fell so thick I could hardly see my cabin anymore. I glanced back one more time to Levi's place.

I made my way carefully back to my place and went straight back to warming my hands in front of the fire.

That was it. No more curiosity, no more distractions. Just finish the article and remember why the work I did mattered.

Levi

"Now, what the hell is she doing?" I glared out the upstairs bathroom window, wiping away the condensation from my scalding shower to see better.

Ripley whined from her bathroom burrow of blankets. Yes, she had a blanket burrow for each room. She was truly living a charmed, albeit codependent, life.

Claire trudged toward the Big Cabin, at least wearing a heavy coat and hat this time.

I glanced down at where I held a towel around my waist and nothing more. I swallowed as a chill went over my body.

My heart hammered, but instead of the panic that visitors usually caused me, a small thrill shot down my spine. I wouldn't have time to get dressed to get her out of the cold…

I shook my head.

What was wrong with me? I just left her because I couldn't be around her without wanting to bare bits of my soul I kept locked safely away. This had to stop.

I dropped my head to the cold glass and took a steadying breath.

Claire stopped in her pursuit, and my frown grew.

She pulled out her phone and started to rapidly text.

"No gloves," I grumbled.

The snow fell so hard now the black of her coat and the glow of her screen were hardly visible.

"I'm two seconds from opening this window and yelling at her."

The snow collected on her hat, hair, and shoulders. She was like a holiday card, so pretty even in the snow.

"I just got her out of the cold. Does she have a death wish?"

I had to wipe the glass again to keep watching her. I would just make sure she got back to her place okay.

"She's probably checking in with her dad. She was the one who assured me when she agreed to my terms that not having internet wouldn't be a problem, but here we are again."

Ripley whined softly.

"For those keeping track at home, she's already broken about half the rules of my listing." I huffed loudly.

Ripley sighed and burrowed further under the blankets, tired of my ranting, it seemed.

"Okay. She's going back. Ridiculous woman."

I got dressed, grumbling the whole time to myself about rules that nobody else managed to follow. "The rules are there for a reason. Why even have rules?"

I tugged on my boots, heaviest coat, gloves, and hat. "Things should be done a certain way, and I'm the only person who cares."

In the extra closet, I found the white cylindrical device I hadn't needed in a few years. With my mallet and the stake I used last time, I made my way to the halfway point between our houses.

The rain from earlier caused a sheet of ice under the fresh powder, the most treacherous of conditions. I slipped in my efforts and almost fell on my ass twice. But soon enough, I'd set up the weatherproof Wi-Fi extender, and the flashing lights indicated it worked.

I trudged down to her house, in the now dark, to slide the pre-written note under the door explaining how to connect to the internet. I didn't wait to make sure she saw the note. I did my part. I certainly wasn't going to do it for her.

Just show her how to do it.

I hesitated just outside her door for only a fraction of a moment. But long enough for that voice deep down inside to find an excuse to knock. I could help her with the Wi-Fi. I could go back in and—

No.

That was enough.

I barely made it back to the main house without injury. I stomped the snow off my boots and laid out all my outerwear by the fire to dry. Even with that short excursion, I was soaked through to the bone.

"For the second time today, thanks to that ridiculous woman."

Ripley had moved to her living room den and had long stopped acknowledging my ranting.

"Now she has no reason to go out in the snow anymore." I crossed my arms, legs spread to warm by the fire. "And good. She has no reason to come up here, either. No more visits or chats."

I grunted. "Good."

I slumped back into a chair. The flames of the fire danced, mesmerizing me for hours. I was alone, which was just how I wanted it.

I didn't think about Claire's dimples when she smiled her huge grin. Or how her eyes moved and widened as she listened intently to me. Or the flashes of Claire's smooth skin as she slid down her pants.

I groaned and dropped my head to my hands, scrubbing them through my hair.

I was so fucked.

CHAPTER 15

Levi

The only good thing about the early winter storm was the built-in excuse not to interact with Claire at all. She would have enough food and wood to last weeks if needed. The snow continued through the night, and we woke up to almost a foot and a half. I had to put Ripley in booties and a puffy vest before she even deemed it enough to sniff the air outside the door. Then I had to carve out a few cubic feet in the deep snow for Princess Feather Butt to use the facilities.

Things were settled with Claire. There would be no surprise visits to use the phone. She had her own internet now. And if she tried to go out and hike in this weather, well, there was only so much a man could do.

This was all good. Freedom from her was exactly what I

wanted.

I leaned against the counter the next morning, waiting for my coffee and mentally planning what I could get done in this weather.

My phone vibrated on the counter, and I glared at it. Claire sent a message.

I'd forgotten that she had my number from the listing, and we'd messaged for instructions all those days ago. It hardly seemed like we were the same people. It vibrated two more times before I sighed and finally picked it up to read her messages.

"Thanks for the internet!! You're a lifesaver!"

"Now I won't bother you anymore, I swear."

"I will finish this article any day now!"

She had a problem with using too many exclamation points.

"Ridiculous woman," I muttered, but when I looked up, I found half my face quirked in a smile in the reflection of the microwave. I fixed that instantly.

I didn't respond.

For the next couple of days, she was true to her promise and was locked away and silent. I went out to work on my new piece, waiting for it to tell me what it needed, and got back into the groove of life. It was almost like I'd never met Claire at all.

After that initial storm, Colorado did its thing, and the sun came back out the following day. Within twenty-four hours, most of the snow had melted except for the shadowy areas that never got direct sunlight. I went around the property to check for felled branches or any other issues caused by the heavy snow.

The first time I had to pass the guesthouse, Claire was hunched over her computer typing. The next time, she was leaning all the way back in the chair, arms flung out to the side, pen in her mouth as she stared up at the ceiling. The last time I passed, she was hunched again and typing furiously, the pen now in her hair and her features creased in focus.

Not that I was checking on her.

When I got back to the house, I had another text from her. I grunted as I picked up to read.

"Tell me that was you that just walked past my window."

Before I could even get my thumbs ready to respond, two more messages came through rapid fire.

"Follow-up question: do you have a gun?"

"Second follow-up question: can you teach me to use a gun?"

I scrubbed at my chin. My face on the reflection of the screen was doing that thing again. I scowled to fix it back into place.

"I was checking the property for damage," I typed.

"Yeesh. Warn a lady next time."

"It's my land."

"I think you like scaring me."

"Did you turn in your story?" I asked.

She didn't respond.

A couple of days later, I was finishing up in the garage when I felt my phone buzzing with another message. A thrill went through me when I saw her name on my screen before I could catch myself. At least with text, I didn't have to see her smile. This was slightly better.

"There is an insanely loud bird outside my window."

"It's black but not a crow. I think it's possessed."

"It will not SHUT. UP."

Once again, her texts came rapid fire instead of as one cohesive thought. She blurted whatever came to mind.

"Constant interruptions must be so annoying," I typed back, wondering if the dry tone came across. Would she pick up on my teasing or think I was just being a jackass like so many people often did?

I watched the little dots, indicating her reply.

"Just so you know, when you admit that I'm annoying you, it only makes me want to do it more. I WILL CHARM YOU YET, SIR."

I moaned out loud. Little did she know...

"Please stop yelling." I typed. "Those birds are grackles. Their calls can get annoying."

This time, I didn't bother hiding my smile. My mother often complained about the same thing.

It sounds like an old grinding, rusty gate all the time.

"Unrelated to the gun thing, do we know if grackles are a protected species?" More texts followed instantly.

"I'm just kidding."

"Mostly."

I chuckled loudly. I couldn't help it. At least nobody was here to see me.

"You don't count," I said when Ripley raised a hairy brow at me.

"I think you're just avoiding your work," I typed to Claire.

"I'll have you know I turned in my story."

My heart stuttered. She was done? Did that mean she was leaving? She signed for two months. She paid for those two months. She was responsible for fulfilling her end of the deal. My jaw ground together. If she thought she could get out of that contract—

"I'm boooored," she wrote.

"I never thought I'd say this, but I miss peopling."

"Think the road to town is okay? I think I need to interact with a human before my reflection starts talking back to me."

"Do you always text in threes?" I messaged instead of answering her questions.

I couldn't answer. I didn't want her going into town alone and couldn't explain why. An offer was on the tip of my tongue. A much more unbelievable and awful idea gained momentum and moved through my mind. It was now mid-October, and Cozy Creek did autumn up in a big way. The town drummed up tourism outside of the ski season, and that meant *all* the fall things: hay rides, carnivals with caramel apples and kettle corn, costume contests with cute kids, and a pet parade with even cuter animals. If it was fall-themed in any way, Cozy Creek did it.

And I was avoiding it at all costs. So then, why was my thumb twitching to text her all about what the town had to offer? Why bother planting the seed?

There was a knock on the door. I jumped so hard, my phone flew in the air, but I fumbled to catch it in time before it crashed to the ground.

I looked around the room in panic, verifying that nothing incriminating was lying around. I scoffed at myself. It wasn't like my thoughts of Claire had jumped out of my brain and lay strewn around the room like dirty boxers. It was probably just Pace. Regardless of sending texts, the man felt obliged to drive up every so often, especially after a storm under the ruse of some flimsy excuse. Last time, he said he missed Ripley and wanted to make sure she wasn't missing him too much. I pretended to go along with it, secretly grateful that anybody was left that cared enough to check in after I'd been so shitty the past few years.

Nevertheless, I glanced at myself in the mirror and ensured I was properly dressed in jeans and a flannel. I ran a hand over my face and smelled my breath in my palm before finally opening the door.

It was her. She flashed a large smile, dimples popping as my blood started pumping. The sun shone brightly today and haloed her in light.

"Hi," she said.

I opened my mouth, then closed it and swallowed. She was in simple jeans and another Henley, this one a light lavender that made her expressive brown eyes pop even more. Her long hair was down in waves that went past her shoulders, looking soft enough to sleep on. I held her gaze, fighting to keep from memorizing her figure.

"I just thought this would be easier than texting. You don't seem like a big texter," she said.

She was right about that, but seeing her after managing almost four days without direct contact well and truly assured me that I was crushing on this woman. And hard.

Her smile did something to my brain.

I had *missed* her.

Her gaze flicked behind me. "Sorry to just drop in, though. I know 'the rules.'" She did air quotes as she said the last bit. It occurred to me that she texted exactly as she spoke. All the thoughts, none of the filter. It didn't bother me, though. I appreciated her earnestness. Better than game-playing or subtle manipulation tactics. "I was just worried about Ripley. You know. Maybe she wanted to go for a *W-A-L-K*," she whispered as she spelled.

I used the opportunity to look for Ripley to hide the smile, trying to break through.

A flimsy excuse if I ever heard one.

I hadn't spoken a single word yet. Speak, man!

"She's not a walker. More of a couch potato," I said.

Well, that wasn't the warm introduction I meant for. I could have gone with "I've liked texting with you. Even if it is mostly one-sided." Or how about, "How are you? If you're done with the story, then what?" Or maybe even, "I like working and knowing you're just down the hill. I can't stop thinking about you ..."

But my short rebuff of her offer was great too.

I should take her into town. It wasn't that hard. People did things with people all the time. That was how this living thing worked.

"Ha. Okay. That's true. It is pretty cold still." She rocked back on her heels and thumbed back to the cabin. "Okay, well. I'll let you get back to it."

Any second now, the words would come out of my mouth.

Oh, for crying out loud, just ask her out.

I pointedly ignored the exacerbated voice of my mom in my head.

"Actually—" I said.

"Yes?" she said, instantly stepping closer, eyes bright with hope as they looked up at me.

I cleared my throat, heat burning the back of my neck. "If you're bored, I-I—uh—"

We both stepped closer at the same time when my voice came out much quieter than I meant. It was like it took too much emotional energy for me to form words at a normal, socially acceptable volume when I was nervous like this.

Her gaze flicked to my mouth, most likely to understand what I was saying. "I am bored. Dreadfully, incurably bored," she said.

Her eyelids grew heavy; her mouth parted as her head tilted back to wait for my response. My whole body was too hot, my skin too tight. Why had she said "bored" like that? Why did it feel like she wasn't talking about boredom at all?

I lowered my head a fraction of an inch. Her cheeks were so full of color, her lips softly parted and pillowy. Those dimples were barely visible. She smelled freshly showered, warm, and floral. A hint of toothpaste. If I kissed her lips, she would taste amazing. I wanted to kiss her so bad.

At that moment, her eyes widened at the sound of tires crunching up the drive. Claire stepped back, putting space between us as she tucked her hair behind her ear. I stepped back too, my heart hammering against my chest.

We'd been standing so close, breathing the same air. Had she wanted—? Was I about to—?

My brain was a maelstrom of hypotheses as Pace parked his truck. Claire looked at me but furrowed her brow at my unreadable features.

Pace skipped up the steps, and his eyes flickered with glee when he registered Claire. For some absurd reason, he wore his firefighter uniform pants and suspenders under a light jacket and baseball cap.

He scooped off his hat and ran his hand through his hair. The gesture was one well and truly rehearsed. "Well, hello." He extended a hand toward her. "I'm Pace Leigh. This goober's best friend."

Claire's dimples came back out as she shook his waiting hand. Her gaze flicked to his pants and suspenders peeking from under the coat. I wanted to pull them all the way out just to snap them back and whack his nipples.

"Hi. I'm Claire. I'm renting the cabin." A small blush crept along Claire's collarbone.

"Well, how about that? You are the illustrious C.L. Wells?"

"Oh." She nodded, tucking her hair behind her ear again. "Yes. That's me."

"I read your piece about the oil fracking in Texas. Fascinating." Pace had turned to her, his shoulder to me, almost his whole back.

Why had he looked up Claire? What was he trying to prove? The suck-up. I'd also looked her up and read everything she ever published, but you didn't see me gloating. With every word of their exchange, a low, simmering tension started to bubble, pushing impatience closer to the surface, close to overflowing. Pace had his charm turned up to eleven.

This had to end now. If she fell victim to his personality, I had no hope.

Hope for what? I wasn't ready to process that yet. I needed to get him out of here. I'd lost most of my friends at this point. Honestly, what was one more?

CHAPTER 16

Claire

This was an interesting turn of events. Caught between two incredibly handsome men, what was a woman to do?

I wasn't sure what urged my feet up to Levi's place. I was bored now that I'd sent off the article. Maybe bored wasn't the right word ... I was itching for something. Restless with pent-up energy. Normally, I had my next project lined up, or at least a new fixation, to catch my attention. But being up here had me secluded, and aside from the room I was most assuredly not going to break into, I didn't have anything currently piquing my interest.

Except Levi.

When he opened the door in his jeans and flannel, I was reminded just how handsome he was. It wasn't boredom that drew me to him ... it was something far more primal.

When his gaze lingered on my lips, my body grew heavy with his direct focus. My lips tingled with the need to feel his pressed against them.

Then his friend had arrived. Thankfully?

Pace's dark blond hair had hints of red when the sun hit it and looked curly but was cropped close when he pulled off his cap. He rocked a mustache that seemed to be swinging back in trend that few people could pull off. He was one of the lucky ones. If the suspenders were any indication, his job as a firefighter made him even more filled out than Levi. Not that it was a competition. They were both good-looking men but in different fonts. And actually, Pace was almost too handsome, the sort of attractive that everybody was aware of, including himself. The sort of handsome that made me leery.

Levi had an attractiveness that grew with time. Every time I looked at him, I found a new striking feature to study, like the hard bump on the bridge of his nose before it sloped down or the gentle strength of his long sculptor fingers. He was far more interesting and distinguished.

I could only imagine what the ladies of Cozy Creek thought when these two went out on the town. Although it was hard to picture Levi going out to peruse for women. In fact, I didn't care to think about that at all.

I realized I'd been lost in my thoughts of women throwing themselves at the sensitive and caring artist who was hosting me when Pace cleared his throat. I think he had asked me a question, but my gaze looked like it was locked on his shoulders. A blush burned my cheeks, and when I flicked a look at Levi, his eyes narrowed, and he crossed his arms.

"I'm sorry, my mind wandered. It does that." I waved my hand through the air.

Pace chuckled in a perfectly handsome way that almost felt rehearsed. "I'm used to that with this one." He clapped Levi on his shoulder. Shoulders that tensed closer to his ears. "I was just telling Levi that tonight is the great pumpkin hunt. I was heading down there to help now. You can get your pumpkin to carve for the season and the winner of the largest pumpkin is announced."

"Fun!" I clapped excitedly.

"Plenty of seasonal gourds competing for the big prize," Pace said.

"And who doesn't love a massive gourd?" I said without missing a beat.

Pace froze, and his gaze flicked between the two of us. I bit the inside of my cheek.

Levi sighed. "Ignore her. She's got the humor of a teenage boy."

Pace let out a cackle, far more authentic than his practiced laugh had been. "Wouldn't you know, so do I? So what do you say, Miss Claire Wells? Would you like to leave Recluse Ranch and make a night of it?"

I wasn't notorious for reading subtext, but I got the impression that Pace was laying it on a little thick, even for the natural charmer he seemed to be. This was Colorado, not the South, yet any moment, I expected him to start to call me ma'am in a thick Southern accent and wink before mounting a horse that appeared out of nowhere.

I snorted out loud at the visual and quickly covered my mouth. "Sorry," I mumbled.

To my surprise, instead of being hurt by laughing in his face, Pace just shrugged his shoulders and laughed it off. "Never hurts to ask."

"I better get back to—" I started to make an excuse that would bring me back to my fortress of solitude.

"Let's go," Levi said loudly.

Pace's expression surely matched my own, eyebrows high, mouth forming an *O* of surprise.

Levi cleared his throat. "To town. The three of us, I mean. We've been cooped up because of the snow. It'll be good to walk around a little."

"For the love of gourds," I said, unable to hide my giant smile.

Levi's gaze snagged on me; it bounced from my neck and chin and lips, before returning back to my eyes, softening some of his hard edges as it flitted around my face.

Pace shifted, creaking a board on the deck. Levi and I blinked, unlocking our gazes, and looked at him. "All right, sounds like a plan." Pace clapped his hands together once.

"I really need to get out of the cabin for a bit." I started talking because the way Levi looked at me was doing something to me again. He had that same lovely, gooey look in his eyes. "I'm as introverted as it gets, but I've begun to have whole conversations with my reflection, and it's starting to feel a little too normal." I was still talking. Why wasn't someone stopping me? "I'll go grab my bag. Should we take both trucks?" I asked, already worrying about who I would ride down with and wondering if I should just drive myself. My car hadn't been driven since my last visit to Cozy Creek, and it probably needed to be started. None of these racing thoughts mattered when, a second later, Pace stopped, abruptly snapping his fingers and sucking in a breath.

"Dang. You know what?" he said.

Levi stilled. The smallest flare of his nostrils was the only indication he'd heard his friend at all.

"I just remembered I told Ruth that I'd go help with the Aubergine Room before I went down to the fire station."

Levi opened his mouth to speak.

Pace held up a hand. "Yes. It is a funny story, Levi. You'll have to tell Claire about it."

Levi turned to me and shared the story with little emotion. "It used to be called the eggplant room, but too many people were making jokes about it. When Ruth found out what the emoji meant, she changed the name."

"I would have had a field day," I said.

"You would have loved it," Levi said at the same time.

Our eyes met, and we shared a quick smile before we both looked away. "That's it. That's the whole story," he finished.

Pace looked between us, his eyes bright and smile almost as large as mine could get. "Yeah, well, sorry to suggest it and dash like that. But you two go. Have a great time." He was already backing toward his truck to leave. "Give Ripley a smooch. Wait. Better yet." He pulled his lip and made a high-pitched whistle.

"Why don't I take her for the night so you don't have to worry about her in the crowds or getting back too fast? Plus, she loves the attention she gets down at the station."

Before Levi could answer, Ripley bolted out of the house and right into Pace's arms. "Good girl." He laughed as she licked all over his face. Once he wasn't trying so hard, I found I liked Pace much more.

Levi was motionless. His eyes narrowed on Pace, but he didn't stop him.

"Thanks, Pace. It was nice meeting you," I said.

He waved as he and Ripley got in his truck.

I didn't want to worry if this was pushing Levi outside his comfort zone. If he was still pretending either of us was following his rules. The rules would need an addendum soon.

Levi

The drive to town felt light-years longer than normal, and every second, dread gripped me tighter with its talons. I didn't do "hanging out" in town. I wasn't part of the Cozy Creek crowd anymore. It wasn't that anybody was mean or judgmental; it was the opposite. They adored my mother. Their pity rolled off them in waves, drowning me in a tsunami of memories I wasn't able to process in public. Lily Carmichael was stamped all over town from the origami cranes she made for Betsy that still hung in the display window of the store to her photographs that lined the walls of several of the establishments. They wanted to talk about her contagious laughter or recall the stern flare of her nostrils when Pace bullshitted her. They wanted to find peace in her memory. They wanted to share the bits of her before they were truly lost forever.

And I just couldn't. I wasn't at that stage of grief yet, and I wasn't sure that I ever would be. The memory of my mother was so drenched in anger over the injustice done to her that I couldn't think about one without drudging up the other.

I gripped the steering wheel tighter and glanced out the driver's window away from Claire.

If the growing tension felt stifling, Claire was oblivious. She chatted happily down the winding roads back to Cozy Creek, one stream of consciousness thought melting into the next. She hadn't stopped chittering since the moment we left the house. Claire didn't need to suffer for my sins like the rest of them. She was passing through this town and deserved to see it in all its autumnal glory.

"And honestly, I think that's what's so weird about memories. They're all as real and as fake as everything else. Like, what if your whole life was an illusion and a lamp was the thing that broke it? You had a wife and kids and were happy, only to wake up and find out you had a traumatic brain injury, you were eighteen, and none of that had happened."

"That would suck," I said as I parallel parked on Main Street. I had zoned out somewhere about a mile back, so I wasn't sure what she was talking about.

She unbuckled her seat belt. "But then, really, what is the culmination of our lives but memories? It's trippy to think about. Wait. What were we talking about?"

"Be more specific," I said, glancing at her quickly.

"Wasn't I making a point?" Her nose crinkled in concentration.

"When we left the house, you were talking about cheese sticks. Now, we are talking about parallel universes and timeline hopping. Or faulty memories." I wasn't entirely sure.

"Oh right. Anyway. Are we here already?" She leaned forward to look out the window. "Whoa. I didn't think places like this actually existed outside movies," Claire said. Her smile was as wide as her eyes as she took in the setting. "It wasn't like this when I got here." I turned off the truck and looked at her as her brow furrowed. "Or maybe it was, and I'd missed it. I was a little distracted that day." She shot me a wince at the reminder of our first meeting. That felt like a million years ago. It was hard to even think of her as that same person.

I went around to help her out of the cab like the proper gentleman my mother would have wanted me to be. She gave me an amused but questioning look as she took my extended hand.

"Thanks," she said, coming to a stop at the corner. "Wow."

I gave her a moment to take in our Main Street in all its kitschy delights. I imagined it through her eyes, seeing it for the first time, instead of these local eyes that had grown accustomed to the breathtaking sights. The streetlamps were wrapped in fall foliage garland, and many storefronts had hay stacks with scarecrows or sunflowers. Brightly colored marigolds and mums sat with pumpkins in the flower beds lining the road. And behind the old buildings of "downtown" were the great snow-capped Rockies, watching over the town of Cozy Creek.

This was pretty picturesque Americana at its finest.

"Where should we start?" she asked, her focus bouncing from one spot to another and never stopping.

I shrugged, wishing I had my tool chest and safety goggles on to slip by unnoticed. Already, Gigi and her visiting granddaughter, Madi, had noticed me and waved cheerily. I lifted my shoulders up to my ears. Billy Mackenzie warned me that there had already been a couple of offers on the storefront on Main Street and that I needed to give him an answer soon. Claire shot me a puzzled look with the interaction but didn't comment.

"Usually, the town square is where the action is, but the whole town seems to be into the event."

She nodded, listening but also highly distracted. "Oh my God, are those hay rides?"

"It's much bigger than I remember," I said. "Lots of tourists."

I didn't look but felt her studying the side of my face. "Then we're both playing tourist today too."

"More like the helpless being led by the clueless."

"I can't imagine there's a bad place to start," she said, ignoring my bad attitude. "This is gonna be fun! Look at us, both leaving the house, among the people."

At that moment, Mack McCreedy came around the bend, steering his tractor down Main Street, pulling a hay-lined trailer full of grinning children and adults.

"How about there?" I pointed at the tractor, thinking at least if we were moving, nobody could talk to us.

"Yes!" She started in the direction where a small queue had formed at the next stop for hay rides. "Is that an apple cider stand?"

Her head whipped to the right, and her feet stopped mid-step, causing me to bump into her backside. I grabbed her shoulders to steady us both, and for just a flash, the full length of her body pressed against mine, and a pulse of nerves flashed through me.

"It is," I said with gruffness.

"Okay, I want that first." But even as we started toward the cider stand, she grew distracted by a small dog passing by dressed as a stormtrooper.

I ran a hand over my smile as she spun in the new direction to crouch to pet the dog. She was making it very difficult to wallow in my misery. It went on like that for a while. She bounced from one side of the street to the other and I followed right behind her. She visited several of the shops, and when she spotted one of my pieces, she raised an eyebrow and pointed at it questioningly.

I nodded and looked around, hoping not to be caught looking at my art. "Okay, I'll stop torturing you." She looped her arm through mine and dragged me away to the next delight.

A thrill shot through me.

"Stop. This cannot be real." We rounded the corner to where the fire station sat next to the town hall. The old building had a vintage fire truck parked in front, decorated with pumpkins and children clambering up its sides. "This is *the* Cozy Creek Fire Brigade." She whipped out her phone to take another hundred pictures. "My dad will absolutely love this."

As we got closer, several of the local firefighters, including Pace and some of the guys from poker night, like Cole Sutter, were out front in their tees and fire pants with suspenders, handing out candy to the kids. Blatant pandering. Pace was not, in fact, helping Ruth as he said. Ripley was in the passenger seat of the fire truck, curled in a bright yellow coat and hiding under a hard helmet. She pretended not to hear me when I whistled for her. The little traitor.

Claire stopped in her tracks, arms out to the side as she took in the sight. "This looks like a calendar photo shoot for October." She shook her head, her cheeks bright and her smile bigger.

"Not you too," I mumbled.

"Me too, what?" she asked.

"Falling victim to the firefighter syndrome."

Pace was holding a baby now that clapped happily on his cheeks as he laughed.

"Where did that baby come from?" I grumbled, rolling my eyes.

Claire followed my line of sight before laughing. Back to me, she made an "oops" face. "I'm but a mere mortal. It's not really something I can control. I think it's hardwired into DNA. Man in uniform. Children playing happily. Parents watching on with smiles." She bent her arms at ninety-degree angles and moved robotically. "Beep boop. Alert, alert." She made a powering-up sound. "Now ovulating."

A surprised laugh burst out of me. Looking down at her, she

studied the goofy, jerky movement, unable to hide the joy she dragged out of me. Her erratic gestures slowed to a stop as she blinked up at me. With her body still, her face lit with joy as her gaze moved to my mouth and around my face, and her smile grew bigger.

"I like seeing this." She poked my cheek where my smile was still beaming.

I was on display, raw and vulnerable, but she made me feel so many things. Yet I couldn't turn it off. I couldn't make it melt away. I didn't want to.

"Who are you?" I asked her, or maybe the universe, for bringing this weird, curiously funny woman into my life.

Her arms fell to her sides as she shrugged at me. "I'm just Claire."

And she was disarming me piece by broken piece. I swallowed and held her gaze. My body leaned toward her gravitational pull.

"You're not *just* anything," I said softly.

Her smile melted, and she swallowed. Why couldn't I stop staring at those lips of hers?

"Hey, there you are!" Pace strolled up with his, as ever, impeccable timing.

Claire waved, shifting to face him. I narrowed my eyes at him. He pretended not to notice.

"This is great," Claire said, gesturing to the scene around us. She had dropped my arm at some point, and I noticed the absence of her more than ever. "I feel like a background character in a Hallmark movie."

"It's pretty neat, huh? Cozy Creek doesn't mess around when it comes to fall," he said.

"Apparently."

"You should see it at Christmas."

She laughed nervously. "I wish I could, but I'll be long gone by then." She elbowed me lightly. "But probably not soon enough for this guy."

I grunted as I crossed my arms and widened my stance. That had been what I wanted, to scare my renter away to have my place back. I wasn't sure when the opposite became true. The thought of her being gone was ... unsettling.

"I somehow doubt that." Pace looked at me closely with a shit-eating grin plastered on his features.

He seemed to look pointedly where I stood slightly ahead of Claire, blocking her from the full blast of his charm. This desire to protect her from him was simply instinctual. The flirtatious playboy was all an act to pretend he wasn't still hurting. Pace had given his heart to someone once, and it was never returned.

"Well, so far, he's had to save me at a grocery store as I unloaded my recent drama onto him, put up with me accidentally dog-napping Ripley, saved me from a winter storm, and set up internet in the cabin despite the arguments that he never would. I'm sure he's just about at the end of his tether," she finished with a huff of laughter.

Her face melted as she spoke, like she understood in real time what a nuisance she'd been. Weirdly, as she listed things out, I found myself recalling the memories with dewy sentimentality.

Huh.

"You went in the cabin?" Pace asked me happily, eyebrows high with hope, obviously not hearing any of the other details.

I blinked at him once. "Yes."

"Yeah." Claire chuckled nervously. "He had to get me out of my clothes when I hurt my knee when I was all wet." She stopped and put out a hand. "Saying that out loud, I hear how that sounds, but it wasn't like that."

"We're going now," I said and began to steer her away. Pace all but vibrated with the need to ask more questions.

"I'll see you for poker night," he called after us.

"No, thank you," I said.

"Oh, that's not nice," Claire whispered.

"Wednesday it is," Pace yelled. "See you then!"

I gave him a sort of salute, much more PG than I wanted to give him, but was conscious of all the families around.

"Aw, that's nice." Claire waved goodbye one more time. "You guys are cute together."

My social batteries were running low, and I needed the safety of my workspace. Claire, too, seemed to be wearing out. The sun was almost down, and the town glowed orangy-pink. I was about to suggest leaving when the next obstacle popped up.

Kathy Wilson spotted me and was making a beeline right for me. I froze in my tracks.

"Oh, my sweet Levi. I am so glad to see you out and about." Mrs. Wilson was the Cozy Creek County clerk and would never relinquish that role because of the firsthand access to gossip.

"Hello, Mrs. Wilson. Nice to see you as well." Not really. If ever there was a person who loved to watch people squirm, it was her.

"You know, I was just thinking about sweet Lily this morning. Gosh, I still can't believe it's been over a year already. I swear I can still smell her gardenia perfume sometimes in the street, and I'll think oh, I just missed her, and then I'll remember."

My Adam's apple lodged in my throat. I felt like I was drowning and having a heart attack at the same time. I couldn't—what was I supposed to—What was anybody—

Claire's hand found my own, warm and stable, as her fingers linked through mine. She gently squeezed my hand, and the tension melted from me as I squeezed her once in return. An arm looped through mine. Only after being held by Claire did I realize my body had been trembling. I couldn't admit how much strength I took from that simple action. Her other hand extended out.

"Hi. I'm Claire Wells."

The older woman took us both in. She stared pointedly at Claire's arm through mine. Claire's thumb brushed over the back of my hand, soothing with our palms pressed tight. I had been there for Claire in her most vulnerable state, and now she instinctually knew how to show up for mine.

"I'm renting out Levi's cabin, and so far, making a total nuisance of myself," she said before Kathy could ask the question on the tip of her nosy tongue.

"Is that right?" They shook hands. "And what are you doing up here in Cozy Creek?"

"I'm a reporter."

The older woman seemed to feel like that necessitated straightening up and fluffing her short yellow-blond bob.

"Are you writing about Cozy Creek?"

"Should I be?" Claire asked in a co-conspiratorial tone.

"Every town has their secrets," Kathy said, looking at me as if putting together pieces that weren't there. Pieces that shouldn't be uncovered. I stiffened, then shifted on my feet. Claire said something in response that my ringing ears couldn't make out.

"Is Levi being a good host?" she asked, still trying to sniff out salacious details to spread through town.

"He is. This whole area is beautiful."

But as the awkwardness grew, so did Claire's momentum. She simply could not stop talking. Maybe I should interact with her more. Perhaps she had some sort of word quota for the year and had lost mileage to make up for. Maybe I should be down at the cabin talking to her more so this could be avoided.

Eventually, I dragged Claire away, insisting we had much more to see. We left a stunned Mrs. Wilson behind as Claire stiffened.

"Was I talking about breast exams with that woman?" she asked when I gently led her into an alley between shops for some privacy.

I nodded, unable to hide my smile now. The secret was out, so no point in locking them down. If anybody should get to see them, it should be Claire. I wouldn't need to avoid the town and talking with people if Claire was here at my side.

"It's like I black out when I start talking. Whatever they say lights up parts of my brain, and my mouth just spews it out. We skip the whole 'is this an inside thought/outside thought' filter on the way," she said with a defeated sigh.

It was true. I had thought something about myself initially made her talk so honestly, but that was who she was. She was genuinely so earnest and open.

"You need to nudge me. Or we need to establish a code word when I start to go too far," she said.

"Absolutely not." I couldn't help my chuckle. She had completely turned my mood around. I had been dreading every moment of that interaction, and by the end, I wanted to pull up a chair with some popcorn.

"You love my humiliation." Claire hid her face in her hands. "My ex would give me a look so I knew when to stop."

I ground my jaw.

"I really hate my brain sometimes," she added.

"I really love your authenticity," I countered. "And your ex sounds like an idiot."

The words came out. I, too, lacked a filter, which was another reason I hated coming into town. But I loved it on Claire. I loved that from the second I met her, there were no games or pretenses. She was exactly what she presented herself as. I thought maybe it was just me who saw this side of her, but that was who she was. In every interaction, she was just a little too goofy and a little too earnest. People didn't know what to do with her.

I knew exactly what I wanted to do with her.

I could kiss this woman senseless. And as soon as the thought formed, it grew and implanted itself deep in my brain tissue, where it would only be removed by a lobotomy that made me forget everything. I wanted this woman. I wanted her with every fiber of my being. And not because she saved me from Kathy Wilson, but because of every real thing about her.

Her head shot up, and her eye contact zinged down my spine. "Oh," she said eventually. "That's good. Because I don't have any control over that."

"Good."

The back alley was quiet in our bubble of honesty.

"Thank you," I said before I did something that might get me slapped. "For intercepting Kathy."

I didn't have to elaborate. Her cheeks went red, and she shook her head. "I'm a pro at dealing out dead mom diversion. Been doing it for a decade." As soon as the words were out, she winced. "Shit. Sorry, that sounds so crass. I just meant—"

My hand cupped her chin and lifted her gaze. "Thank you," I repeated because, again, the desire to kiss her muted all other words.

She placed her hand over mine and nodded softly. "You're welcome."

After a moment that held too long, she dropped her hand, and I released her. Determined to give her a good time, I led her out of the alley and back toward the festivities. She buzzed to a few more places, and by the time we reached the town square, my arms were loaded with bags of souvenirs for her dad, kettle corn, fried food, and other various "irresistible" snacks.

She sipped her cider, humming happily as we rounded into the center of town. The town square had transitioned into a nighttime spectacle with hundreds of jack-o'-lanterns glowing along fake flickering candles and white fairy lights. She gasped as she took in the pumpkins that filled every square foot set up for the competition. She found a bench and sat, that ever-present smile still on her face. A few musicians were set up and playing an acoustic version of a song I recognized but couldn't place. A group of kids were right in front of them, shaking their little bodies out of rhythm and without a care in the world. A few couples danced hand in hand just outside the kids, laughing and rocking to the light tempo. I groaned at myself and set down all her treasures.

"All right. Come on then," I said and stood.

She frowned up at me. "We're leaving?" Her brows contorted in the saddest expression I'd ever been victim to. Even if leaving had been the plan, it wouldn't have been anymore.

"You're wiggling so hard, you're shaking the bench."

I held out my hand. Her jaw dropped. "You want to dance? Out here? In front of God and everyone?"

I huffed. "You're quickly talking me out of it."

She set down her paper cup of cider. "No. No. This is happening."

She bounced up so fast that I had to step back. She dropped her hand into mine and squeezed. It was dark and crowded enough that I didn't worry too much about being seen. Also, what would my mother think if I didn't dance with this beautiful woman? As we stepped to the makeshift dance floor in front of the musicians, the song transitioned from a fast beat to a slow, soft melody.

Because, of course, it did.

CHAPTER 17

Claire

Levi cleared his throat and brought me closer as the music shifted. My right hand slid into his left as his other hand moved to my waist. It was perfectly innocent, but for the way every nerve of my body lit up. I held his shoulder and wished I could close the last bit of distance between us.

Levi smelled incredible. A masculine woody scent with soap and the hints of apple cider still in the air. How many times could I take deep inhales of his chest and neck area before I weirded him out?

Chances were, I'd passed that line the moment I met him.

The soft music playing was an acoustic guitar and a man and woman gently harmonizing a love song about traveling the world. Their voices were lovely and fit the mood as the exciting events of the day melted into the luxurious softness of the fall evening. All around the town square, portable metal firepits were jumped to life, surrounded by little groups of people wrapped in blankets.

I held on to Levi, not ready to let go of him or end this perfect day. He had done well, too, though the strain around his eyes spoke of how taxing this day had been. I would let him get back to the safety of the cabin.

Just one more song.

It was so nice to be held. I couldn't remember the last time I enjoyed it without counting the appropriate number of seconds until it would be over, or worse, feeling like it led to an obligation. So much of what I thought was normal with Kevin, I was starting to understand that maybe it wasn't healthy. Something was wrong with me and the way I behaved in our relationship, so I made up for it by being *obliging* in other areas even when I didn't necessarily desire to. I never actively wanted a physical connection. I didn't hate it. I just wouldn't have chosen it.

I'd been delusional in thinking he left me because of the story. This breakup was coming long before that.

I dropped my head to Levi's chest, letting the steady thump of his heart smooth my jumbled thoughts.

Bump-bump. Bump-bump.

"You've gone quiet." His voice rumbled through my ear and down my spine.

I lifted my head to meet his gaze. "Have I? It's loud as ever up here."

His focus flicked over my features. His thumb lifted to smooth the tension between my brows that I hadn't even known was there. My breath caught at the action, but he dropped his hand again to wrap it around me.

"Are you okay?" he asked softly.

Boldness had me releasing his hand to swing my arms over his shoulders under the guise of better speaking in hushed voices. After a beat of hesitation, his hands came to rest just over my hips.

"I don't think I was a very good girlfriend. Or at least, not very good for my ex."

He frowned, and his body tensed as he missed a step. "Why do you say that?"

"Just thinking about things toward the end." When I felt him tense, I decided this wasn't the direction I wanted this night to go. I wouldn't let Kevin ruin this moment. "Anyway. I don't want to think about that right now."

"Tell me what else is on your mind," he said.

"I forget it's like this sometimes," I said, eventually focusing on the more positive direction of my tailspin.

He hummed a questioning sound.

"The simple sweet humanity of it all." I looked around at the easy joy that surrounded us, and he followed my gaze. The friendly smiles between neighbors. The glow of children loaded up on sugar in the brisk air. The tired but happy eyes of their doleful parents smiling on.

"I'm so in my head all the time. I'm deep-diving into some

new topic, usually something awful, the underbelly of the worst of humanity. I get so set in the truth that people are inherently greedy and awful, but then, and maybe this is silly—I come out, and I see these little pockets of love and think, aw, maybe we aren't so bad. Maybe most of us are just doing our best. We're just a messy little collection of cells and matter given a conscience, and perhaps we're doing okay with the chaos of the fact. Considering how hard it all can be. You know? Humans are cute."

His jaw clenched, and his eyes went all hazy in the way they did when I spoke a lot at once. "Yeah," he said. "It's ... nice. I should probably get out more."

I wanted to pry into why his hometown seemed to be just as strange and new to him as it was to me, a visitor just passing through.

"Me too." I sighed.

"But not too much. We've seen what happened when I try small talk." I squeezed him into an unexpected hug, and he stopped our movement to hug me back. Here we were in the center of town, hugging like it was nothing. I wondered if it bothered him to have the rumor mill seeing this. "This is the happiest I've been in a long time. Thank you," I said.

He stiffened in my arms and made a soft sound of understanding. He didn't need to speak, he just needed to know that I was thankful for his kindness.

"Are *you* doing okay?" I asked, looking closer at him.

"I'm okay." I waited for him to expand. He looked around the town and collected his thoughts. "It's been a while since I came down here to hang out. Nothing more than a quick job to help someone or get groceries."

"A lot of people seem happy to see you," I said. It was true. He'd been treated like the prodigal son.

"This town cared about my mom," he said.

"What was her name?" I asked, hoping this question was okay. He was so reluctant to talk about her. He pulled me a little closer with no excuse given, just mutual comfort.

"Lily. She was one of those rare people who was genuinely kind. Genuinely unbothered by the trivialities of life." He started rocking me to the slow tempo again. "Not like me." He added the last sentence like a confession.

"Not like me either," I admitted. "My whole life, I feel like I've shown up for a class halfway through the semester. I'm so envious of people like your mother. It's like they understand some big secret and are waiting for the rest of us to work it out." I smiled.

He nodded, his throat bobbing as he looked over my shoulder. "Yeah. Exactly." He cleared the tightness from his throat before asking, "What are you working on now? You said you finished your story?" His voice stilted with repressed emotion.

I studied him for a moment but decided to allow the subject to change. "I don't know actually. I'll probably get some edits back here soon, but that won't take too long. I need to find my next project. Usually, I don't know I'm into my next story until it's too late."

"Too late?" he asked.

"Sleepless nights. Obsessive research." My fingers tapped a wave pattern on his strong shoulder. "You've not seen me at my worst. Don't make that face," I said when his eyebrows shot up skeptically. "You're catching me at a pretty even keel time. This is 'normal' Claire."

"You're far from normal," he said. I must have frowned because he added, "Thankfully. Anything inspiring you here?"

"Not unless Farmer Nelson has a secret racket of cheating for the biggest pumpkin prize," I teased.

He tensed and forced out a laugh.

"Oh my God, does he?" I lowered my voice and got close enough that his exhales brushed my cheek. "Because if there is some secret injustice, I will sniff it out and bring it to light," I added faux menace to my voice.

"I don't doubt that." His forehead wrinkled when I leaned back to study him. "How about we just dance?"

I lowered my head to the planes of his hard chest with a dramatic sigh. "If I must."

His chuckle rumbled through me. He pulled me closer yet. The front of him was pressed warmly against me. A heady heat spread through me, making my breasts feel heavy and making me want to press even harder against him. He smelled so good. Being held by him was *so* good. I was all melty inside and wanted to just spread my body all over his. I wanted to taste him and be tasted by him. I wanted to hear what sort of noises I could get him to make and find out the secrets of his desire.

God, I was really, really *bored*.

When the next song ended, we broke apart, and after collecting my souvenirs, he led me to a firepit on the outskirts of the town square instead of toward the truck. A small family, with sleeping kids in their arms, spoke quietly that they were leaving.

I settled next to the fire as he stoked it back to life. To my surprise, yet again, instead of seating himself on the opposite side of the fire, he took the spot right next to me and covered us both in a blanket that had been left on the chair. We were close enough that our elbows touched. Maybe because of the hushed environment, or perhaps because he was enjoying our closeness as well, but Levi hadn't seemed in any hurry to leave.

My heart raced like we were teenagers about to share a first kiss. This attraction to Levi was intriguing and refreshing. Maybe he was just as "bored" as I was.

It was Levi who broke the silence first. He mumbled something that sounded like "at your worst."

"What?" I leaned my shoulder into him and looked up with wide eyes until he was forced to turn his head to me. Our faces were so close. "Ex-squeeze me, baking powder?"

"Claire." He shook his head. The smile melted off his face as his gaze moved over my features. He glared back at the fire with a swallow. "You said that you're at your worst when you're into your work. I was just curious who told you that?"

"Oh." My silly mood abated. I watched how the light of the fire sharpened the line of his jaw and strong nose. He was very lovely to look at. "Nobody, I guess. I just get so focused that the rest of the world fades away. I'm not a very good partner."

"Do you stay like that forever?"

"Eventually, I crawl out of my cave," I joked. "Unshaven, blinking back at the bright light, grunting for food."

He smiled, and it was so full and genuine that my heart flipped in my chest.

"I was just thinking about my art," he said slowly. "When I lose myself to my work, nobody tells me that that's when I'm at my worst. In fact, people usually get excited and support me."

It was my turn to frown at the dancing flames. "Yeah, but you create beauty," I pointed out. "I just uncover the ugly."

He made that soft sound of processing information. "You find the truth, right? Share it with the world?"

"I try," I said.

"I've read your work. That's what you do. You shine a light on the truths of the world, no matter how they look."

I smiled into my clasped fingers. To know that he had read my work filled me with pride.

"I want to make a difference," I admitted, but I didn't add that I felt like I was failing.

"When I make art, all I'm trying to do is unearth some version of truth. What's more beautiful than truth, no matter in what form? It's that human connection."

Inexplicably, my chest and throat tightened with undefined emotion. I felt seen and understood. That was what I wanted to believe about myself, but lately, I wasn't so sure. I leaned more of my body into him, still unable to voice my appreciation for his words.

My gaze moved around the square at all the pockets of people. Eventually, I organized my thoughts. "Kevin. My ex. He said that I'm ruthless," I whispered. "That all I care about are other people because I don't want to deal with my issues."

Muscles flexed in his clenching jaw.

"He wasn't wrong," I added. "I have this drive for information. I don't stop. Even when I know I'm going too far. Even when it's destroying my relationships." I wrapped my arms tight around my middle. "He made me feel like helping people was greedy." I narrowed my eyes and spoke softly in the quiet night. "My whole life, I grew up thinking I was meant to change the world and help people. I read stories where heroes sacrificed everything for the moral good to make the world better. But I don't think he really wanted that. Maybe he did at first, but not recently. Recently, he wanted the security of money. I get that. But it wasn't the most important thing. As much as he said he supported me, I think he just wanted me to fit into the role in *his* story. Kevin wanted to be the main character, and I messed with that."

I thought about Kevin's incessant desire for money. His desperate need to ensure he would never have the poverty he perceived as a child.

Levi remained thoughtful at my side. He picked up a poker to fuss with a piece of burning wood. I sighed and slumped back. I was too much. I opened up too soon and too wide. I was a gaping wound oozing all over the place, ruining the moment.

"I'm sorry. I don't even know how we got here." It was the car ride into town all over again. I talked and talked and took his lack of speaking for listening. But all I did was lasso him into the thoughts that tied me up.

Levi slowly leaned the poker to the side of the pit and grabbed my hand. He watched with a frown as he intertwined our fingers. My heart raced, the sting of those unshed tears replaced by an overwhelming awareness of where our bodies connected.

Warmth. Sturdiness. Comfort. Longing.

"Kevin sounds like a tool bag," Levi said.

I coughed a surprised laugh. I clasped his hand to my chest as I bent forward, half with humor, half with relief I hadn't freaked him out.

Should I argue? Defend the man I gave years of my life to because didn't it make me less somehow for staying with him? Wouldn't I bear the weight of that bad relationship by staying in it for so long? But I found I couldn't argue with Levi's assessment.

"You aren't lacking, Claire. Not even a little." Levi tugged his hand free from where his knuckles brushed against the tops of my breast. He turned so our knees bumped on the low log. "You carry an entire universe in you. Every time you speak, I'm excited to hear what you'll say. You make me feel things in a way that I haven't felt in years. You make me see the world in a different and exciting way."

My dry mouth closed slowly. "Oh." What did you say to the ultimate compliment? How could I even be expected to function again? All I wanted to do was prick his words over and over my body until they were tattooed on me forever.

"If somebody told you at any point that something was wrong

with the way your mind worked, they were simply incorrect. Or jealous. Or motivated by their own wants. I've seen the beauty of that machine"—he brushed his thumb along my temple—"and there isn't anything wrong there. It's all magnificent."

I closed my eyes and turned into his palm before he could take it away. We were here in this private moment in a public place. I didn't want to be here anymore. I wanted to go back to our little spot in the woods, where we both felt free to be exactly who we were.

In all our naked glory.

"I'm getting a massive ego," I said, trying to joke. But really, my heart was jackhammering against my chest. I'd opened up fully and truly to this man, not quite a stranger, but not what I ever thought he would be. Could it be this easy to talk to a person? To let yourself open to them? To want them? If it felt like this for normal people, then I understood. I understood it all.

"Good. You deserve a massive ego. Anybody who made you feel lacking is an absolute idiot."

He lowered his head to mine. I think he was aiming for my cheek or my temple, but at the last moment, he lifted my chin to press the gentlest of kisses against my mouth. It didn't linger, and it didn't demand. It was a small gift of comfort.

It wasn't enough. I wanted and needed more but would accept that for now.

"Wait," I whispered, and he stilled in his retreat. "Wait," I repeated before I straightened my back and pressed my lips back up and into his.

He exhaled in a sigh of relief and cupped the back of my head. We held there, rubbing softness against softness. Breaths hovering. I memorized the shape of his soft lips, the way his exhale brushed against my skin. I tilted my head, opening my mouth—

He pulled away abruptly.

"Claire, I—" He grabbed my shoulders and held me in place. Mortification slithered down my neck as determination narrowed his eyes.

"I'm sorry. I got carried away." *As always.*

I was embarrassed. I thought the heat between us was tangible, but this was a hard stop.

"It's not that. Trust me, this is—" He looked around. "I just—not here." He groaned in frustration.

"It's okay. I shouldn't have assumed." I shook my head, then bent down to collect our stuff.

He lifted my chin to get my focus back. "Please don't apologize. It makes me feel like shit."

I closed my eyes so I couldn't see the sympathy in his face. "You just said all those sweet things, and I—"

"You don't owe me anything because I was kind to you." His words came out frustrated—a grumpy and familiar Levi.

I winced and felt even more humiliated. Was that what he thought? That I kissed anybody who wasn't confused by my verbal onslaught? That wasn't what this was. This was the purest form of want I'd ever experienced.

"It's fine. We can just pretend it didn't happen," I said, getting back to collect our stuff. I stood, and the cold air seeped in, causing a shiver.

"Really. It's not that I didn't want that." He took a breath and held up a finger in the air, so I sucked in my lips to keep from speaking anymore. I could still taste him there. I still wanted him. He sounded as frustrated as I felt embarrassed.

Well, this would be a fun and not-at-all-awkward ride back to the cabin.

"I wanted it. Trust me." He stood, and the evidence of that was clear as day, based on that bulge currently trying to distract me. Speaking of aubergines, I'm pretty sure he had one stuffed down his pants. I blinked up at him, my lips still clamped tight.

Absolutely nothing needed to come out of my mouth right now.

He took a breath as he lifted and dropped his shoulders. His fingers splayed as he collected himself. "Can I show you something?" he asked.

It took all of my force of will to keep my eyes locked on his when he said that. "I, uh—"

"Not here. Back at the house."

Back at the house? Was he going to continue this kiss? Was he trying to end this next level of physicality? Was he going to take me to his shed and show me his wood? *I would not make a wood joke. I would not make a wood joke.*

I bit my bottom lip harder and nodded.

"Oh, man." He chuckled. "You are trying so hard not to say something inappropriate right now, and I'm not sure I want to know what it is."

CHAPTER 18

Levi

The moment her lips touched mine, my growing suspicions were confirmed. I had fallen for Claire, and I had no way of coming back from these feelings.

I wanted more from Claire, and I couldn't do that without her understanding bits of me. She'd been so open and honest. It was time to share part of myself in return before things went any further.

The drive back to the house was the exact opposite of the ride into town. Claire sat in contemplative silence. Although she was quiet, when I glanced her way, wanting to simply look at her through the flashes of streetlights, she gazed at me with heat in her eyes, her teeth chewing on her bottom lip, watching me with an intensity that made sitting in jeans difficult. Each time

I caught her heated stare, Claire would turn to look out the window as my grip tightened on the steering wheel until my knuckles went white.

She sat up, surprised when I parked in front of Little Cabin. "We don't have to go in there," she said with patient understanding.

"I want to show you something," I explained.

She glanced at the cabin and back at me. "Okay."

I went around and gave her my hand to help her out of the truck. This time, it was met with a soft smile instead of skepticism. I wound my fingers through hers as I led her up the deck and into the house. Our hands fit naturally together. She was smiling when I glanced over at her.

I took a deep breath to steady myself as we walked into the house. The nerves were still there, but they weren't incapacitating. More like the lingering chill in your fingers when you come in from the cold to warm by the fire. The desire to be near her and share with her was stronger than the tragedy of this house that still plagued me.

When Claire was around, she demanded all attention from my senses, so there was no room for anything but her.

I'd taken two steps forward to the extra room when her hand slid from mine.

"I think we should kiss more. Make out, actually," she said.

I stopped in my tracks. I turned as slowly as possible so I could collect all the thoughts that had just exploded through my brain.

"Unless you don't want to. Obviously. But that kiss." She whooshed out a deep breath, fingers twisting in front of her. "It was like—" She made a gesture that I think was supposed to represent fire. "And you are just—so I think we should. Make out. Yep." She nodded, apparently pleased with that proposal.

I chuckled, feeling more nervous than I would have ever thought. Now, I was fully distracted from the reason I brought her here. She wanted to kiss me. I took one large step toward her. Her eyes widened, and she sucked in another breath, lifting her breasts closer to me.

"It's just that I don't do subtext. I don't really get body language. Unless it's very obvious." Her gaze flicked to my groin, where I had been sporting an erection like a randy teenager at the fire, and back up to meet my waiting eyes. Color burned her cheeks. She was adorable. "I just really need to know one way or the other."

"I do want to kiss you more—"

"Okay, great." She slammed into me before I could finish the sentence.

I caught her shoulders with my palms as her lips pressed into mine. I had been about to say something else, but when we collided, I didn't remember how to speak. Whatever thin thread that had been pulling me through the house snapped, mission forgotten. My desire for her was a simmering pot, and the press of her lips against mine was the heat to bubble over. She was delicious and warm and soft against me.

All there was were her lips moving softly against mine.

It took fractions of a second to realize I hadn't responded to her yet. Far too long. She had been taking the lead, but no more.

My hands went to her luxuriously soft hair, threading through the thick locks. I moved us so that I could press her against the door and use my thigh and hip to grind into her, hold her up. I slanted my mouth across her, using my tongue to press into hers. She moaned in relief.

I couldn't settle myself. I couldn't kiss her enough. I was shaking and out of control. I lapped at her. I pawed at her. Hands moving to her waist from her hair and back again. But too risky to leave them there. My thumbs were desperate to worm their way under her shirt, under the hem of her jeans. I moved them back to her head and cupped her head gently as my hips jutted into her. My cock needed friction in any form. Needed her to feel my want.

She gasped out. Took gulping breaths of air into her lungs. I used it as an opportunity to suck and kiss at her neck. I wanted to take her here. I wanted to bend her over that desk of hers where I'd seen her working so many hours and tease her until she was dripping for me, until I could slide in all the way to the hilt and feel her wet heat clenching around me.

"God, Levi," she gasped out.

My hand had somehow moved back to her hip, my traitorous thumb working its way under her shirt, rubbing in slow circles across her heated skin.

"Fuck." I tore my mouth away. I mumbled thoughts without thinking. "Fuck. I knew it would be like that. I knew it would be too hard to stop once we started." I backed up until I was against the wall opposite her. I bent over with my hands on my knees and my now intensely painful second erection for the night. Taking gasps of breath in.

I lifted my head to check in on the woman I'd all but devoured.

Claire leaned back against the wall, a smug smile on her red plumped lips, chest heaving. She ran a hand across her chest and brought her fingers to her lips, a sort of daze slowness to her movements. "Okay," she said. "Okay."

I pushed myself against the wall, letting the corner of it dig into my back, trying to distract my body with pain.

I blinked at her, my breaths still coming too fast. Confusion as to who I was and what I was doing there. My gaze focused on her nipples pressing against her shirt, and my mind wandered to wonder if she'd be wet if I slipped my hand into those jeans.

"Levi?" she asked.

"Claire."

Her smile widened. "You wanted to show me something?"

"I wanted to show you something," I agreed.

"And it wasn't just to make out?"

"It wasn't just to make out." I cleared my head with a rough shake. "No. Right. I wanted to show something to you. In the room." I ran the back of my hand over my mouth. I tasted her. Fuck, I still wanted her so badly.

In a daze, I went to the room in question. I heard her soft laughter as she followed. I unlocked the door.

"This was my mom's darkroom," I said, flicking on the light of the once-forbidden room.

It was a soft yellow light that cast us in film noir shadows. It cleared the final haze of lust from my mind, and I was able to focus. An understanding passed over Claire's features.

"Oh." The way she said it made me wonder if she'd already guessed the purpose of this room.

She was a very convincing liar if she had been in there already.

"You left it unlocked the other day when you were in here," she admitted.

"Ah." I sighed, not easily hiding the hurt I felt. "You already saw everything?" If I knew Claire, she hadn't waited five minutes before her curiosity got the better of her.

"No," she said quickly. Then added, sheepishly, "I thought about it. Trust me. But it felt wrong." She tucked her hair behind her ear. "It felt personal, and it's better seeing it this way. With you showing me. I want to learn about Lily, but I want it to be on your terms. When you're ready."

Her gaze held mine, and I swallowed. "I'm ready." Her ex-boyfriend had been wrong to call her ruthless. This was not a ruthless journalist. This was a woman who cared deeply.

"My mother was an incredible photographer. Mostly portraits. She would have been the next Anne Leibovitz." I took her to the first box as I spoke.

"So art runs in your blood."

"She was the talented one. She could have been huge," I said, and a hint of bitterness came through.

She gave me a questioning look, but I didn't expand. I turned my back toward her while I opened the box and pulled out some of the prints. I waited for the familiar pain of shock and sadness to hit. But it didn't. I only felt pride as I pulled out each photo and held them reverently to Claire.

Her mouth parted as she took them with equal gentleness. Her gaze flickered over every one, not rushing. Really seeing. "These are amazing."

"She was unbelievably talented." I stepped back to give her space. I had seen all these photos a hundred times.

"I can't believe I've never heard of her. She could have had exhibits. I've worked with many photographers over the years and learned a little about the skills required to be good. Did she maybe go by another name?"

"No. She never had success in that sense," I said stiffly.

"Why not?" she asked, appalled, and I narrowed my eyes. She closed her eyes with a frustrated huff of air. "I'm sorry. Don't answer that. You can tell me as much or as little as you want."

"It's okay. I don't like to talk about it. She never wanted fame. She—" I skirted around the full truth by latching on to others. "She liked living here in Cozy Creek. She liked raising me. She said that was all she ever wanted."

"That's lovely." Claire smiled, her gaze drifting as she thought. After a moment, she went back to the photographs. A little crease formed between her brows before a massive smile split her face open. "I recognize these little guys."

I knew before I looked exactly what picture she had found. It was a picture of Pace and me. We were eight years old and had just come back from exploring in the woods. We were covered in dirt, jeans ripped, and hair a mess, but we wore the biggest grins you'd ever seen. Our front teeth were a little too big, with summer freckles on our noses as we slung arms around each other. I clearly remembered that moment, stepping out of the trees and onto the driveway. My mother's face was obscured by the lens. I had rolled my eyes, but Pace was ready for his close-up. The lighting somehow looked ethereal and sentimental all at once.

More than that, it was an incredible photograph. My mother deserved to have it all, and that choice was taken from her.

I couldn't talk about that with Claire yet. The rawness of being here, of our kiss, the day in town talking about Lily and seeing the pity, it was all catching up. I felt bone weary. I felt the darkness creeping in around the edges.

"Thank you for sharing this with me," Claire said.

I nodded.

"Are you okay?" she asked, carefully setting down the photos back into the box. "Is this too much?"

"It's a lot," I said honestly.

"Let's leave it for now," she said simply. She quickly flipped through a few more before gently lowering them back into the box. "Maybe, one day, you can show me the rest of the photos? I think I recognized some people from town."

I nodded and headed to the door. "You can come look at this stuff. I won't lock it anymore."

"Thank you," she said.

It hit me then. The real reason I wanted to show Claire this room. It was about sharing a part of myself, but it was also my way of showing myself the truth.

When you fall for a woman, it's going to hit you like a train.

It had felt like a warning when my mother said it. I felt things too deep and wanted things too much. My mother always recognized my sensitive nature. I was sure I had inherited it from her. But where it made her patient with the world, understanding the ebb and flow of nature, it made me scared and hard. She said that the softest insides have to develop the strongest shells. It wasn't easy to be an artist male with squishy insides who cried at movies and got goose bumps at musicals—yes, we watched musicals—living in a small town.

She never made me feel bad about it. She tried to teach me the balance of it.

Too soft and too hard for this world.

This time, I heard Claire's voice.

"I just haven't had the heart to clear this stuff out. Or see if this medical equipment could be donated. I keep meaning to," I explained as we moved out of the room.

"I understand. I was often told that there is no timeline for grief. It doesn't just stop one day. That room can wait." She reached for my hand and squeezed.

We went silently back into the main area, but she didn't let me go. She stepped closer. Questioning. I cupped her cheek and kissed her forehead. My heart raced, betraying my head. Or maybe the other way around.

It would be so easy to kiss her. To peel off her clothes like I had before.

I stepped forward to reach for her. I felt lighter having shared.

"Thank you for sharing this with me," she said. "Really. I feel honored." She held my eyes for a beat and smiled wide.

"Thank you for listening." I wanted this woman. I wanted to share more with her. The day was catching up, but being with her didn't drain me. It filled me up. I wanted to tell her that. I wanted to tell her so much more.

"I know I'm just passing through and am practically a stranger. I understand now why having someone stay here would be so difficult."

Just passing through.

I nodded at her feet. "Yeah. I just—"

"It's okay. You made the rules very clear." Her tone was light and understanding, but how could she think she was a stranger after I shared this with her? "You don't have to explain," she said honestly. "I know I've been a little pushy, but you're a good man, Levi. I like spending time with you. I understand you have rules in place, but if you ever want to spend more time with me ... if you get *bored*." Her gaze met mine, pupils dark with subtext. "I'll be here. In Little Cabin."

I swallowed with difficulty. There was no doubt in my mind that I wanted her. I had wanted her and thought about her every moment of every day, even when I told myself I wasn't.

Fuck the rules. They were in place to protect me, but now they were hurting me.

"Having the rules is important to you?" I asked.

"I like clear boundaries and expectations," she said with a nod.

Nothing about my feelings for her was clear. I would have

probably followed that desire if I hadn't started to develop feelings. I would have let myself get lost in her body as a distraction from the grief I was still processing in a way I hadn't allowed myself to do in the past few years. But then, she enraptured me. She spoke in a way that made me anxious to hear what she'd come up with next. She had such a special way of seeing the world.

I couldn't take her up on her offer as much as I wanted to. I wasn't content to only have her for a night or a few weeks while she was *passing through* town. If only I didn't feel things so deeply, if only I was able to take things in stride like everybody else seemed to. But now, having kissed her and spent time with her, my meeting Claire felt monumental and crucial. Everything I thought I wanted and knew had changed.

I didn't want to know what these feelings for her were, or if I did, I wasn't ready to admit them. It was like the empty shell I had been living in was now too small to contain everything I had experienced. I would never be able to squeeze myself back in now.

No.

I would have some self-control.

For now, I would just avoid her and let things simmer before they boil over. My blood was too hot around her. My control was a hair trigger, and that kiss proved it. I didn't want to give in and risk her thinking she wasn't important to me. We were more than hookups based on spiked cider and "good vibes."

I waited too long to speak. She sighed and tossed her hands out to the side. We were walking to the front door. "It's been a long day. You have shared a lot and been around a lot of people. You go get some rest," she said.

"Good night, Claire," I said at the door.

"Good night, Levi." She hesitated, body tense, but didn't move.

Right when I was about to turn to leave, I bent to gently lift her chin. I kissed her forehead, brushing my thumb along the dimple that appeared. I searched her eyes, hoping the right answer would come to me, but I only found my feelings for her growing every second.

I didn't look back as I walked up to Big Cabin. I needed help from someone who could talk me through this.

CHAPTER 19

Claire

After our toe-curling, panty-melting, incendiary make-out session, I decided that the only next right course of action was to fall into my next project. I'd made my intentions clear. It was up to him, but in the meantime, I needed to keep my mind occupied. And *hands*.

The ball was in Levi's court.

Both balls. *Heh*.

The strangest thing was happening to me. Since Levi's first accidental brush, and especially since that kiss—though *kiss* falls short of describing the experience that was making out with Levi—I was lustful. Well and truly full of lust. I'd find myself daydreaming about the feel of the warm comfort of just riding in Levi's truck and then suddenly imagined sliding across the seat to straddle him and kiss him senseless. Or I'd be thinking about his passion as he spoke of his work, that serious blaze in his eyes that matched the fire we'd been sitting in front of at the pumpkin measuring contest, and remember how good his lips tasted. I'd elaborate on my fantasy to run my hand up his thigh and test that hardness I had witnessed firsthand.

My body was a live wire. My bras rubbed me in ways I wasn't used to, and my hand drifted under the covers into my panties every night. But it wasn't near enough. Like scratching an itch on a knuckle, it provided no relief. I was insatiable. I had never been this restless and wanting before in my life, and quite frankly, it was humiliating because now, more than ever, Levi finally seemed to be sticking to his rules. Picture my dramatic eye roll here. When I had mentioned the boundaries, I'd sort of hoped he'd dash them out the window and say *fuck the rules, take off your shirt.*

But alas, he was well and truly a gentleman. And because I was leaving soon, it was best.

I wasn't sure about his hesitation. Was it some old-fashioned and misplaced sense of chivalry? Was it that maybe his body was into it, but the rest of him wasn't? That made my stomach hurt, so I didn't think about it. But what else could it be? It was times like these when I wished people could just have blunt conversations, but then I imagined his pity as he rejected me and the gurgle in my gut was back. Best not to think about that.

This would be so much easier if he just listed out every single thought he had on the subject matter as he had in the listing.

"Ugh," I groaned.

"Are you okay?" Levi asked from the driver's seat.

"Ah!" I jumped and gripped the door handle.

He chuckled and looked over at me disbelievingly. "If I had a nickel every time I scared you by simply existing..."

"Who carries change these days?"

"Did you really forget I was here?"

"Ha." I chuckled good-naturedly. "No, of course not." Honestly, yes. I was so lost in my thoughts I forgot he was right next to me, driving us to town. "Just thinking," I added.

"Anything you want to share with the class?" he asked in a gravelly growl.

Why haven't you kissed me since the pumpkin night last week? Why weren't we locking lips with the little time I had left? Why won't you show me to *your* aubergine room? I'd say that last one with bouncy, suggestive eyebrows. Why haven't we updated the rules to include mild groping? After all, what's a bit of friendly groping between neighbors?

"No. Just thinking about my new story." I settled on.

I had made it clear that I was interested. Anything more would be pushy or clingy.

He straightened. "Oh. Anything interesting?"

I hadn't told Levi at the time, but something about his mom's art had rung a bell in my brain. In that way I hadn't felt in a while. That incessant buzz of a new story taking wing and beating against the inside of my brain. He gave me full access to the formerly locked room. And what a room it was. The life of Lily

Carmichael was remarkable.

And so I chased the serotonin and lost myself to this new lead for the past few days. When he mentioned he had to go into town to meet Pace, I latched myself on to his plans in the hopes of searching the library for stories or chatting with some locals to get more information and maybe another story for the online journal I was still playing around with.

"I'm not sure yet," I said.

He glanced over at me with a little bit of worry.

"Don't worry. I'm sure you'll be the first to know when I'm hooked on something real." I patted his shoulder. "Whether you want to or not," I teased.

He parked the truck behind the Cozy Creek B&B and hopped out. I knew the drill by now and waited for him to come around and assist me.

A girl could really get used to this. "Thanks," I said, smiling up at him and tucking a loose strand behind my ear as I looked up at him. I searched his hard-to-read expressions for any sign of thoughts of groping, friendly or otherwise.

He swallowed audibly, squeezing my hand once before releasing me. Move over, Mr. Darcy and the hand flex. We had a new contender in town.

"I shouldn't be long helping Pace," he said.

"Honestly, take your time. I've been dying to check out Cozy Creek Confectionery ever since I had a caramel apple from them the night of the pumpkin fest."

"Just avoid the coffee," he warned ominously. "Okay, I'll come get you from there. I shouldn't be more than an hour," he said before he bent and kissed my cheek.

Kissed. My. Cheek.

Like we were a couple saying goodbye. We stared at each other for what was easily a millennium. His mouth and eyes were wide. Mine were probably the same.

"Oh," I said awkwardly and lifted a hand to my cheek. "That was nice."

"Sorry. That was—I didn't mean—"

"It's okay," I said, even as my heart cartwheeled in my chest. I shook my head and began backing up, ready to turn away. "No biggie."

"Right." He cleared his throat. "See ya."

"Yep," I said in a voice a few octaves higher.

It was far more innocent than our last kiss, but I found myself pressing a hand to my chest as I walked away, sucking in my lips to keep from smiling. I couldn't help how charmed I was by the whole exchange.

Forget groping; let's get more slightly awkward but wholesome PDA.

"Well, isn't that a sight to see," a woman's voice said as I crossed over to the opposite street's sidewalk.

An older woman was sitting, one leg in a cast propped up on a chair outside Cozy Creek Confectionery.

"That was—I think he just—We aren't really—I don't know what we are, to be frank," I said. "Hi. I'm Claire Wells. I'm staying up at Levi's place."

"I'm Gigi. This is my shop. I'm currently laid up, but my granddaughter is in town helping out." She gestured a hand to where Levi had just kissed my cheek.

Remember that? Remember how he kissed my cheek like it was the most natural thing in the world?

"That's none of my business, doll. I'm just happy to see Levi come down from that place and not all by himself. It is what Lily would have wanted."

"Were you friends with Lily Carmichael?" I asked as curiosity mobilized my feet in her direction.

"I was. We all were," she said with a smile.

"Levi showed me some of her photos. I'd love to know more about her."

"Did he now? Well, well." Her eyebrows lifted higher in surprise. "Why don't you come in and tell us about it, and I'll answer your questions about Lily."

Inside, I was introduced to Gigi's granddaughter Madi, a stunningly gorgeous woman my age with perfectly manicured nails, highlighted hair, and designer clothes. I tried not to be hyper-aware of my oversized sweater, undone face, and hair in a messy bun, but there was no need to feel self-conscious. Both women welcomed me warmly, and we sat and chatted like instant new-old friends. We talked over each other, bouncing jokes and rapidly changing topics in the best way. And neither of them seemed to mind my stream of consciousness oversharing. They gave me several more story ideas for my online journal and the people I could talk to in town, and I was excited at that prospect.

Not in the same way I felt about a new story but like a little sugary treat for my brain and the few regular readers I now had.

It was nice to sit and chat with these women. It soothed a part of me that I didn't know needed soothing. I loved my father, we were close as could be, but there must have been something on an evolutionary level that made sitting around chatting with these two feel so comforting, so natural.

We talked about Lily and all she meant to the town and how devastating the loss was.

"I still wish there was something we could do," Gigi said. "But Levi won't talk to anybody. He barely talks to Pace."

As they spoke, more information came to the surface about the less charming aspects of Lily's past. Of course, there had been a man who had swept through town and broke her heart.

At some point, I decided this was the sign I needed. I was eager to get back to Little Cabin and learn more. An idea was forming, and I needed focus and quiet.

I glanced at my watch to see that an hour had flown by.

"He's been pacing back and forth," Madi said. "For the past ten minutes, at least."

Outside the shop window, Levi looked up from where he'd been striding by, only to look away again quickly.

"That's my fault," Gigi said. "Last time he came in here, I tried to talk to him, and now he's avoiding me."

I frowned but stood. "I better get him home," I said jokingly. "Before he leaves me."

"The way he's looking at you, I doubt he'd leave you alone

anywhere," Madi said.

I tucked my chin and shrugged in my coat, avoiding the implications. I couldn't even say what was happening between Levi and me, let alone try to describe it to these strangers.

"Come back next week?" Madi asked.

"I'd like that." I smiled.

Maybe it would be nice to chat again. Maybe I could chat with some other people in town too. For now, I was anxious to get to work and find out all I could about Lily Carmichael.

Levi

"I thought you were fixing the Aubergine Room?" I asked Pace as I gestured for him to hand me the Phillips screwdriver he twirled lackadaisically around his fingers.

We were at Ruth's B&B, in the aptly named Aubergine Room, named not only for the deep purple that colored the walls but for the surprising amount of porcelain eggplant figurines. Even after finding out the truth about the eggplant euphemism, Ruth refused to remove the phallic art.

"Oh yeah, must have gotten distracted." Pace handed over the screwdriver with a lazy flick of his wrist. "You can thank me now or later."

"You know this isn't a two-man job." Sure enough, after pulling off the light switch, the disconnected wire was obvious.

It should only take maybe three minutes to fix without interruption. Ten with Pace here.

"Sorry, I wanted to see you. How annoying friends are."

"I just saw you last week at the pumpkin thing."

"Then you blew off poker night. There's a new guy in town, Noah. I think you'd hit it off with your surly silence." I gave Pace a pointed look. He shrugged innocently. "I would have just come by to visit, but the last few times I've texted you to come up, you've been too busy for a visit," he said. He said the last bit, making air quotes.

Maybe this would take twenty minutes.

I sighed and ignored his implications even as a blush burned up my neck. I hunched my shoulders under the guise of peeking into the socket cutout to hide from Pace and his stupid, smug expression.

"Now, what could be keeping you so busy up in that cabin all by yourself?"

"Enough, Pace." I grunted.

He snapped for dramatic effect as if he wasn't leading up to all this. "Oh wait, that's right. You have your beautiful brunette tenant now."

"I have been busy. I started a new piece." That was the truth. Had I been hiding because of my complicated growing feelings for Claire also? Maybe. Had I been finding excuses to come check on things at the Little Cabin just to spend time near her? Also maybe. "You turned off the breaker to this room, right?" I asked.

"Of course." He leaned against the wall next to where *I* was doing all the work, likely to get a better look at my face. "So, can I safely guess that my not-so-subtle tactic worked?"

I carefully unscrewed the loose connector. It had burn marks like it had been the victim of a power surge. "Hand me that extra wire." I pointed at where the coil of black wire sat on my tool bag. The actual bag, not Pace, as he asked me all these questions.

"You're welcome." He handed it over. "Tell me you're tainting every surface of that place."

"Pace."

Now, there was a heat flushing over all my skin, burning under my collar, making my pits sweat. Because even though he was wrong, he was close enough to the truth. I had been imagining taking Claire on every surface. After that initial kiss, I couldn't keep my fantasies locked down. I thought about her sprawled on the floor in front of my fireplace, naked and wet for me. I imagined laying her out and devouring her like a feast as she pulled my hair, ground against my mouth, coming so hard her whole body shuddered.

I cleared the vision as I cleared my throat. If I kept down that route, I'd end up getting a hard-on and never hearing the end of it from Pace.

"Man, I love seeing how red I can make you get." Pace shook my shoulder, my screwdriver slipping off the head of the screw into the wires. I glared at him. "Sorry, sorry. But it's freaking nice to see you into her. I'm messing with you. I know you never kiss and tell. Which, in its own way, confirms my suspicions."

"No. It's not like that. She is just a tenant. Passing through. She likes rules and boundaries." They were the same truths I'd been repeating to keep the distance.

"You're truly a match made in heaven," Pace said.

I paid close attention to my hands, and I found the words to work through my feelings. "I really like Claire," I admitted. "She's wildly smart and thoughtful. She's kind and inquisitive. And obviously, she's gorgeous."

"But she doesn't want to cross any lines? Is that the issue?" Pace asked.

"No. The opposite actually."

"But you don't want to?" Pace asked with a frown.

"She'll be gone before Christmas," I said. "I really like her," I repeated, cringing at how juvenile that descriptor felt for the massive knot of feelings currently tying me down.

Pace leaned back as understanding dawned. "You don't want to get caught up in anything, only for her to leave."

"Basically."

"So, then, maybe she'll stay a little longer if you're having fun."

I shook my head. "Her ex made her choose between her career and him. That didn't go well for him."

I wasn't about to derail her life. I wasn't going to make her decide between her career and me. I already had one woman I loved give up everything for me.

"Make her choose? Levi. You hardly know her. Now you're talking about serious life changes." His voice grew tense with incredulity. "You've only known her a few weeks."

And it only took a few hours, I thought, but didn't say.

An image of her flushed and laughing next to me, her deep

dimples on full display, had my heart thump hard. He didn't understand. I didn't understand. How could I express what I was still working through?

"You didn't even want a tenant, and now you don't want her to leave?" he added.

"That's not what I'm saying—"

"Because take it from someone who knows, it wouldn't do any good to go and fall for someone set to leave," Pace said flatly.

My screwdriver slipped and connected with something, causing a loud pop and bright spark that zapped my finger and set all my hair standing on edge.

I swore and dropped the screwdriver, cradling my hand as I winced.

"Oh shit. Sorry, man!" Pace covered his mouth as he looked at me. "Are you okay?"

I shook out my hand. "I'm fine. Just scared the shit out of me."

"Fuck. I'm so sorry. I must have flipped the wrong breaker."

I took a minute to collect myself and assess for any major damage. Mostly, my heart had a scare, and my finger was tingling, but it could have been a lot worse. "Now who's distracted?" I asked.

Pace looked sheepish and apologized again. There was a metaphor here: Pace's carelessness leading to my pain. He was lucky he made up for it by being a great friend. "I know, man, I'm sorry."

I looked at him closer now. It had been what I needed though. I jolt of electricity to get my head on right. I couldn't go and fall for a woman I just met. I was building it up. I was just ... lonely and projecting all sorts of shit on her.

I looked at Pace, really looked at Pace. There was a noticeable tension in his jaw and bruising under his eyes that spoke of a lack of sleep.

"Hey. For real, are you okay?" I asked.

Pace tugged off his ball cap and scraped his hair. He hesitated only a minute; something warred behind his light blue eyes. Finally, he slid a smile back in place. "Nah, I'm good. I just got off a shift and am tired, is all."

I held his gaze and waited. Sometimes, if I remained silent, I could wait him out in the awkwardness, and he'd break first, spilling whatever it was that was bothering him.

He flicked his eyes to the side, breaking the eye contact.

I waited, still watching him closely.

He cleared his throat and chuckled. "Really, man. I'm fine."

"If you need to—"

Ruth popped her head in. "The power went out in the downstairs parlor. Hi, Levi." Ruth flashed a wide smile at me, her gaze snagging, distracting her from whatever she'd been about to say. "Look at how flushed you are. Must be that pretty brunette chatting with Gigi across the street. The one I saw you dancing with?"

Pace gave me a look, fighting a grin.

I bent to pick up my stuff to leave. I'd had enough.

"I was wondering, if you have a minute, I'd love to ask you about some photos of your mother's?" she asked me.

I shook my head. The adrenaline still bolting through me. This was too much. It was all too much.

"Maybe next time. I have to head home. Pace is going to finish up here, Ruth," I said.

She gave me a long look that almost made me back down before she nodded. "Okay, sweetie."

Pace opened his mouth and closed it tightly after I pointed at the black spot on the wall switch.

"Yeah. I'll finish up here," he said.

This had been the reminder I needed. No leaving the house. Definitely, no falling for the tenant.

CHAPTER 20

Claire

For the next week, I lost myself in research on the life of Lily Carmichael. Aside from the Dad daily check-ins, I felt myself hardening into a Claire-shaped mass hunched over the keyboard. Some nights, as I worked late into the night, Levi was there in his workshop, blaring weepy indie rock. My favorite nights.

I text him occasionally, but without anything important to say, it felt like desperation.

"The bird is back," I texted him one morning.

"I'm starting to understand his language."

"He said, 'Put the slingshot down, lady.'" I sent in my patented rapid-fire series of texts.

"Lol," he replied.

"Oof," I said to Ripley, who was at my side. "El oh el, no punctuation. Even I can read the subtext in that." I stopped texting after that. Maybe I had my answer.

I couldn't even use Ripley as an excuse to text or visit because as we worked and throughout the days, she'd wander between Big Cabin and Little Cabin when attention became too lacking. I tried not to get stuck in the circular loop of why Levi ran so hot and cold. It did me no good.

When my phone buzzed with a text this morning, I'd had a moment of hope, thinking it might be Levi, at least checking in.

It was Kevin.

Instant stomachache.

He was all moved into his home in New York. It was swanky indeed. I knew that because he sent a grinning selfie of a luxurious-looking apartment with skyscrapers in the background window and a caption that read. "Never thought I would make it."

I didn't really think we were to the "sending selfie updates" phase of our breakup, so I left the message on read.

A few minutes later, he sent another message asking me how the article was going. I genuinely couldn't tell if he was being passive-aggressive, looking to see if I was failing or actually interested in my status. Regardless, I continued to ignore him.

My stomach churned. I had finished the edits and sent the final story out. It would be printed before Christmas. I will have done my job. Then I would start the next phase of my life. Whatever that may be. I thought of my stuff in storage and lugging it back to my childhood home. It was the best plan because it was the only one. But with each passing week, I regretted committing to it.

I'd feel better once the story was out. One step at a time.

I stood staring at how happy Kevin looked in the selfie, debating with myself until I heard the crunch of Levi driving away. I made it to the window in enough time to see him driving with Ripley. He turned onto the road heading in the direction of town.

I rubbed the knot amassing between my neck and shoulder blade. The guest shower was small and often freezing, even after warming up for ten minutes. The gorgeous deep-seated, clawfoot tub in Levi's bathroom. He said I was welcome to use his shower anytime. Surely, that extended to the bath too. I imagined lighting some candles and looking at the foliage from the massive bathroom window.

The dust in the road was still settling from where his tires had kicked it up.

"I would easily have an hour," I said to my reflection in the glass. "Even if he's just going to town, the round trip will be at least an hour. If not all day if he's doing a job."

"I could take a good half-hour bath, and he'd never even notice," I said.

I frowned at my reflection. "I thought we weren't doing this anymore." My reflection stuck out her tongue.

I grabbed some bath essentials and made my way to the Big Cabin, sprinting because the weather had officially turned and it was chilly. Also, my nerves made me jittery and rushed.

Levi was never gone less than a few hours when he left. There wasn't anything nearby that necessitated quick trips so when he left it was an event.

Nevertheless, as the filling tub clouded the bathroom with steam, I wiped the condensation from the window and kept watch to make sure there was no sign of his return. I lit some surrounding candles and poured some lavender bath oil "to help relaxation" according to the bottle.

I smiled to myself, thinking of this big, gruff man pulling out all the stops to have such a luxurious bath.

The sky was gray with clouds, but that only emphasized the color-changing trees. I dropped my clothes and stepped into the tub.

As soon as the silky, warm water ran through and over my body, tickling and teasing the areas so rarely touched, a heat burned through me. Instantly reminded of that incendiary kiss. My hand went to my collar to trace over where his short facial hair had rubbed. It moved to my neck, where he had laved my skin with his lips and tongue.

It was those hot, ragged breaths of his as he tried to compose himself that were burned into my mind. I heard them whenever I closed my eyes. He was always so quiet, so tightly wound. Hearing that lack of control was like glimpsing a secret. I kept hearing his harsh, barely tethered breathing repeat in my mind, wishing I could hear all his sounds.

It was so incredibly, thigh-clenchingly hot.

I replayed that kiss for the thousandth time. Kiss didn't even feel like enough of a word for what our bodies were doing. With Levi, it was like being pampered or cherished by his mouth and hands. That rawness when he broke away from me, putting space between us because he was wrecked. I had wrecked him.

All I wanted was to be fully wrecked in return.

My hand ran over my knee and traced down into the water. I had taken off my clothes in front of him before. I had caught the stare we both pretended not to notice. What would he think now?

What would he do if he watched the way my fingers slipped below the water to explore myself? Heat burned across my chest, the hot water and desire making the air stiflingly warm. I was lost to the momentum of my touch. I burned with shame, but I couldn't stop now. I was so far gone, so tightly coiled a few more brushes of my fingers, and I would release.

The quiet sounds of water splashing filled the peaceful space, soon matched by my breaths picking up as my hand moved under the surface. I sighed deeply, letting my head fall back. My right leg slipped over the lip of the tub, balancing behind the knee, as I rocked my hips up to get a better angle.

I groaned. My cheeks burned from the heat and shame at what I was doing.

I imagined him walking into the room. Finding me naked and sprawled out before him for the taking. He would take me rough and greedy or maybe torturously slow. He would leave my skin splotched and tender from his strong hands. My eyes closed tight, imagining every way he would use me, tease me. The way that same tongue would lick all over, lavish me, his gorgeous mouth sucking on my breasts and lower. He would bury his head between my legs and adore me for hours.

Levi had the confidence of a man who knew how to go down on a woman.

"Levi," I gasped out his name, luxuriating in my devious fantasy.

"Claire," he groaned.

God, it was like I could hear him in this room over my panting and moaning.

"Claire," Levi said louder, choked and short.

I gasped my eyes open, my leg slipping back in the water, causing a large splash of water over the edge. My hands flew out and gripped the sides of the tub. My heart that was already racing so fast, was out of control now.

"Oh my God!" I shouted.

I was no longer alone. Levi stood on the edge of the room. His pupils were blown out and locked on my face. Red bloomed on his nose, cheeks, and the tips of his ears. Bits of mud were splattered across his arms and face and in his hair. I hardly noticed the dirt when I was dirty enough for both of us. His neck and shoulder muscles were strained, and he was wrapped in a white cotton towel, gripping it at his hip like it was holding him together. His cock was tenting the material into the air, a very large area, out and up almost to his belly button.

My mouth went dry.

We stared at each other. I sank deeper into the water but didn't bother covering anything at this point. If anything, I fought the desire to arch my back and press my breasts up with every passing moment.

I opened my mouth to speak but couldn't come up with a single coherent thought. I felt embarrassed at being caught, but only mildly. Mostly, I felt like I had manifested him. I created this. I wasn't even entirely sure it wasn't still part of my fantasy.

Just how long had he been watching? Why did the idea of him watching me make me clench around where I wanted him to fill me? Maybe this had been my plan all along. Perhaps a perverted part of me wanted nothing more than to be discovered.

Even with his features frozen in shock, he was fucking gorgeous. All hot masculine energy, he practically throbbed with it. In the muscles of his shoulders and the smattering of hair on his broad chest to his solid core flexing a six-pack. His waist was narrow, the hair leading to his length.

I looked away to his still-shocked face. Then looked back. His bulge twitched when I looked again.

His free hand moved to cover it. Not like I could even see anything. Not really. And I was really looking. His large veiny hands and forearms covered enough but not the flexing of his thighs and definition of his calves not covered.

He was beautiful.

Couldn't we both give in to all the thoughts and fantasies?

After what could have only been years, he shifted on his feet, muffling a swear.

He said, "I wasn't—I didn't know you were in here."

"Sorry. I wasn't expecting you," I said at the same time.

I nodded, my chin dipping into the warm water, eyes locked

on his. A creeping sense of understanding filled me. Whatever was happening here was too far past the point of no return. We wouldn't be able to brush this off or ignore it like when we kissed. Maybe I just wouldn't let us.

"I'll just go." He ran a hand through his hair.

"Or ..." I suggested. "You can stay?"

CHAPTER 21

Levi

Claire was a fantasy come to life. Hot and pink from the water, no bubbles, all soft flesh and blurred heat. Her leg had been slung out of the tub, her nipples hard and poking out of the water when she threw her head back in silent pleasure. Eyes clenched tight as her hand worked under the water; I could only imagine what she was doing.

I came back to grab a quick shower after Ripley decided to roll in a puddle and then demanded to be carried back to the truck. There was no way I could have possibly expected to find the object of all my dirty dreams, soaked and waiting for me in my bathtub.

When I realized she was in there, I had already walked in.

When I realized what she was doing, I froze.

When I heard her gasp my name, I almost came.

I had called her name.

I had tried. I didn't mean to watch for even the seconds that I had. But she had been so beautiful, and my body was frozen with surprise and indecision.

My balls were so high and tight, my cock so hard; one brush, and I'd explode.

Now she offered me to stay. Claire studied me with heavy-lidded eyes, waiting for an answer.

What was I supposed to do here? My entire body felt like it was burning from the inside out. How could I feel like I was going to burst into flame and still be frozen in place?

I could stay. I could stay. The possibility of that short-circuited my brain.

"Well," she said after a long silence. "You do what you got to do," she said.

I swallowed with difficulty. Any second, my feet would carry me out of here.

"But I was sort of in the middle of something." Her long, silky leg lifted out of the water. At the same time, she rested her head back with a sigh, and one hand trailed down her thigh as the other luxuriously crossed her collar, causing water to collect and pool in the little dip I wanted so badly to lick.

Fuck. *Fuck*.

Leave! I screamed in my mind.

"I don't mind you watching," she said, giving me one long look as her hand began to work under the water. Had she really just said that? I groaned and somehow got even harder. Even the cotton of the towel against my cock was close to making me come.

What I wouldn't give to see what she was doing and memorize it so I could do it for her every day.

Her cheeks were flushed with color, but she never broke the bold gaze moving over my body. I felt my cock twitch again, as though if it tried hard enough, it could pull the towel away. My hips jutted out as I rocked forward on my toes, none of which I consciously did. My body was drawn to her.

Her back arched on a sharp gasp, pressing her breasts up and out of the water. The hard nipples broke the surface tension first, followed by the full cups, water streaking around and down them. I wanted to drop to my knees and suck them into my mouth, really make her scream.

"Jesus," I gasped.

Her gaze challenged, taunted. She was really doing this. She was moaning more frequently, louder, soft little inhales growing closer together, as her arm worked a steady motion.

She stared so hard at my towel; it was like she was trying to catch it on fire.

It was a challenge, and suddenly, I found myself feeling competitive.

Tentatively, questioningly, I moved my hand under the towel. Her eyebrows lifted, mouth parting as she watched me. Was I really doing this? Were we really doing this? It felt decided already. There was no leaving this room now. Not when we were locked in this dirty dare.

I kept my gaze riveted to hers as I widened my stance, decision made. I found my cock. I kept the towel in place with the other, allowing the tease to be enough. Like she was doing for me. *To* me.

I sucked in a sharp breath as I wrapped my hand around it and pumped it, once long and slow. I felt harder than I'd ever been; the skin burned. My precum dripped over onto my thumb and onto the towel.

Her mouth fell open, her gaze focusing on the motion of my hand.

"Yes," she whispered.

Her hand teased as the tension grew and grew. The elegant slope of her neck into her shoulders was captivating as the water splashed around them, creating rivulets at her jerking movements. Her eyes didn't close this time, they were open and locked on me. They also seemed to struggle to remain in one place. She looked at my face and hands and …

"I've imagined this. You," she said. "And so much more."

I ground my jaw. She had to stop talking or this would be over too fast.

"You're so hot," she said like it was painful. "I wish—"

"No. Don't," I said instantly.

Whatever she was about to say, I couldn't hear. I was already using all my strength to not come. I had to wait for her to come first, even if it killed me.

She whined, her legs rubbing together, the flush on her chest spreading up her neck. God, what it would be like to fuck her.

To make her moan like that while those thighs wrapped tight around me, while her perfect tightness clenched me deeper. I bit hard into my lip, squeezed hard around the base of my cock, to keep from coming. It was dirty and the hottest fucking thing I'd ever seen, and I wasn't even touching her. But it was her. It was her when I did this and thought of her. It was her that was getting me off now.

"Levi." Her legs shifted, she called out, almost in pain.

"You're so beautiful like this," I told her honestly, worried that the rawness in my voice might give too much away. "Please show me how you come. Claire, please," I begged.

"Oh, God." Her head fell back, eyes squeezed tight as she called out loudly. "I'm—"

She stopped when her whole body froze at its peak. The tendons of her neck were strained, nipples rock hard, water sloshing all over as her body went rigid, breath frozen after being sucked in. Under the water, her muscles would be clenching repeatedly and I wished I could feel it. I imagined stepping closer, releasing on those perfect breasts. The mark of me on soft skin and hard nipples.

Fire burned up my spine, and I came, shooting rope after rope of cum into the towel.

I grunted the last aftershock, even more thankful for the decision to keep the towel in place. A light wind would knock me over as I gathered my breath and waited to find some stability. Claire also panting, collected herself in the now silent—except for our breathing—room.

Eventually, she shifted and made a sound of distress as she brought her leg back into the tub.

"Are you okay?" I asked, panting, the heat of the moment giving way to awkwardness.

"Yeah. Rough angle. I just don't think I did anything to help the knot I came here to get rid of." She sat up in the tub, breasts on full display, no shame, as her head stretched side to side. Her arm was wrapped to rub at a spot between her shoulder blades, making them move in a hypnotizing manner. "Are you okay?" she asked gently. "I hope that wasn't too much."

Too much? Not nearly enough. And I was so far from okay. My whole body hummed with release and some parts shame, but mostly, I just wanted her even more. I wanted so much more. I gripped the dirtied towel tighter, anxious to get out of it, anxious to shower and have a few minutes to analyze all that I felt.

"Ahem, no. That was good," I said before my silence could go on too long.

Her gaze quickly flicked over me. She smiled. "Okay, good."

She leaned forward and pulled the plug from the drain. With no warning, she stood and got out of the tub, her entire front revealed. Water traveled down her shoulders and collar, making rivulets under her nipples and around her belly button. Her smooth belly, hips, and the swollen lips of her vulva were perfectly on display. I almost fell to my knees then to worship every inch with my tongue.

I turned away before my hard-on came back. Not that it had gone away completely.

She stepped closer, and her finger picked at something on my chest. "You're so dirty," she said.

"What?" I gasped out.

"The mud?" A slow smile made her dimples pop. "I'll let you get to your shower. Thanks for that. It was fun."

She reached across me, arm brushing my chest and bicep, stealing my breath, to grab an extra towel on the sink.

I clenched my jaw so hard, tension popped it. I would not look at that perfectly round ass tempting me. If I grabbed her hips and slid a finger into her, she'd be wet and swollen from her orgasm.

"Bye, Levi," she said, shooting me one last look. "I'm around if you ever want to do that again."

My nostrils flared as she sauntered out of the restroom.

CHAPTER 22

Levi

Life was a ticking clock. Every second since she came apart in the tub was another moment closer to our inevitable collision. As transparent as always, Claire made her desire clear. *Claire* as ever.

"She'd like that pun," I said out loud as I sanded an edge.

It had been three long and hard days, with emphasis on the hard, since I watched her get herself off. The most wonderful sight in the world. Not true; the most wonderful sight would be watching me sliding in and out of her tight body as my fingers got her off. That would be the only thing that could top it. Once I'd admitted the fantasies—and to be fair and very mature about it, she started it—it was like they couldn't be contained. In the past seventy hours, I had imagined every possible position we could put our mouths and bodies in with the tenacity and creativity of a teenage boy.

And every second of every day stretched longer and longer. Every morning, I woke up rock hard and spilled into my hand with hollow satisfaction. Every night, I worked until I passed out. I purposely pushed myself physically so no thoughts were possible. So I wouldn't march down to the Little Cabin to ask for what she offered so easily.

I had to make a decision soon. I picked up my phone. Or maybe I didn't. I put it back down.

Pace. If ever there was a time I needed the opinion of the man who was arguably far better with women, it was now.

But then. There was a part of me that cherished what had happened in the bathroom. Watching Claire had been gifted to me, her brazen forwardness always a gift but a private one. Plus, I could almost hear his warning; having had his heart broken before, Pace wouldn't understand how I could fall for Claire so simply, an instinctual decision that had been made without me. It was a decision that couldn't be changed. The feelings I had for her weren't rational or easily explained, and Pace hadn't understood. My friend cared that I would be hurt when she left. Now, it was a matter of how much hurt could be avoided. How would I get out of this alive?

I preferred to be stuck in this state of immobilization. I was better here. No quick movements to scare her away.

We wanted each other; that was not the problem. The problem was, I wanted more than that.

There was a knock on the workshop wall, even though the

metal door was open.

As always, my entire body became more aware the moment I saw her.

"Hey," she said when she must have observed the tension gather in me. Big strong man, so afraid of the little brunette with a larger-than-life smile. "I come in peace," she added and just like that, like always, I was disarmed by her.

I smiled at my planer as I set it on the bench and pushed up my safety goggles. "Come on in."

I wouldn't have to make the decision after all. The moment I saw her, it all became obvious. She was here. And for once, all of me was on the same page.

I was tired of fighting my desire to be near her. She moved to one of the stools near the tall bench, tugging her sweater down over her hands and wrapping herself up. She wore tight leggings and a sweater despite the cold. I went to the main door and tugged it down to keep out most of the chilly air. It always got hot when I was working, but the temperature at this time of night dipped low.

My feet brought me to stand in front of her. Her focus was blurred, eyes wide in a thousand-yard stare.

"Claire?" I asked.

She straightened and blinked, turning her head in my direction, but her eyes still locked on some distant point. I frowned, noticing that she was more disheveled than I'd seen her. Her eyes were bloodshot, her hair piled on her head, and a pale pallor to her cheeks. She had warned me that she was different when she was in research mode, but it was startling to see firsthand. An air of anxiety hummed in the air around her, in the jumping of her leg and the short nails bitten to the quick. Her gaze kept moving around the room, avoiding me.

"Claire," I said more firmly and rested my hands on her shoulders.

She finally met my eyes. They cleared their haze, and she took me in for the first time. I was aware that I only wore my loose work khakis and a white tee, clinging to my sweating body. They moved over me and she swallowed.

"How are you?" she asked, voice high and tight.

Whatever was on her mind, she was trying hard to delay the inevitable. That made me nervous. There was no conversation Claire wasn't perfectly willing to barrel straight through. I stepped back, crossing my arms to lean against the workbench opposite her.

Maybe she hadn't come here to take things to the next level; maybe she was here to stop us from going down the physical path that seemed inevitable only seconds ago.

I wished I hadn't set down my tool so I could keep my hands busy and avoid making eye contact.

"I'm fine. I haven't seen you around much," I said and cursed myself for the stiff and awkward small talk. This was why we both agreed it was a waste of time.

"I've been working," she said, eyes going foggy again as she checked out to wherever she went.

I nodded. "I wondered where you disappeared to." Then I

wondered if that gave too much away. So I quickly added, "New story?"

She straightened, a hint of her usual clarity returning to her distracted and rapidly moving eyes.

"Yeah. That's why I'm here." She tugged her bottom lip in to chew on it. "I actually found out something, and it's a lot to take in."

"Ah." I gripped the bench behind me.

Claire's stomach made a loud rumble, and she quickly wrapped her hands around her middle.

"Are you hungry?" Had we even shared a meal since the fall festival? That didn't seem right. That's what she was missing. Wining and dining. That's what she deserved. "Want some food?"

Her face went slack, like the mention of food made her nauseated. "No. I'm just—ignore that. It's nerves."

The visits in town, the nervous fidgeting, the researching; it all clicked into place. All at once, I knew why she was here. I knew what she discovered.

I ground my molars as grim determination sharpened her features, and she forced herself to meet my gaze.

My palms grew sweaty, and the edges of my vision blurred.

"I found out something." I shook my head as she started talking. "I thought that there was something familiar about Lily's, uh, your mom's work. I couldn't shake it."

I turned my back. I gripped the edge of the workbench. I felt the earth tilting. *Come on, get it together.*

Distantly, Claire's words filtered in, though I tried to block them out. "There's this guy who's famous in my world, well, my world adjacent. I know he's a travel photographer who built a name for himself. Richard Stanley."

The ringing in my ears began then. The muscles of my shoulders were high and tight. "Claire," I growled.

If she heard me, it didn't stop the obviously rehearsed words. "He-he first popped up around the same time that your mother was starting to make a name for herself in the art world. It's become obvious in my research, albeit still in its initial stages, that this *man*"—here, her words sharpened with disgust—"plagiarized not only your mother's work stylistically, but in some cases actually stole some of her shots. Based on some negatives that I have uncovered. Levi, I'm so sorry."

My eyes were squeezed shut. I winced away when her hand came to rest on my shoulder. "Did you hear me?" she asked lightly.

"I heard you." My voice cracked.

"I know this is probably awful to hear about your mother. The injustice of it all makes me sick. This-this sleazebag has gone on to have a career riding the coattails of works that are not his own. Yet he continues to use that earlier success to this day, no doubt financially as well, for these past thirty years."

I took steadying breaths in and out. "Leave it," I growled out the words. My throat was raw with the restraint I used.

"But the silver lining in all this is that I have started compiling a pretty credible case against him. I think, with a few more weeks, maybe more, of work, I can really have something here. I already pitched the idea to my editor."

"You what?" I spun, barely reining in my anger as the words burst out of me.

She blanched, reeling back. "No names or details, of course." She held her hands up in a soothing gesture. "I wanted to talk to you first."

"You need to leave it, Claire," I said slowly and flatly.

Her eyebrows contorted in hurt confusion. "Didn't you hear me? I have proof. I could write the story. Your mother deserves justice."

"Jesus, Claire, I said leave it!" This time, I did shout.

Her shoulders rose and fell in anger. "Leave it? Are you kidding me?"

"I should have known the second I showed you that room that it wouldn't be enough to share this part of myself with you. You couldn't just accept the piece of myself that I offered. You had to keep going and going."

Her eyes were moving all around, trying to put pieces together, trying to catch up. "I wasn't trying to pry. I recognized something about her style. I thought—I thought you would want to know this about your mother. I thought you would be upset, sure, but you want me to leave it?"

"That is what I said." The fear. The sadness. The helplessness. They all clawed up my throat. It made me feel like I'd swallowed scalding coffee, burning me from the inside out. But more than anything, the anger, the pure unadulterated rage that lit up every cell, making me want to scream and flip the workbench, rip it from the hardware securing it, and throw it across the room like something out of a horror movie.

"Just like that?" Her head was shaking as she spoke. "I thought you would want to know that this snake of a man was stealing her work. I thought you would want to know the truth."

My chest was hammering; I imagined my features were twisted in a terrifying snarl as I spat the next words out at her. "I know who he is. I know all about everything he did." I tossed out my arms. Hands flexing to keep from grabbing and breaking something. "I know because he's my bastard father." I huffed a humorless laugh as her eyes went wide in horror. "Or I guess it's more realistic to say I'm his bastard son."

CHAPTER 23

Claire

This wasn't happening. I had rehearsed this scenario a hundred times in the past few days, thinking of exactly how I would break this awful news to Levi. Never, in any reiteration, had I imagined him already knowing and wanting me to stop my search for justice.

"Your father?" I said, but it was mostly to myself as I processed this information. I certainly hadn't accounted for that.

His father. That couldn't be right. But the dates lined up, and even looking at his strong jaw and that patrician nose, the hints of Richard Stanley were there. But still. Why would he ever want me to stop? He loved and cared about his mother. My brain couldn't make sense of it.

I looked around at the workshop and thought of his gorgeous

cabin with all the top-of-the-line furnishings. Had that *man*, that thief, funded this life for Levi? Was this another case of man looking out for man? Was this like Kevin wanting to protect his job over my story? Was he protecting this life? I'd managed to find yet another man who wanted to conceal a horrible, awful truth rather than deal with a modicum of discomfort.

I would have never thought in a million years that Levi would be like that. He seemed to be unconcerned with the things the rest of capitalist society cared about. Then again, only people who could afford to could easily say they wouldn't be a cog in the machine.

"Forget the research. Forget the article. Let. It. Go," he said when I remained quiet, processing.

I looked up to find the man standing right in front of me. His nostrils were flared, red flushed up his neck as he narrowed his eyes, boring them into me.

He had the audacity to be mad at me?

"I don't need your permission to write this article. I came here as a-a friend, or whatever, to tell you because I thought you would want to know. Now I see I misread the situation." Again.

I felt sick, worse than the nerves had made me feel. I felt lied to, cheated once again by a man I thought I understood, thought I shared some of the same incorruptible scruples. I couldn't even think about the feelings I'd been harboring for him right now without another wave of nausea. How was I so naive? How was I so susceptible to this type of man? How did I miss the signs around me?

Betrayed. That was the word. The familiar feeling that I fought so hard to protect myself from. Thinking I had all the information only to feel like the ultimate idiot.

Hot anger burned the back of my eyes as I twisted to shove past him and get out of there.

"You've got to be kidding me!" He spun and kicked a large plastic bucket across the room.

I yelped, shoulders to my ears, racing now to the exit. He wasn't violent, but I wouldn't stay and play witness to his pouting either. Thank God, Ripley was still up at my cabin. I could only imagine how she would react to such an immature display of temper.

"Where are you going? We aren't done talking," he called after me.

"We really are. You don't need an audience for your tantrum." I was proud of myself for concealing my nerves.

"You always have to go too far," he spat.

It was enough to get me to stop in my tracks, spin on my heels, and spit right back, "Excuse me? Just because I have a spine!"

"You have no idea what you're talking about." He stomped toward me, but this time, I held my ground.

Even now, I wasn't actually afraid of him. I had once watched him carefully place each one of Ripley's paws in a bootie even as she struggled. Despite his size, he was not a brute.

I couldn't understand him, understand this rapid change in him. My arms flopped to my side in defeat. I wasn't going to publish a story he explicitly told me not to. I was just so angry and helpless. "Don't you want justice for your mother?"

He scoffed, eyes searching the ceiling for some answer. "Of course I fucking do! You don't think this eats at me every single day? Why I couldn't even go in that cabin for the last year? You think I chose this life of cowardice?"

"I-I don't understand," I said, feeling that I lost my footing the second I walked in here, like I was trying to walk up an ice-covered hill.

"I know you don't, which is why I am telling you to leave it." His words were more even-keeled, but the rage still pulsated out from him in his shoulders and clenched jaw.

"If you would only try to explain—"

"Leave it."

"But wouldn't she want—"

"No!" He tugged at his hair, eyes pinched tight. "It was her choice. Lily's. I tried to get her to do something about the plagiarism. We all did." He waved an arm toward the direction of town. "But she wouldn't have a word of it. It was her choice to let him take her credit and run with it. She never tried to stop him. She didn't care about the notoriety. More than that, it was her dying wish that I didn't do anything posthumously. She never wanted to give him any of her energy. Her words." He scoffed, and his jaw clenched on a tight smile. As the last wave of anger retreated, I could see now that all that was left was a desolate shore of sadness. "She swore the injustice didn't matter. That she was happy. She still held this silly fucking idealism, even as she was wasting away from the illness that ate her from the inside out."

He sharply turned his head away as his eyes glistened. My mouth parted in shock. His words restructured all the thoughts I had filed away.

"I'm so sorry," I said softly.

His Adam's apple bobbed on a loud, tight swallow. "He left when she got pregnant. He never cared about either of us. He took what he wanted, and he left."

I slumped back, realization draining blood from me so fast I felt dizzy. My fingertips and lips tingled from the shock of his revelation. "I-I didn't know."

And a minute ago, I had assumed the worst of this man when all he'd done was help and protect me since the moment I arrived. What was wrong with me?

"Why couldn't you just leave well enough alone? Why did I have to show you that fucking room?" His voice went soft, and his head dropped, looking so hurt and vulnerable.

"I will. I'll stop. I'm sorry," I repeated.

This was what happened when I didn't have all the information. People got hurt.

He finally lifted his gaze to mine, raw sadness etched in every line of his features. "It's my fault. I should have known what the curiosity would do to you. Pandora's box and all that."

I winced as he looked away. Because I was a machine that never knew when to stop. I was the bad guy in this story, well, one of them, picking at an almost healed scab until it was raw and bleeding again.

My apologies felt empty. I wanted to tell him that I thought I was helping, that this had all been a deep dive in some backward way to try to help him heal.

But had it?

Had this been about me, once again seeking out the truth under the guise of righteousness when, really, I just wanted to be the one who figured it out first and put the pieces together? Did I want justice, or did I want validation?

My head spun from the adrenaline rush of the argument and the day of anxiety leading up to the confrontation. I felt buzzy and weird and unsure of all the swirling things in my mind.

Levi shifted and let out a sigh as he slumped into the chair.

This wasn't about me. Not right now. I would process my complicated feelings later.

"Levi," I said and stepped forward to place a hand on his arched shoulders.

With his head down and his strong shoulders wrapped in the soft material of his tee, he looked like a marble statue of a defeated demigod.

I couldn't apologize enough, so I slowly stepped forward until our knees brushed. His breath stuttered, but a moment later, his legs widened. He grabbed my wrists and tugged me forward until no space was left between us. His forehead pressed against my chest, and he let me cradle his head. I could comfort. I could only give and not take.

"I think about it every damn day," he said, letting himself exhale deeply, the warm air seeping through my sweater.

"How could you not?" I brushed the hair from his temple to

run my fingers through.

"I don't know what the right thing is in this situation." His arms were looped behind my back, resting on my bottom. "I feel like I'm failing her. But it was her choice. I couldn't dissuade her. She was so stubborn about this. If she didn't care about justice, then anything I could do would be for my benefit. It would go directly against her wishes, and I just can't."

I inhaled and exhaled deeply. His words settled into me. If the person didn't want justice, then any action would be done for selfish reasons. That resonated with me, and I tucked it away to process later. There would be no article about Lily Carmichael written by me. This family's history was their own.

"You're not failing her. You're respecting her wishes. You just have to own that choice and make peace with it. It's the fighting yourself that's causing you trouble."

He nodded against my sternum.

"You're a good son," I said.

His body tensed as he nuzzled deeper and pulled me tighter. "Thank you." His mumbled words rumbled through me.

This was not how I thought this day would go, yet even now, knowing what I did, a part of me was disappointed that I wouldn't get to finish the piece. That I would have to shift gears and find another trail to chase. A new plan. The entire prospect of starting all over again made me feel weary. I wanted to go to sleep for a week to make up for the frantic high I'd been existing on. As it quickly drained out of me, it left behind a void that felt dangerous.

Minutes passed, and Levi hadn't released the tight hold on me. Actually, his thighs squeezed me closer. His forehead had started rubbing back and forth slowly. The awareness of that pebbled my nipples, and I stilled to see where this was going to make sure I wasn't misreading the situation. His nose brushed against my breast, and a tremble of desire raised the hairs on my arm. I didn't come here for this. I hadn't meant to tease him after our last meeting, but I had gotten carried away in the work.

I wasn't sure when the air shifted so drastically, but a heavy tension filled it now. I was all too aware of how his scent relaxed my shoulders, how his hands had moved at some point to grip my hips. His thumb moved in small circles, sending a tingling electricity to my core. There was so much want, so heavy and tangible in the little bit of space between us.

My hands gently pushed on his shoulders until he released me enough to look up at me.

"Are you okay?" I winced, biting my tongue to keep from apologizing again.

I didn't want to cheapen it with overuse.

"Yeah." His features were clearer and more relaxed now. "I shouldn't have lost my temper like that. I'm embarrassed," he said.

How marvelous that he could identify his feelings so easily in the moment. It would probably take me a week to work through the past ten minutes. This poor man. All the things that I couldn't understand before slid into place. Every time he went to town and they spoke about his mother, all his insecurities and doubts were thrown back in his face. Every time he stepped foot in the Little Cabin, he would see those final moments with her, begging her to change her mind. The anger at a man he didn't know who started his life and stopped caring there. It was why he had been hiding in the safety of his home, and I had dragged him out into the cold kicking and screaming.

"I would have never—"

"I know," he said. "If I had just been honest from the beginning, we would have avoided all this."

"It's a lot to unload on an almost stranger. Here's some food. Also, here's all my trauma."

He chuckled softly. "Yeah, I guess."

"Not everybody has a full-on episode and shares their current chaos upon first meeting," I said, pulling a face to show my own awkwardness.

"Only the special ones." He smiled up at me. It was criminal how handsome he was.

I bent and dropped a kiss on his temple without thinking. More tension melted from him. It was nice to be able to make somebody relax instead of clench with worry at my arrival. I kissed his other temple to keep things balanced, lingering a moment longer. His thumbs had worked under the fabric of my sweater and now brushed against the skin of my stomach, causing heat to settle heavy and low in me.

"You know," he said slowly. "When you first showed up, I thought you were here for an entirely different reason."

"And what reason was that?" I asked boldly, breathily.

His eyes darkened as he watched me, causing a swoop in my stomach. "Boredom." His rumbling, heated voice was delicious.

"What a terrible bait and switch."

He laughed before he cleared his throat. "And the funny thing is that I had just finally decided I wanted to stop holding back."

The swoop swooped with even swoopier gusto. "Holding back?"

"From all the things I wanted to do to you. With you." His eyes seemed to go completely black as they held mine. "Make a few addenda to the rules."

A soft squeak came from me. He had to hear how loud my heart beat against my sternum.

"But I could understand if—" Here, his face grew pensive again, almost regretful. "If you're no longer *bored*."

"It was a very riveting turn of events." I used a finger to lift his chin and lowered my mouth to hover just above his lips. "What I'm feeling is anything but boring."

He closed the distance, and our lips met in a soft exhale. He pulled back too quickly.

"Claire, if you don't leave right now, I won't be held responsible for what happens."

"Why would you be? There are two of us here. Don't be so old-fashioned."

"Nothing I want to do is old-fashioned," he said before our mouths met again.

Nothing was stopping him, he'd said. But what had been stopping him before? What held him back that was no longer an issue? Was it the shame of his past? Or this final secret? This and other questions were quickly relocated to the back of my mind as his greedy tongue pushed into mine, making me moan in pleasure.

His fingers gently brushed my cheeks as his head tilted to kiss me deeper. He held me like I was something delicate and precious. At the same time, his hard length pressed against my hip. His tongue brushed mine so confidently, seductively. He took his time. His long, gentle kiss said he could do this forever. In contrast, I squirmed in impatience. I wanted to climb up on top of him or drag him up to his bedroom. I wanted him so bad. I wanted to feel him fill other parts of me, press me down, and feel the weight of him on top of me. I wanted every sense to be overcome by only him.

"Levi," I gasped his name, surprised by an aching surge of tenderness in my chest.

I wanted to take care of him too. I wanted to remove his pain and long-suffering until he only felt my desire for him.

CHAPTER 24

Levi

Claire shifted impatiently and pressed herself harder against me with a frustrated groan. Sitting on this chair with her standing between my legs wasn't nearly enough.

I smiled against her mouth. "Something wrong?"

Her hands moved restlessly, never ceasing as they clawed and gripped up and down my arms and shoulders and back. I wanted to touch her everywhere too. I was quaking with the need. But more than that, I wanted to drive her wild. Wanted to show her that there was no rush for me. I would spend hours just holding her delicate chin and kissing her pretty mouth. I wanted her melting and on the edge of combustion when I finally touched her.

"I need more," she said.

"So impatient."

She growled. "You started this." It was bordering on a whine.

"Hmm. It really doesn't feel like that," I said.

I kissed her deeper, allowing my hands to thread through her hair, thinking of the thousands of times I'd dreamed about just this. I wasn't going to have it pass too quickly. I tugged her hair a little to break the kiss and have her meet my eyes with her dark, heated gaze. Her lips were glistening and swollen. She seemed half out of her mind already.

"If we recall, it was you who kissed me first. You who—" I swallowed with difficulty. Bringing this up again made my control slip. "Touched yourself for me to watch."

She groaned another whine. "Levi."

I lowered my mouth to just below her ear, brushing my lips up the column of her throat. I nuzzled my nose along where her hair met the smooth skin of her neck. I whispered along the shell of her ear. "You were so wet that day, weren't you?"

She gasped out and collapsed so that I had to stand quickly to capture her. I hefted her up and carried her to the only cleared-off surface in the workspace, a small table where I'd sometimes take breaks to eat. I don't think I'd ever be able to eat my lunch at this table the same way again. Not without remnants of Claire infiltrating every thought.

I set her down on the table and stepped back to take her in.

"I just need to look at you," I said.

She leaned back on her hands for support, her breasts hard under the sweater. Her neck was flushed, and her chest was rising and falling rapidly as she watched me with heated confusion at my retreat.

"You want this, don't you, Claire?" I asked, adjusting myself.

She watched the motion before she nodded seriously. "Yes. I want you, Levi." Straight to the point as ever, my sweet, earnest Claire.

"Before we go any further, I want you to understand why I've been holding back," I said.

Her gaze flicked to the side before coming back. "Okay."

"I've wanted this for some time. I've wanted you. And I know that once I let go of this restraint, this thirst won't be easily quenched. When I want something, I want it with my entire being. I don't really half-ass anything in my life. When I finally have you, it's going to be fully. Repeatedly. Ruthlessly."

She'd been nibbling her bottom lip as I spoke. It popped out of her mouth now. She swallowed, legs rubbing together once. "I'm wondering where the warning is?" Heat and determination lit her eyes. She wouldn't be backing down. If anything, my suggestion that she couldn't handle my advances only riled her up more. She never backed down from a challenge.

She would never let the unexplored go so easily.

I shrugged and stepped back to her. "Consider yourself warned." I brought my mouth just above her collarbone and sucked hard and quick.

She gasped, and a tremble went through her body.

"What is it that you want, Claire?" I moved to her other side and dragged my nose up the column of her neck, barely grazing her skin, a contrast to the rough sucking. She smelled so addictive. She was perfectly created to muddle my senses. "What will finally quench your thirst?"

She arched her back and pressed her hips forward. She brushed against my jeans, and my half-erection hardened, pressing painfully against the zipper. I grunted as I pushed forward and against her core, hot even through the layers of fabric.

She gasped and threw her head back.

"Is that what you're curious about?" I teased.

My hand tangled into her decadently soft hair, and I pulled until she met my gaze. Her pupils were blown out, lips parted and wet. "Is this what you want to know? How full I'll feel inside you?" I lowered to run my tongue along those lips that have been driving me absolutely crazy. "Or maybe how my mouth will be on your body?" I pulled her bottom lip into my mouth to suck on it lightly before releasing it.

She gasped, and her tongue went to taste and bite where I had been.

"You aren't alone in this search for knowledge," I said since her words seemed to be missing for once. I was happy to do all the talking, thrilled to list every dirty thing I wanted to do to her. "I think about these lips all the time. I think about sucking and licking them. I think about how they will look—"

I cut myself off. My thoughts spilled out unfiltered and vulgar. I checked her to make sure I hadn't gone too far.

"How?" she gasped, grinding herself heedlessly against my bulge. "How my lips will look doing what?"

I licked my lips and grinned at her. "Wrapped around my cock. I'm so hard for you." I pivoted my hips to rock along her. "I think about you all the time. I watch you work, and it drives me crazy. I see your breasts in that shirt, and I want to squeeze and tongue them. Every inch of you. God, when I saw you take off your clothes, I thought I was going to lose it."

"Yes. I-I want to know it all too."

"Good." I yanked her hips up and off the table, signaling she should wrap her ankles behind me. She obeyed so perfectly. "I'm going to get these out of the way." I tugged on the elastic hem of her leggings.

She nodded, shifting to balance on one hand to help as I held her ass up with one hand and worked with her to tug down the leggings. I wanted to fall to my knees and devour her on the table right there. I collected myself. With her panties still on, I brought her ass back to the table. With both hands free, I coaxed her knees wide apart and ran my hands up her thigh.

"Fuck." The fabric of her underwear was darkened from her dampness. I softly ran my finger over the material, knowing that she was going to be so hot and swollen when I finally pressed into her.

Instead of ripping off the only thing that stood between us, like I was desperate to, I brought myself back to her mouth, kissed her, memorized her, hands sprawling under the back of her sweater, thumb grazing her rib cage and up to the bottom of her breast. I pushed the sweater up and out of my way so I could fully look at her.

"Okay?" I asked.

"God, yes."

I took the permission and ran with it. I tugged down a lace bra to cup her breast. She groaned louder as I tweaked her nipple and ran my other hand up her thigh to brush my thumb against the growing wet spot.

I pulled back to look questioningly.

"All stations go." She gasped. She met my gaze. "I'll tell you if I want you to stop."

I nodded and carefully used my thumb to pull the edge of her panties out of the way. I was panting and sweating when I looked down at her glistening and exposed core.

"Gorgeous," I mumbled. Slowly, I dragged my thumb up and down. "Look how perfect you are."

"Levi," she groaned, gripping me tighter and trembling as I brushed over her swollen bud.

Her spine arched, legs trying to curl up, but I kept her spread wide.

I swirled my finger into her and felt the silky moisture growing as I gave her all the information she needed.

"I think about how wet you'd get. All the time. Just like this." I pressed her moisture hard into her clit. "I think about how tight you'd feel around me."

Her knees had a viselike grip on my hips, her body rocking out of pure instinct as it begged to get closer. I had to help her. Centimeter by centimeter, I pushed my middle finger inside her, where her walls clenched, and pulled it deeper.

She was feverishly hot and trembling. Her folds were slick as I worked to continue to tease everywhere.

"More," she said between pants.

I slid another finger into her, my thumb circling, testing softer or harder, fingers strong and working hard. "I want to slide down these panties and bend you over this table. I want to bite it and suck bruises on the inside of your thighs. I want to make you scream. I want to make you delirious."

I said every dirty fantasy that had come into my mind since I'd met her. I thought about how badly I'd wanted her for weeks now and how much I'd been lying to myself. Every thought had been her. I've imagined her in my bed, on this exact workbench, in the bed of my truck. I've thought of her everywhere. "All I want to do is fall to my knees and eat this dripping pussy until I make you come over and over and over."

Tension burned through me, and my groin ached. I had to hold on. Had to get her there before I broke. It felt nearly impossible. But the only thing more important than my release was hers. My other hand cupped and squeezed her breast as her head flew back with a mighty moan of pleasure. She came on my fingers, clenching and spasming, drenching me. "Fuck," I swore as I watched her come apart. "Fuck. You are so fucking beautiful."

I waited patiently as she came back to herself. Felt a few aftershocks spasm around my fingers, slowly pushing them out of her.

"Does that answer your questions?" I brought my fingers to my mouth and sucked.

She leaned forward, holding herself up on a shaking arm.

"Not even close." She tugged me by my shirt until my mouth slammed against hers again. Her fingers slid down my chest until she palmed where I was painfully hard. "I have so many more questions."

She fumbled for the buttons of my jeans. I couldn't take it anymore. The tease of her taste was still in my mouth, her greedy hand brushing against me. I needed so much more. I needed to release this before I exploded.

"I need to—" I gasped out.

"I've got you," she said, panting, forehead pressed to mine as she focused on her work.

She unzipped me and pulled me free as I gasped in pleasurable pain. She wrapped her hot hand around me, and I groaned and gripped the bench behind her, worried I was going to come right there.

"Fuck, I'm—"

"Good." She pumped me three times, and my hands went back to her breasts.

I kissed her neck. I touched everywhere. I was lost. I wasn't thinking. My body thrust into her hand, rough and hard. She held on tight and took it all.

"So good. So good," I mumbled.

She had to brace herself to keep up with my out-of-control pumps.

"Can I come on you?" I gasped.

"God, yes. Come on me."

Fire shot down my spine and exploded my vision, whitening

everything out. I looked down in time to watch as I spilled along her soaked panties and thighs. I came harder than I ever had. I shuddered another jerking release at the gorgeous sight of her.

I ran my free hand down my face as I took in the sight of her, leaned back on her elbows, chest flushed, breasts out, legs sprawled and dripping from both of us. She was incredible. I ran a finger down her core, causing a spasm in her as she watched me watching her. I leaned forward and kissed her again. She met me back with a greedy kiss.

"I'll get something to clean up. Stay here," I said.

She fell back against the table with an exhale. "I just need a breath. Then I have so many questions."

I smiled as I reached for the soft blue workshop towels. "I have no doubt. I'm here to help."

CHAPTER 25

Claire

Cozy Creek Confectionery was fully decorated for fall as Madi flitted from table to table, helping tourists and locals alike with an easy smile and friendly chatter. I'd become a sort of regular these past few weeks, chatting with locals and learning all the hot gossip. Sometimes, Dad joined in from my computer on a video call, falling for this funky little town as much as I was.

Did I know about the one and only Huber car service? Did I know a billionaire was in town?

"No! Tell me everything," I'd said, and Madi did between customers, Gigi filling in pieces for me.

The journal I'd started keeping when I first got here about the stories of Cozy Creek had even started getting some traction online. Not a lot, as it wasn't as exciting to read as watch videos these days, but enough that it kept the side project alive. Even though I wasn't changing the world with these hidden treasures, I found I couldn't get enough of them. They kept me occupied as I waited to hear back from my editor. I had emailed her to tell her that I couldn't do the Lily story but pitched a few others that I would hopefully get excited about when the time came. For now, I interviewed the locals and learned about the Ruby Ridge Art Retreat, just outside of town.

"Only one more week, huh? I feel like I'm just getting to know you," Madi said. "Then again, I'm leaving too." Her voice held the same sad realization that settled in my bones.

"I know. It doesn't feel real. Time is going so fast," I said.

We sat for a beat in silence, both staring without saying what weighed on us. Neither of us voiced it out loud.

I couldn't think about how Levi and I were obsessed with each other. How we'd fully given in to our desire for each other. How we hadn't talked about what any of this meant or if we had a future. I tried to think of a plan where I could move on from here but found it hurt too much, and the plan was already decided. He hadn't mentioned when my rental was up either.

Maybe I should make a PowerPoint presentation to clarify the boundaries and expectations of this newly budding situation-ship?

But then, what if I imagined things that weren't there? He typically shared easily. If he wanted to see me after my time was up ... it wouldn't matter. I had a storage unit of all my stuff waiting for me to come get it, and my dad had already booked his flight.

My phone lit up, and I reached for it, instantly wondering if Levi was ready to head back. Not to sound like a teenage girl, but maybe we would finally go all the way tonight.

Instead, I winced when I saw it was Kevin. Again.

"Hope you are doing okay. Heard the news. Call me if you want to talk." I stared at his confusing text for too long. What news? Was he stalking me? Had small-town gossip about Levi and me somehow made it up to his fancy New York condo? I highly doubted that.

"Oh, that's a face I know too well. Either the milk is expired in that coffee or an ex-boyfriend?" Madi said.

"My ex," I said, shaking off his confusing comment. The coffee *was* bad, milk or not, but I kept that to myself.

"Ew."

"I don't know why he continues to talk to me. I haven't even been thinking about him at all," I confessed.

"I wouldn't be either if I spent that much time with Levi Carmichael." She smiled suggestively, but I didn't spill the beans.

"I think my ex is just toying with me. I don't know."

My phone lit up again, and it was my editor this time. This call I would take. "Excuse me."

I stepped outside and despite the cold fall day, the sun shone bright and felt good on my face.

"Hey, Claire." Melanie's voice was tight and businesslike.

"Hey, Mel. What's going on?"

She sighed. "Listen. I don't have a lot of time, so I'm going to get this out as fast as I can before the big boss comes down here.

There's no good way of putting this, but I know you, and you like it straight to the point anyway."

A cold breeze had me shiver as a cloud moved in front of the sun. My stomach churned audibly.

"Okay," I whispered, slumping into one of the metal bistro seats.

"You're about to get an email saying you've been let go. The Finance Scheme story has been pulled from next month's schedule too. They're threatening legal action if we publish it. I'm so sorry. I *really* am. I fought for you."

"What—no. That can't be because every source was sound. Triple verified."

"I know. It's absolute BS. Shit, he's on his way down. He just messaged me. The short reason is claiming budget cuts, but it's bullshit."

"But all those people—" My fingertips went icy numb. The single mom and her ceramic beads. It was almost Christmas. My ears rang so loudly that I couldn't fully process what Mel told me.

"I know. It's a bullshit reason. The truth is, one of our last advertisers is a subsidiary of his company. They would pull their ads if we ran the story about him. Crap. I hear big boss. Gotta go. I'll call tonight. I just wanted you to hear it from me before you saw the email. I'm so sorry. I did try, but my hands are tied. It's been great working with you. I wish you the best of luck, and you will always have a reference with me."

The call ended without so much as a click. Just like my career. Soundless. Without fanfare. All these years of working hard, searching out justice, trying to make a difference ...

I couldn't think about it for another second—

I stared unseeing for so long. Distantly, I registered my brain was in shock. It wasn't dissimilar to the days that followed Kevin's departure. I was numb. But not numb in a physical sense, numb, as though I floated outside my body. My stomach clenched with a viselike grip cramp, and my fingertips were icy. I registered it all but absorbed nothing as my brain became a maelstrom of endless looping fears and anxieties.

People talked around me, but I heard nothing. I needed to get out of here. I needed to figure out what the hell I was supposed to do now. Jobless. Soon-to-be homeless. I was a disaster. But I worked so hard to avoid this. I did all the things I was supposed to. And just like that, everything was gone.

"How long has she been like this?" Levi's voice pierced the fog.

"About twenty minutes. She isn't answering us. Just mumbling that she's okay. As you can see, she's catatonic."

"Thanks for getting me. I'll get her home," he said.

Home. I snorted as Levi scooped me up and carried me to his truck. A rational part of my brain would be embarrassed about this coddling later. It was lamenting how poorly I was handling the situation, but then I remembered Kevin's cryptic text and blurred into oblivion again.

We made it back to the driveway somehow. Ripley whined and circled on my lap.

And how could this be happening? When I'd been feeling so good, very much in the physical sense, thanks to the past week. From the day Levi had given me the most spectacular orgasm of my life, and lucky me, every day since then. Every day, I texted him and met him up at Big Cabin or in the work shed, and every day, we came together literally and figuratively to explore each other with our hands and mouths. I never offered for him to come to my place since it was still so tied up in memories. But every day, we would lick and kiss and bring each other to orgasm. I was in heaven.

I was resting regularly and relaxed for the first time I could remember. From college to my career, I'd never felt like I'd taken a single breather. It was always the next step in the plan, the next story consuming my mind. I had never luxuriated in the touch of another person, woken up late, only to fool around and go back to sleep without a care in the world.

Maybe that was why I was paying the price now. I was caught unaware.

Levi carried me up to his room and tucked me in. The sheets smelled familiar now. It felt like comfort.

"Just sleep. We will talk tomorrow," he whispered as he tucked me in. I registered the worry creasing his sharp features, but it was like the sound of a distant train, noticed but unregistered at the same time. He pressed a light kiss to my temple, and the first tear formed behind my clenched eyes.

I fell asleep instantly, even though it wasn't dark outside.

I shot up, slamming awake. My heart raced as I remembered it all. From Levi's bedroom window, the comforting glow of his workshop was like a beacon in the dark, cold night. Urgency, like I never felt, moved me forward. There was no time to waste. Nothing was promised. Nothing really mattered. Any effort was pointless.

I pushed into slip-ons and made my way to Levi. It must have been after midnight. I had no idea what time it was. I didn't care. The garage was open as always, despite the cold of deep fall now and the lightly falling snowflakes.

Late fall meant heavy snow, and winter was right around the corner. Winter meant the end of this contract. It meant the end of—

No. I stopped before the thoughts could snowball into each other and bring me right back to what I was not thinking about.

I stood on the edge of the garage, waiting until he reached a good breaking spot. Again, I had that vague and distant awareness that I wasn't wearing a coat as the shivers wracked my body, but I didn't feel them. Levi hadn't noticed my arrival yet, so I watched him work.

He was incredibly, undeniably beautiful. Sculpted in the most extreme example of peak male physical form. It made no sense that anybody so gentle and loving and thoughtful and sensitive could also be gifted with the handsome face and that objectively incredible body.

His long, strong fingers held his tool with a simple dexterity that could only come with years of practice. The more effortless looking a talent, the more skill it required, and the more years taken to hone it. His shirt was off despite the flurries falling outside. His back muscles gleamed under the orange from heated lamps, beads of perspiration at his temple and the back of his neck. Triceps, biceps, and whatever other tiny muscles made up the arms worked and flexed in perfect cohesion.

I needed Levi. Time was running out. I needed him. He was good and nice and lovely and generous and the best man I knew. He made me feel good, and I would feel good before I dealt with the bad.

After another minute of me scrutinizing and remembering how those muscles felt under my palms, how his tongue, currently pressed against his lower lip in concentration, worked itself to exhaustion against my most intimate parts, Levi seemed to notice my hovering. His head shot up, and he pushed off his goggles. Those same goggles he wore the day I first met him, the day I'd spilled my guts to what I thought would be a stranger I would never see again. Now, Levi was the person I came to when my life imploded.

"Hey, Claire." The deep, grumbly way he said my name felt like a soothing pressure on my shoulders. He said it like he was happy to see me and not the other way around. Like the mere sight of him wasn't a soothing tonic on the blistering crisis burning up my throat. This beautiful, kind man. "How are you feeling?"

"Are you busy?" I asked, ignoring his question, and my voice cracked to my deep annoyance and shame.

He tossed his tool onto the bench and headed toward me, large steps quickly eating up the distance between us. His eyebrows lowered and pinched together as he scrutinized me. "Why don't you go get more rest?"

I shook my head.

Whatever he saw in my features made me think I wasn't as numb and out of my body as I initially thought. He grabbed my hands and dragged me closer to the heat lamps. "Christ, you're freezing. What is it with you and appropriate outerwear?"

"I forgot a coat," I said.

Warmth suffusing my shivering muscles was the first sense of feeling that I'd registered in hours. He reached up to crank the heater to a higher setting before grabbing his jacket from a hook and putting it over my shoulders.

"I'm f-fine."

"You're not. You're all pale—"

I jumped up on my tiptoes to plant a kiss on his lips. I've missed him so much. Just since this morning. I needed him. Now.

"Hey," he said, gently rubbing my arms up and down, *not* kissing me as planned. "Are you ready to talk? Tell me what happened?"

"No talking. I'm fine. I was fired. But fine." Even saying the words was too close to what I didn't want to feel. I pushed up to kiss him again. He avoided me, darting my puckered lips like it was second grade and I had cooties.

"Wait, what?" he asked.

"They pulled my article. They fired me." I put my hands up under his shirt, letting the hot skin warm my numb fingertips. I moaned as he sucked in a breath.

"Whoa, whoa. *Darling*. Wait." He spoke between the kisses that I peppered him with.

I leaned my head forward to kiss him, but he pulled back and away. "Don't you think we should talk about this?"

"I don't want to. I don't want to think or feel. If I start now, I'll shatter." My teeth chattered harder the longer he wasn't kissing me.

"Oh, my love," he said it so softly, so quietly. He said it without knowing the impact of hearing that word come from his lips. "I'm so sorry." I closed my eyes to brace myself for his gentle kindness.

"It's fine. You can distract me. I want you, Levi. I want everything. Please."

"Darling, no." He grabbed my wrists to keep them from where my hands were reaching for his buttons. He placed gentle kisses on my fingertips, his face contorted with pity and pain. "I'm not going to make love with you half out of your mind in a state of catatonic shock."

"I don't mind," I said, pouting up at him. He narrowed his eyes, glaring with disappointment. "But. Why?" I asked.

"You need to process what happened. Tell me what you're feeling."

My head fell back, and I groaned at the roof. "That sounds stupid. Let's let our bodies do the talking."

When I met his gaze again, I found him with his arms crossed, showing off his big stupid muscles and an unamused expression. "I won't be a distraction."

"Please?"

He met my gaze and held it for a long moment. I was pretty sure I had him now. This was it. We were going to do the thing. And this was what I wanted and needed. Definitely. I wasn't avoiding anything. What did he know?

"I know just what you need," he said.

I yelped as he scooped me up and threw me over his broad set of shoulders. I had nowhere to go.

"Hell yeah!" I said as he brought me out of the shed and toward Big Cabin.

He chuckled and smacked me on the bottom.

CHAPTER 26

Levi

"This wasn't what I had in mind." Claire's bottom lip jutted out in a pout as she sat cross-legged on my sofa, a blanket draped over her shoulders and cradling a steaming cup of tea.

"But it's what you need," I said.

I stood a few feet away, crouched to pet Ripley but mostly keeping a safe distance from Claire. I was being honest when I said I didn't want to be her distraction from whatever happened, at least not at this point in the process. I could practically hear my mother shouting, *You better not take advantage of that sweet woman in crisis.*

As if I would. Still. Best to keep the space. Claire was determined and had grabby little fingers.

Wrapped in that blanket, looking like a petulant child, Claire eventually let out a long sigh. "I don't know what you want me to say," she said.

"Start from the beginning." I stood and brushed my hands on my knees when Ripley burrowed herself deeper in her blankets, done with scratches.

"It was a sunny day in May at Our Lady of Assumption Hospital in Chicago, Illinois, when my first cries broke through the air. My mother bravely labored for seventeen hours—"

I sat back in the short chair across from her with a loud sigh. "Come on, Claire."

"What? You didn't specify."

I guessed moving on from blind lust to anger and annoyance was a sort of progress. "You weren't kidding when you said you were bad at this."

"My mom died suddenly from cancer when I was nineteen. For all his wonderful qualities, my father is still a Boomer firefighter from Chicago and a byproduct of his generation. We didn't have a lot of big emotional talks." She studied her tea. "Not everybody can just identify what they're feeling in the moment and label it."

"Thankfully, I was raised by a woman who bordered on being a hippie, so I know exactly how to do those things." I scooted forward in the chair until I could reach her knees and rub them through the blanket. "Take your time. You aren't alone, and I want to help."

She set her tea on the side table before rounding her shoulders and stretching her neck. "Ugh. This is itchy."

"What is?" I ran a hand over the blanket.

"Talking about all this. I feel itchy."

I huffed a laugh. "You seemed plenty able to talk about things at the general store when you first arrived in town, if you recall."

"And if *you* recall, that was a week after the breakup, and the creamer was pushing me to the edge with its emotional demands." Her arms wrapped tight around her middle, and a loud gurgling sound filled the air between us. "Ugh. You brought this upon yourself; just remember that."

"I'll take the risk."

"Well. After I left hanging out this morning—"

She met my gaze with a flash of heat, and both of us recalled the fun times of getting each other off earlier.

"I went to hang out with Madi and Gigi, and I got a call from my editor. They pulled my story set to publish next week, and also, I'm fired."

"The story you came here to finish?"

She nodded. "The very one. The one I spent months of my life working on."

"I don't understand. Did they give a reason?"

She continued to nod, but it led to her upper body rocking in a sort of self-soothing motion. "Budget cuts."

I frowned at her. This article was important to her, but she also mentioned earning income from smaller pieces and miscellaneous help with researching and fact-checking. This meant she'd more than lost the article. She lost her sole source of income. More important, she'd lost what was driving her.

"That's the official reason." Her features clouded, and she stiffened. "But I got a cryptic text from my ex right before I got fired. I don't even know how he knew."

My thoughts snagged on that detail, wondering how often she talked to the douche canoe ex-boyfriend.

"That's a pretty heavy coincidence," I said instead.

"I thought that as well." She stopped rocking to run her hands by her temples and tug. "He was set to quit his job. It was only supposed to be temporary. That was the plan, but then he got the promotion and told me I had to choose between the story and our relationship. And now it was pointless. The story isn't going to happen." She shook her head. "None of this makes sense. Every single fact in that article is bulletproof. I had everything triple-checked and verified, and this is utter bullshit."

Her growing anger felt like a relief. It burned its way through her state of shock. Slowly, one layer at a time, I would help her through this.

"Unbelievable," I said.

"That's not even the worst bit. Melanie told me she thinks it's because Slimeball McGee had major stock investments in this company, which, as it happens, has a subsidiary. A subsidiary that is one of the few remaining major advertisers for the paper. I always thought the integrity of the paper was more important than anything. But once again, I had completely misjudged what I thought to be cut-and-dry ethics."

"Fuck." I ran a hand down my face.

"Yep. If I had to guess, there was a 'nudge, nudge get rid of your problem child or lose your paper' situation. Actually, hearing that option feels slightly less awful than the excuse they gave me. Better corrupt office politics than just being seen as useless?"

"I'm so sorry, Claire."

She made a sound of *hmm* before staring into the fire for a long time. She still hadn't cried or shown as much anger or devastation as I would probably be displaying at this moment, but as she said, identifying feelings in the heat of the moment was a skill that required training like anything else.

"I feel like it's a bad dream," she said eventually. Softly. "That I'll wake up and realize that it was a horrible stress dream all along."

Her desolation destroyed me. I couldn't bear seeing her like this; I hated that I couldn't fix it for her. I scooped her into my lap, let her nestle against me, and find comfort in my nearness, if nothing else.

"It's understandable. You put your heart into your work. It's admirable."

"And I just keep thinking about the people I was trying to help. They're just gonna get screwed over as an already obscenely rich person gets richer. I don't know what to do. It just seems so unfair. It's the injustice of it all that is so infuriating. Kevin made me seem so naive for believing I could make a difference, and it kills me that he's right."

"You aren't naive. He wasn't right." I bit out the words, my fists clenched tight.

"All I ever wanted was to make some sort of difference in the world, and now it all feels so pointless."

"It's not pointless. It matters. People need to care," I said, but it felt flat. "But I understand feeling powerless."

"I know," she said sadly. She turned to hold my hand. " I'll be okay. I'll go back to Chicago, homeless. Jobless. And start all over, and I'll be okay. I just feel so tired. Defeated."

The announcement of her new plan made my palms sweaty. "You don't have to decide anything right now." I clenched my fists, hoping she couldn't see the nerves I tried to hide. I wanted her to stay here. I wanted her to know that she could stay here as long as she needed.

Forever.

If there had ever been doubt before about my growing feelings for her, they vanished as I tried to soothe her. If loving someone meant feeling desperate to stop them from ever hurting, then there was no doubt I loved Claire. There hadn't been doubt for a while. I wanted to protect her. Keep her safe and satisfied.

But her restless gaze and jumping leg told me that this wouldn't be the right time to make that offer. "You have a little under a week until Thanksgiving. Just rest and process for now."

She made a soft sound before she retreated back into herself, the fire dancing in her glassy eyes.

"Thank you for all this. I'm not great at feeling things. Blah."

"It's a lot to process. There is time," I said.

"Can I admit something shallow?" she asked.

"This is a circle of trust." I gestured around us.

"I'm so mad about Kevin too. That text was so damn smug." She ground her jaw, nostrils flaring. "This story was everything to me. It's everything I amounted to."

"That's not true. It's an article. It doesn't define you," I said.

She shook her head, and I wasn't entirely sure she was listening. "Publishing this story made everything worth it. I was saving lives or at least helping them not be financially ruined. All the rest wouldn't be so bad if I could just make a difference, but it was all for nothing. Evil will win. Money will always mean power. And in the end, Kevin was right. It really sucks."

"He wasn't right. He might have money, but Kevin lost the best thing, so I can't imagine he's feeling smug right now. He's probably realizing he messed up. Especially if he's still trying to contact you."

She looked confused.

I rolled my eyes. "You, Claire. He lost you."

"And for what?"

"Would you have wanted to be with him still?" I asked, containing a shaking fear that made me feel sick.

"God. No." Her answer was instant and solid, and with it was a wave of relief. "I lost all respect for him the moment he took that promotion. No. We were long over. Honestly, I don't even miss him. Sadly, I rarely ever think about him."

I brushed my lips along the top of her head. Another few moments of silence passed as I continued to hold her.

"I'm devastated," she said. Something came over her features as if she recognized a scent she couldn't previously place. "That's what I feel. Utter devastation. I feel like my whole life I've been working to make a difference, and I'm just like that one mortal suffering for sins of the gods, pushing up the rock, and these big rich people are laughing from their perches above us all as it rolls back down."

Her hands shook as I collected them to kiss her knuckles. "Darling," I said sadly. I hated her pain, but I hated her self-doubt more than anything. The pain would end, but would her self-esteem recover? Her larger-than-life morals were part of what made her so passionate and wonderful.

"I don't even know who I am without that purpose anymore."

"You are so many things. Don't make judgments about your character when you've been dealt a blow. Treat yourself how you would treat a friend in this situation."

Her brow furrowed. "I can't pick apart every choice I ever made to make a case about how awful a person I am?"

"I'm afraid that won't help you from feeling like shit."

She dropped her head into her hands. "What am I even going to do?"

"Nothing needs to be decided right now."

She tilted her head back and met my gaze. "How can you understand that about me so clearly?" she asked with a sense of awe. Despite myself, my gaze moved to her mouth, where she licked her lips.

"I think the issue is that ..." She took a breath and went on. "It used to feel so important to change the world. Now, I fear I was just avoiding something else, but I can't even consider it because I've invested so much into this version of myself. It feels so impossible to change now."

I let out a long, slow breath. "Now that's something I know a little bit about."

She grabbed my fingers back and squeezed.

"I think we just try small steps. A little bit, each day that scares us." My throat was so tight, the words so close to coming out. "And with time, we can be whoever we want."

"I like that, Levi Carmichael." She leaned forward and kissed my temple. "Thank you. For all of it."

I couldn't share my desire to keep her here, not now. Not when she was just starting to relax.

I was a hypocrite and a liar. So much for having the courage to change.

CHAPTER 27

Claire

Levi and I ended up talking well into the night. I was so emotionally drained that I must have drifted off. I remembered being on the couch and feeling the weight of sleep pull me under, but I felt too at peace to disturb the status quo.

I vaguely remember him scooping me up and carrying me upstairs.

Now, I sat up and looked around groggily from Levi's bed. Again. My phone said it was after four a.m. I felt lighter. Not happy. I was still concerned about the future, the article, and my career, but I wasn't spiraling. I had spun out, launching myself to another planet of numbness and denial, but Levi had grabbed me and brought me back to Earth. He'd cared enough and been patient enough to help me work out what I couldn't understand.

As always, Levi understood what I needed before I had.

I went to the restroom before padding down to the living room to find him on the couch. He slept on his back, legs hanging off the couch, an arm slung over his face, and Ripley taking up the other half. She lifted her head and lowered it, unimpressed to find me.

I shivered in the cool air before heading over to him. I gently shook him awake.

"Come to your bed, you sweet silly man."

He blinked groggily. "I wasn't sure."

"Just come on."

The three of us went back upstairs and fell into bed. Well, except Ripley, who burrowed into her little cot on the floor. There was no hesitation as he lifted his arm so I could tuck up next to him. I was back asleep in an instant, sucked into the warmth of him. The last thing I remembered was the soft kiss brushed against my temple and the feeling of safety brought on by his arm around me.

My body woke before my mind.

I knew that because, by the time I had any semblance of being awake, my back was already arching, ass rubbing against hardness. Kisses were being placed on my neck as Levi's rough hand cupped and teased my breast. His heavy leg moved between me, and the thickest part of his thigh ground into me until I was turned almost on my stomach.

My underwear was already damp, and a tingling readiness pulsed heavy in my abdomen.

My eyes remained closed as I focused only on sensation. It gave every touch and sigh a dreamy quality.

His other hand, the one not driving me wild while toying with my nipple, slid between my body and the mattress, finding my core. Expertly, he pet the areas I needed as I writhed, all but humping his hand. Push down, and my clit hit just the right spot. Arch up, and his hard cock pumped along my backside. It was a win-win.

"Claire?" he whispered against my ear.

"Hmm?"

"Are you awake?"

"No. I'm dreaming. Please never wake me up."

His deep rumble of laughter raised the hairs on my neck and had me clench around the air. I needed him in me, above me, filling me. We'd waited long enough.

"I need you awake for my plans." As he spoke, he dipped a finger into my core, and he pressed harder above me, causing me to groan from the exquisite weight of him.

"God," he gasped out. "You're so wet already. How are you so wet already?"

"I think our bodies may have been going at it for a while."

He turned me over so that I faced him as he hovered above me, balanced on his elbows. His tender gaze moved over my face. I studied him in return as intense pressure filled my chest.

"How are you so beautiful in the mornings?" He dipped his head to kiss my neck and chin and that little spot by my ear that he found.

I yawned and covered my mouth with the back of my hand. "You should talk."

He grinned down at me, the gentle light of the early morning softened by the curtains still backlit him enough to make him seem to glow. His dreamy eyes were so entrancing, and his disheveled bedhead was laughably charming. He was the picturesque view. I could get quite used to seeing this every morning. The revelations of last night, the plans to move to Chicago, it all threatened to taint this moment like a storm on the horizon.

Instead, I lifted my head to place a tentative closed-mouth kiss on his. It was a question about where this was going and maybe a little bit on our stance on morning breath.

But that was what was so weird. I was so pliant for this man, so flexible in all things. Qualms and trivialities with anybody else that bothered me so much before didn't matter with Levi. Being with him felt so natural. Where everything else required effort, Levi was easy and necessary.

His tongue slipping into my mouth, his slow lowering of his body on mine, it all felt right and natural. We kissed for a long time, hands intertwined in the other's hair. I broke apart to slip out of my clothes as he did the same. No words were exchanged. Again, a natural understanding and progression.

We kissed deeply, naked bodies rubbing. My nipples rubbed against his chest, luxuriating in the forgiven feeling of his coarse hair against my smooth skin. His calloused hands moved relentlessly over my calves, hips, ass, back, and abdomen. Anywhere he could reach was subject to his exploration, and my urge grew stronger with every new body part memorized under his touch. Toes gripped at nothing, hips rocking forward in a syncopated rhythm.

We both gasped when the motion caused his incredibly hot and hard length to slip between my clenching thighs. I was slick and ready for him to slide into me, but he maintained more self-control than I had by simply rocking back and forth so that his blunt tip teased my soaking clit and folds. It brought me close to a precipice I wasn't ready to fall off yet.

He shifted away, a brief shock of cool air before the sound of a condom being unwrapped and rolled on.

When he returned, hovering above me, his head fell back, revealing his beautiful, strong neck to me. My hands grasped at his body. A frantic energy, racing to that final destination, made me mindless with want.

Spreading my knees wide, I arched my back to pull away from him. I slid my hand between our bodies to find him hard as iron, large and intimidating. I swallowed, holding his gaze, and lined him up.

A tremor passed through his body as I pressed just the head of him to my entrance, already meeting my first hurdle.

"We'll go slow," he said.

I nodded and tried to relax back.

"I've got you." He bent to kiss me again, hovering just where he was until my muscles relaxed again and the need to be filled surpassed anything else.

Inch by inch, my body made room for him. When he finally

pushed to his hilt, we both gasped out.

"You're so good. You're doing so good," he whispered.

Heat suffused me with his tender praise. My body clenched to take him deeper, spurring him on. His words came faster, more muffled and frantic. "You are so incredible. You feel so good, you know that? You're so hot and wet and perfect for me."

My head pushed back into the pillow, and I gripped his hard ass as I met his demanding pace. I pushed us faster, loving how good he filled me, sliding in and out of me. Our frantic breaths filled the air, the sounds of our bodies colliding.

"I've wanted this for so long," he said. "I've wanted to fuck you so hard. I'm going to take you again and again. I'll never have enough." On and on, he spoke all the dirty little things I never knew I needed to hear. He held my gaze and pressed his forehead to mine, sharing my breath as we pushed higher and higher. It was so intensely beautiful I broke away, clenching my eyes shut as sensation ratcheted me up. He filled all my senses as deeply as his hard cock filled my core.

I coiled tighter and tighter.

"Yes, just like that. So good. So perfect. Gorgeous."

His hand slipped between us and slid against my swollen bud. It was the final push I needed to crash into my orgasm. I screamed out, vocal for the first time, as wave after wave passed through me.

Above me, Levi continued with his praise, his hips jerking more erratically after waiting for my final pulse.

"Fuuu—" he called out, and hot pulses spasmed into me.

He stayed in me a minute longer. We both remained quiet, me certainly in a state of bliss. Occasionally, an aftershock would pulse through me, clenching him. He'd groan and mumble something about killing him as he pressed up into me, still hard even now.

It was too good. It was so unbelievably, bone-meltingly good.

I never thought it could be like this. My rational mind always thought people exaggerated the connection that came with this level of intimacy. I'd had tastes of it when he got me off with his fingers and tongue, but this connection was next level. Primal. With him rocking inside me, holding my gaze, as some tender emotion pulled at his brows, I was connected to every atom of my being. I'd never been so in touch with my body or this level of emotion.

I might not ever be able to process this. Too many new things were happening inside my body and mind. It was more than this incredible physical connection that I shared with him after never experiencing anything even close before. It was how he doted on me time and time again. How he took care of me and understood my needs long before I did. How he made looking after me, knowing me, being with me so effortless. He made it seem as though I wasn't strange or a burden to be born. I couldn't understand it. It didn't match up with my experiences so far, and it didn't help me understand the future. It was wild, unventured lands.

Even after I slipped away to use the restroom and come back, Levi's touch was confounding in the multitude of feelings that it brought with it.

Wasn't this supposed to just be for fun? It was fun. But why had that felt so heavy, or maybe deep? Why wasn't I able to just crack a joke and move on?

What the hell was I going to do now? Where were the rules that would help me understand this intimacy?

CHAPTER 28

Levi

By dinnertime, both of us were boneless with exhaustion. Thankfully, we could microwave some leftovers because the idea of cooking was too much for either of us.

Not that I was complaining. It had been the best day of my life. And that wasn't an exaggeration.

After we refueled, we decided to read in silence by the fire, nowhere to be, and enjoying the light falling snow outside.

Peace settled over me for the first time in a long time.

"What was that big sigh for?" Claire asked, looking up from her book and wiggling her feet that were tucked into my lap.

"I don't know." I shrugged. "It was good, though. Contented."

She smiled full dimples. "Good." She closed her book and looked out the large windows facing the trees. "Man, it's really coming down."

"Guess you're stuck here for a few more days."

"Darn."

We drifted into silence again, neither of us talking, but neither of us went back to reading either. I watched the snowfall for several minutes.

A fresh start...

"Yeah," I said, only realizing too late that it was out loud.

Claire tilted her head in confusion.

"I was, uh, talking to my mom." I quickly added, "I still hear her sometimes. It makes me feel crazy. But it's clear as day. Maybe it's my own inner intuition that was sculpted by her words and actions growing up, but Mom's still there."

As she listened, her features softened into understanding. "It's nice that you have that," she said.

"You don't think it's crazy?" I asked tentatively, feeling heat burning down the back of my neck.

"You're asking the woman who has full-blown conversations with her reflection, so I might not be the best litmus test, but no. I think it's nice you still hear her. It's like a gift. And what do we know? Maybe it is some form of her energy, spirit, whatever."

I smiled, wondering if it was true, hoping that it was.

"Do you ever hear your mother?" I asked.

"No. Mostly just my dad rambling about in my head. But if she is still watching me, I'd like to think she's proud of me." After a beat, she added, face falling. "Or she was."

I squeezed her toes. "She hasn't stopped being proud because you were obstructed in justice by centuries-old systematic corruption."

"Thanks. But I'm talked out about the whole thing. Tell me more about what you're thinking."

I rubbed Claire's arches as she leaned back to stretch her legs out and give me her full attention. "I miss Mom. A lot. We were so close my whole life. Even over a year later, I reach for the phone to call her or think of how I'll have to tell her something only to remember." I swallowed. "Sometimes, I don't even feel like she's gone. It's like by avoiding the house, I'm stuck in this limbo. I'm just avoiding all the—" My throat tightened to the point where I couldn't swallow. "Like I'm just delaying the inevitable."

"There's no timeline for grief. You'll know when you're ready to tackle the room and the rest of it." She crawled forward to kiss me on the cheek. "Plus. Once I'm out next week, you'll have your space back. Which, let's be honest, is what you've wanted the whole time."

Her words were light, so I tried to match her levity as I asked, "What do you mean?"

"Well, I may not be a genius when it comes to reading people, but you weren't exactly thrilled to share your home. And now you won't have to. Maybe this was your sign that you aren't ready yet." She smiled. "And that's okay. It's not like you need the money."

It felt like a sucker punch to the center of this nice moment we'd been having.

"Claire, you don't have to go."

"Yes, I do. The contract I signed is up," she said simply. It was unfathomable to me that she could be so casual after what we had shared.

"What I'm saying is ... you should stay." I watched as her gaze turned inward while my words soaked in. "Just for a little while. Maybe through New Year's until you have a plan," I added too quickly, but she must have seen the truth behind them.

"I don't have any income. I have some saved, but I need to look for more work and ..."

"Then stay *here*." I emphasized to the room around us. "I'll rent the cabin to someone else for extra income if you're worried about that."

Her gaze dropped to her fingers now, twisting in her lap. "Levi. I—Thank you. That's a kind gesture, but I already told my dad. And I have the moving truck planned. I just, I have a plan."

"You won't even think about it?"

She breathed in and out. "I-I think maybe it's too fast. Maybe I can make a list of the pros and cons."

"Pros and cons." My words were flat, but my heart lurched, twisting in pain.

What was there to think about? We were infatuated with each other. Wasn't she here the last few weeks while we fell for each other? I shared everything with her, and she wouldn't even consider my offer?

I ground my jaw. "What's all this been?" I asked.

She sat back on her heels, surprise pinching her brows. "This?"

"Claire, you're honestly going to sit there and pretend you

don't have feelings for me? Are you afraid to admit it? Because I will. I'm falling for you. I don't want you to go. I want you to stay here. Indefinitely."

She stood off the couch in a blur. The sudden action caused Ripley to pop her head up and whine. "Of course, I have—of course, I've been having a good time. But sex complicates things. It inflates feelings that aren't ... well, it complicates things. I want to have all the facts before I decide anything. Just a few months ago, I was planning a whole different life."

"Oh right. Heaven forbid you admit to feelings." It was a low blow, and I was defensive. I regretted it the moment I said it.

"Maybe I just don't fall for someone I've only known for seven weeks. Maybe it's not so easy for me to pick up my entire life and move here. That's not fair to make me feel like shit about this."

"I'm offering a solution, but you're being too proud to accept my help."

"It's not about pride," she said slowly, her features going flat, thoughts inward.

I was being an asshat, as Pace would say. But I shared everything with her, every vulnerable nook and cranny of my soul, and she was ready to just pack up and leave.

"What's all this been, Claire? You're just going to leave like nothing? Like we haven't been sleeping together and sharing our lives."

"I-I don't know." She paced, hands to her temples. "I need a minute to breathe. I need to think."

"Was all of this just a vacation for you?" I couldn't understand it. I showed her everything, admitted everything, and she was ready to walk away like it was a hookup.

"No. I don't know. It's been this weird little pocket out of time." She pressed her hands to her temple, eyes squeezed tight. "My life is in total upheaval." Her shoulders shrugged to her ears and dropped. She spoke animatedly. "I have always known what to do next. I have followed exactly the right path, and all for nothing."

"Nothing?" I stood now too. "That makes me feel great."

"Not you, Levi. You've been amazing. Truly. This has been so great. I won the lottery, finding this place and finding you. But it's not *my* life. It's yours that I've been borrowing." Her arms wrapped tight around her middle.

"That's not how it feels for me. I've known for some time how I feel about you." I stood and crossed my arms, putting the couch between us, hating how bad this fucking hurt. "I'm never gonna force you to stay or to choose me. But I didn't think it would be a choice."

Something about my words made her pale. "I didn't know I had to choose," she spoke with a whispered gasp, hands curling around her stomach. "I can't have this conversation. I can't believe I'm back here. You had the rules and the boundaries, and I told you you needed to be clear about that. It's not easy for me to just jump into a major life change after a few weeks."

"It is for me. You're easy to love," I said, not saying the implied. What was left unsaid? Apparently, I wasn't.

"Love? Levi. You're throwing around the love word now?" Her arms wrapped tight around her middle, and she looked sick.

"I don't understand how you're not. I don't talk about my mother with anyone. I don't share that history of my family with anybody."

Her shoulders fell, and her color drained. "I know. I appreciate that you did, but we are two very different people. I can't just be in love. That's—" She sucked in her lips, stopping whatever she'd been about to say.

My chest felt like it was caving in on itself. My head was shaking. "It's just so obvious to me, and it's heartbreaking that you hadn't even considered it."

But it answered everything I needed to know. It was what had made me hesitate this long to share my feelings.

"This isn't fair. I wasn't playing with a full deck. I didn't have all the information. For you to just say all this and make me feel like I'm the one to blame," she said, head tilted.

"You are, though!" I snapped at her, embarrassment making me rage. "It's all your fault I fell in love with you. Do you think I wanted this? You think I even wanted to rent out the cabin? No. I only did it so Pace and the rest of this town would stop harping on me. This is your fault."

"My *fault*?"

"Yes. You completely disarmed me. You wormed your way into my head. I never wanted this. You know it. You just said it. So this was all some game. Make your way in and just leave."

"Oh, because this was all part of my big master plan. Get dumped. Lose home. Lose job. Checklist of every woman hitting thirty."

"Well, stop being so damn charming and beautiful and sexy and smart." Her head shook with a sarcastic laugh as I went on. "Stop listening to me when I speak and being so interested in what I have to say. Stop stealing the thoughts from my head and giving them the voice they need. Stop being so authentic and tenacious and vibrant."

"That was the weirdest compliment I ever got." She huffed a laugh. "I-I think I just need a little space. I'm going back to my cabin. With all the sex and everything, I don't think either of us are thinking clearly. Let's just cool off, okay? I won't make any decisions. But I need to process this. I didn't know you felt so strongly about me. About a future after this."

"Would that matter? If I said it the moment I started to feel them? Or would you tell me you had a plan that couldn't change?"

"That's not fair." She backed up to the door.

"It's like you think you can avoid any sort of feelings if you have enough information. You can't think your way out of pain. Having information doesn't stop the hurting. Trust me, I know firsthand." My words sat heavy in the air between us.

She sighed. "It must be so nice for you to have the answers to everything all the time." She shook her head. "I'm not trying to outsmart feelings, Levi. I'm just not ready to put myself into a position where a man can take everything from me the moment he decides to change the plan without telling me."

She walked out the door with that final blow, and I felt like an absolute prick.

CHAPTER 29

Levi

I swung the axe so hard it split the wood and lodged itself in the stump. I had to rock it several times it was stuck so far into the now split base.

"You seem lovelier than normal. Even for you," Pace said by way of greeting.

I grunted.

"You see that it is snowing, right?" he asked.

I grunted.

"Ah, just like old times. So. How's Claire?"

"I'm in love with her."

"Oh. Wow. I wasn't expecting that." Pace frowned and came to an abrupt stop. "Now that I think about it, I'm not that surprised. You always were a romantic. But why are you mad about it?"

I stood and shivered as the sweat on my neck instantly cooled in the cold air. "I'm mad because I told her and said she could stay here, and she acted like I was insane."

Pace blew in his hands, rubbing them together. "You're gonna need to walk me through it. But first, let's get inside before I freeze my balls off. I do plan to have kids one day."

"God help us," I grumbled, setting down the axe and leading him to the house.

I brought us to the couch but then turned sharply on my heels, remembering that our most recent conversation tainted it. In the kitchen, I remembered the time I bent her over the butcher block and couldn't stay there. We walked in a circle, Pace and now Ripley following silently behind until finally, I settled in the one safe spot, free from thoughts of Claire, at the base of the stairs. Pace and Ripley exchanged a look before she gave up on my antics and went to her bed.

I gave Pace a quick rundown of the previous day's events.

"And then I told her I loved her, and I wanted her to stay, and she ran out." I curled my tongue in my mouth that felt acidic.

Pace listened patiently, nodded, and then grimaced, looking queasy as I came to the end of my diatribe. It was understandable. He had the ultimate heartbreak, and since then, had never been a fan of love or relationships.

"I know, I know. It's not for you," I said.

"It's just really fast. She just got here what, last month?"

"Seven and a half weeks. People have fallen in love in a moment. Not that fast." Not fast enough. The lead-up until I finally got to kiss her felt like much longer, like years. Lifetimes before we finally made love.

Pace looked a little green around the gills. "What did she say, exactly?"

"She told me she wasn't aware of how I felt for her or that I wanted her to stay. Or something. I offered her everything. A home until she landed on her feet. And no charge."

"And you offered her that after you slept together?" Pace raised an eyebrow.

"You make it seem shady when you put those facts together in that order. It wasn't like that."

"Yeah, but you have to understand that may not have felt like the amazing offer of a lifetime you thought," he said, crossing his arms.

"Why?"

Pace ran a hand down his face. "Shit. I don't know what women want. Each one is different. Maybe some women would want that, I'm sure. But does that sound like Claire? Is she easy with big changes and going with the flow? Does she always know what she wants right away, or does she take more time to think things through? I guess what I'm asking is, does she make choices from her heart or her head?"

Had she been serious about the pros and cons list? She did mention the rules a lot. It was my turn to feel queasy. "I guess it could feel a little fast for her. It's so obvious to me, though. She has to be feeling the same. How could she not?"

"Is it possible she is but is also confused? Both things can be true. I do think she was very into you. But you have to think from her point of view. What if you just decide that you're done one day? Then she's back where she started, dumped and homeless."

I slumped back against the wall, the corner cutting into my spine. "Shit."

"So maybe she just freaked out. And does need time. Which you should give her. A little time to sort yourselves out wouldn't hurt."

"Fuck." I scrubbed at my eyes.

"It sounds like you guys have really made a connection, so just, you know, have a little faith." He said it like it tasted bad.

"Okay. Yeah."

"Yeah." Pace kept nodding and debating with himself. He was really bothered by something now that I looked at him. He tugged his cap off, his reddish-blond curls sticking in all directions. "So then. The only other thing I wanted to ask then, I guess, you know that she's been going around town? Interviewing people about Lily?"

A sinking sensation started in my gut. "What do you mean?"

Pace took a deep breath in and out and slumped back. "Judging by how all the color just drained out of your face, you didn't know. Shit, man. That's what I was afraid of. Especially with all the, uh"—he gestured at me—"waxing poetic and whatnot."

"Tell me exactly what you heard."

"A few of the matrons of the town were talking. Overheard them. They said she was interviewing them about Lily and ... about her life and relationship with your father. When I got closer to listen, they gave me the stink eye and told me to mind my own business."

My eyes closed as I processed the information. "She told me when she found out about Richard. When I explained everything to her, she said she would stop. She hasn't mentioned it since." I opened my eyes to meet his.

He nodded.

"When was this?" I asked.

Please let it be before. Before we talked. Before I fell this hard. Maybe it was all bad timing and a misunderstanding.

"Two days ago," he said.

My head fell forward. When was she even doing it? When did she find time between all the sex and talking and exploring each other's bodies?

"I'm sorry, man. I came here to find out what was going on. I know I had been pushing you this whole time. To rent the cabin. Then, pushing to have a night out. I just wanted you to unwind. Maybe fool around a little." He rubbed his brow until the skin turned red. "I'm sorry, man. I mean. We still don't know anything for sure. I say, talk to her. Maybe she doesn't get how private you are? Or how fucked up the whole situation is."

My jaw clenched, and I nodded. "I told her. I told her everything." I felt humiliated. Strewn out. Was it a coincidence that this charming, completely beautiful woman rented my cabin? Did she somehow know the truth the whole time, and I played right into everything?

"Just talk to her. Nobody would be that vindictive."

"Maybe this was why she's so eager to leave. Why she rebuffed this whole offer? Maybe she'll offer this article about my mom to try to get her job back?" A dozen thoughts, each worse than the last.

"You don't really think that. Trust what you know about her. Talk to her."

I didn't really think that, but I also thought we were on the same page regarding our feelings for each other. What did I know?

Claire

"Have you heard about pickleball, Claire Bear? It's all the rage." My dad, sweaty and red, waved to me from what looked to be an indoor tennis court.

Several of his friends ran around yelling in the background. I was happy to see them doing something other than eating sausages and drinking beer.

"I have. I'm glad you're trying it," I said.

"Yes." He panted for several breaths. "I think. Maybe. I need to get the ole stamina back up."

"You will get there. Take it easy on yourself."

"Man, my thirty-year-old self would be pissed to see how much I've slacked off." He moved to a hallway, much quieter. "How are you?" His face moved closer to the screen, and he squinted. "Why have you been crying?"

I blinked back in surprise. I really tried to make sure all evidence was gone before I called him. "How can you tell?"

"How can you tell when you've got to burp? You just have the look."

"Thanks?" I blinked to clear my mind.

"How are you holding up? Any more news?"

I called the next day after the best and worst day. How Levi and I could have such a wonderful night after the worst day of my life still plagued me.

"I'm at a crossroads, Dad. I don't know what to do."

"What do you want to do?" he asked as if that was just the easiest thing in the world. Who really knew what they wanted? How did one become a person who just knew things without looking at them from a thousand different angles? Seemed like a sort of magic I just did not possess.

I was back at my cabin. I had packed up the car that had remained unused for weeks and very little of my own stuff remained. I held Ripley on my lap in the kitchen.

"You know how I've been working on that project? I finished it," I said. I'd spent weeks collecting information about Lily and her life to write something for Levi. It had filled the time between the stories for the online journal. "I wanted to give him something as a thank you. But I think it might be deeper than that."

"What do you mean?" he asked.

"It felt necessary for Levi to see his mom and this life from a different point of view. And in writing her story and the stories about other people in town, I really liked the personal touch. I can't explain it."

"That might be worth exploring."

I groaned and felt my brain pulling in so many directions. Fighting with Levi was awful. I hated being so close to him and feeling his hurt and frustration. But I also couldn't put myself in a position to lose everything again. I missed important details and suffered the consequences when the world shook around me.

"I have no idea how to figure out what I want," I said.

"What would you do if you could do anything?" he asked.

"I want to go back in time and—" I cut myself off. I was going to say, "Never ask Kevin to quit," but then I could go back further than that. Never come out here? Never write that article? Never meet Kevin? Just how far back would I go until the person I was today was erased completely? I wouldn't want to forget Levi. I wouldn't want to lose these past few weeks.

"And not hurt Levi," I finished.

"How can you guarantee that you'll not hurt him? What happened?"

I explained, not in so much detail, the offer Levi proposed and his love confession.

"And. You don't believe him?" my dad asked.

"It's not that I don't believe him. I think he *thinks* he's in love. But Levi is like that. He's emotional and artistic and … just very *feely*."

"And we know how that upsets you?"

"I know you're joking, but I'm super sensitive about that right now. It's not that I don't have feelings. I just can't always express them well. I'm not some unfeeling robot." My voice cracked.

"Oh. I'm sorry, Claire Bear. I know that. I thought that was our joke." My dad looked pained, and the guilt ate me up.

"I know. I'm sorry. I-I just feel awful. He looked so pitiful. Not unlike you're looking right now."

"Well. People are going to get their feelings hurt. And not that you hurt mine, but I would like to point out that you said something to me about my teasing that I don't think you would have said before," he said.

I thought about that. It was true. I never would have been able to tell my dad that I was feeling touchy about a subject, let alone even identify that that was happening in the moment. "I guess he rubbed off on me a little."

"It's good that he's emotionally intelligent. It's a skill set that, I'm ashamed to say, I haven't always had." My dad scratched at his head. "But I don't think that it's insane to think he'd be in love with you. You're very lovable."

I scoffed because *dads*. Their opinions couldn't be trusted.

"I'm serious. You have this thing where you think that your passion makes you unlikeable. But I think it's a great part of who you are. My biggest issue with Kevin was that he said he supported that side of you but it never seemed like he really did. It mostly seemed he knew how to pay lip service to it. When push came to shove, he never challenged you or encouraged you to flourish. I think that Levi senses your strengths."

I focused on petting Ripley and thought of the times that Levi said exactly that. He had really made me feel special.

"He did. He liked that about me. He said that I had an entire universe in my brain and that it fascinated him. Or something. It was really sweet." My bottom lip trembled. "It's just that when things burn too hot, they burn out fast."

My dad sat thoughtfully for a moment. "Do they burn out? Or do they change their chemical makeup to something else? Fires demolish, but they also provide life, warmth, comfort, and protection."

I nodded. "It would be pretty insane to love somebody after knowing them for a few weeks, right?" I asked, chewing my lip.

"I think I'm the wrong person to ask. I loved your mother within minutes."

A cough-sob choked out of me. I tried to tease around a tearful voice. "Ugh, men. So simple." But this was all me projecting because, really ... really, there was something more scary than Levi loving me in just a few weeks. That was, I was pretty sure, I loved him right back. And that ... that couldn't and didn't make any sense. "It took me forever to feel like I could let my guard down with Kevin." *And I was still completely blindsided.*

"I just don't think there is a timeframe to these things. I think when some people know, they just know." Dad rubbed his forefinger over his lips. "There's a bravery to that sort of blind feeling. It's easier to rationalize and compartmentalize rather than feel."

"Oof. That sounds familiar."

"The feeling is where the bravery comes in. Recognizing it and acting."

Then Levi was so brave. He wore all his feelings; he seemed to live and marinate in them. Whereas, I caught a whiff of a feeling cooking and I ran out of the house into a different neighborhood.

"Levi is so brave."

"What's the worst that could happen if you admit that you want something?" he asked.

"I could let down my guard and at that moment, the worst could happen? He could decide I'm not actually enough. I could blink, and the whole world could shift because I missed the signs." My voice cracked. "Like what Kevin did to me. And I didn't even feel a fraction of what I did for him as I do for Levi."

His brows shot up at my confession. "Interesting. But you were okay, right? You are okay?"

I nodded. "But what if Levi is just using me to avoid the pain of the loss of his mother? What if he's latching on to me instead of processing his grief?" I blurted the biggest fear and wished instantly I could swallow it back down.

"You know what? You'd still be okay. Life would still go on. You would surely have to sit in some awful, yucky feelings for a while, but eventually, you would be okay," he said.

"God, that sounds terrible."

"But you aren't alone. And you are loved, and you will be okay. No matter what. Repeat it to yourself."

"I'll be okay." Inexplicably, I felt the tension release from my shoulders.

"I know your mother's death blindsided us both," he said,

holding my gaze, "but knowing it was coming wouldn't have made it hurt any less. You couldn't have changed it. It wasn't your fault that it happened because you weren't paying attention. You were starting college; you were doing exactly what you needed to be doing. Her passing didn't happen because you got caught up living," he said.

"Okay," I gasped out a sob. I understood that to be true, rationally, but hearing it out loud, I realized that's exactly what I had been doing. I thought I wouldn't get hurt if I knew everything all the time. Turned out, that was impossible.

After I collected myself and smoothed my breaths, I met my dad's gaze, waving a hand at my drying face.

"We're both okay now? Aren't we?" he asked.

I nodded, chin quivering.

"I love you," he said.

"I love you too." It spurted out wet and gaspy. I sucked in my lips to keep from crying any harder.

Once you started to register how you felt in the moment, everything sort of spilled out all over, like a punctured can of biscuits. I wanted to ignore this last thought and pretend it wasn't always there at the back of my mind, but the soft, doughy truth spilled over.

"And-and what if I've been using work to avoid feeling anything ever? What if I don't have a job now, and I'll just have to sit and think and process things." I held his gaze, and we both knew what I was referring to. That Levi wasn't the only one still processing the loss of his mom.

"Can't imagine where you get that from." His throat tightened on the words. "Let someone with that sort of emotional intelligence guide you through, then? Let someone else have more knowledge in an area and be okay with that," he suggested.

"God, I don't like any of this."

He chuckled. "Yeah, welcome to the club. Club human. It is a wild freaking ride."

I made a loud, pained sound. "I guess I'll just go talk to Levi and tell him how I'm feeling, then."

"Good luck, kiddo."

After I hung up the call, I went to the living room. Levi stood there, shoulders hunched, faced away from me. Shaking and still filled with adrenaline from crying, I took a deep breath to go tell Levi that, despite all the facts, we were two fools in love.

"Hey. I was just going to come to apologize and tell you, I've been thinking—"

He turned around; his face was ashen, and there was a tension in his brows I'd never seen before. "What is this?" he asked.

I looked at where he held my story in his hands and realized I was too late.

CHAPTER 30

Levi

"What is this?" I asked roughly, refusing to accept the words I'd seen.

Claire set down her phone; she'd been talking to her father in the kitchen. When I first came in, I debated indicating that I was here so I wouldn't surprise her, but then I found the neat stack of papers on her desk. On top was a Post-it that said *to Levi*.

After that, their conversation was blocked out due to the sound of blood rushing in my ears. I stood staring at the papers for too long. I finally picked up what appeared to be her newest article when she walked into the room.

"It's what I've been working on. I was going to give it to you before I left," she said.

Like I hadn't seen her loading up her car all day. Like I hadn't come back to her just running away as she had when she arrived in Cozy Creek all those weeks ago. Maybe in time some hapless soul passing by will have to hear the story about how I ruined her life. My jaw was tense. My heartbeat was still so loud in my head that I struggled to focus on anything she said.

I tried to find what I wanted to say. Pace had been right. "You've been working on a story behind my back?" I tossed the papers on the ground between us. She flinched back. "'The True Legacy of Lily Carmichael.' I told you to leave it."

"I couldn't. Her story spoke to me, and now I know I was right." She lifted her chin.

Even now, even after everything, she looked at me like I was the one who didn't understand.

"Right about what? Jesus, Claire." I ran a hand down my face. "Did you get your job back with this, huh? An exposé on a celebrity photographer who wronged the woman he loved would surely be enough?"

At that, her color drained. "How could you even think that?" She reached her hands out and took a bracing breath. "You should read things before you jump to conclusions. Actually, I've been thinking about what we talked about. About your offer."

She had to be kidding. "And you just decided to go against everything I said?"

She shook her head, looking at me like I was the one out of line.

"That's what I want to talk to you about. I realized after I finished it why I couldn't stop researching her story and why it was so important to me. It just took me a little longer to understand what I'm feeling."

"I know why. Justice. Retribution at all costs, right? It's all that's important to you. Or whatever you think this sense of justice is, no matter who it hurts," I said.

She looked at me for a long moment. "That's what you think? You won't read it, then?"

I shook my head. "There's nothing in there that I don't already know," I spat. "You forget that this is my life. It's not some key to the next step in my career. Do you even care who gets hurt?"

Her mouth hung open. "This conversation feels so familiar." She mumbled it to herself.

"Oh, yeah. Now you paint me with the same brush as your ex. This is why you didn't want to stay here with me? Because you couldn't just leave it, couldn't do what I said were her dying wishes. Because everybody else is wrong. But not Claire. All facts, no fucks given."

Her hand went to her mouth. Her eyes closed for the briefest moment, and the soft skin trembled. "I came here to tell you I was sorry for reacting to your offer the way that I did. And to tell you I l-love you too." Her throat caught. "But I don't think you can love me. Not really, not if you are accusing me of all this. Not if you even think me capable. I thought you knew me better than anybody else. Recognized truths in myself before they revealed themselves to me."

I was seething, I couldn't even look at her. The words I was so desperate to hear before fell flat. Useless. Hollow. A means to an end. But something started to sink in, started to make me doubt myself even now.

"I see what I see. And what I've heard around town," I said.

She frowned. "I asked them not to tell you. I wanted it to be a surprise."

"I'm surprised." I didn't drag Pace into this. She didn't need to have him in her sights next.

"You aren't listening. I see I'm too late." She closed up her laptop and slid it into her shoulder bag. Her eyes were glistening as she spoke. "I'm not sure what I did that made it so easy for you to see me as this awful person. But I'm sorry if my reaction to your offer to stay hurt you. But the story is for you. I wanted you to have a proper memorial of your mother. I wanted you to be able to see her as the world saw her and not as the victim of your father. She chose you. She chose love. She was the winner in all ways. She got you. I just wanted you to see that, so hopefully, you could finally mourn her. I wanted you to see yourself the way she saw you and not as some huge cost she had to pay."

I shook but couldn't speak. The fears and the pain caught up with me. I was frozen.

She walked to the door, her laptop bag over her shoulder. Her smile was sad and brittle. The pain in her eyes palpable, the first tear falling and quickly wiped away by her hand, like she didn't want me to see her hurt. She glanced back toward the room, then fleetingly at the scattered papers, before her watery gaze fell back to me.

"I wrote that for you, Levi. It's not for any paper or magazine.

Just for you. That's the only copy outside my computer. I would never publish a story like that without your consent. I know that sometimes my morals come at a cost, but I wouldn't do that. I would never hurt somebody I love so intentionally." She took a deep, shuddering breath. "I do think you should read it. I wanted you to have a story about your mother that was beautiful to replace the one in your head."

She walked out. I didn't stop her. I couldn't think when she was near me. She made me doubt everything.

For a long time, long after her car rumbled away, long after Ripley came out of her hiding spot to lick my hand, I stood there immobile.

Had I really fucked up?

The sun had set. The house was dark.

I listened for her voice. Here I was, in the space that was so hard to be in, the space I avoided so long, and suddenly, Lily Carmichael's voice was nowhere to be heard.

"Have I disappointed you?" I asked the quiet and dark house.

I didn't need to know her answer. I felt it in my entire being. Claire wouldn't do the awful things that I accused her of. I felt hurt and rejected and wanted any reason to think she wasn't the woman I fell in love with, so maybe her leaving wouldn't hurt as much.

Eventually, I grabbed the story and Ripley and walked out.

I locked the front door, not sure I would ever open it again.

I had tried to open my heart to someone like I had tried to open the house to her.

And it was pointless.

I stomped back up to the main cabin.

I paced. I made a fire. I glared at the story, wrinkling in my damp grip.

"I don't want to read anything about that man. I don't want to give him any more of my attention." I spoke out loud to Ripley. She whined at my side, licking my hand even more. "I've already wasted so much time thinking about justice and his happy life."

I held the paper to the fire. The heat of the flames started to curl the edges of the sheets.

Ripley barked. With her ears pressed back, crouched down on her hind quarters, her little backside sliding as she whined, tail smacking the hardwood floor.

"Fine. I'll read until I see his name. Then I'm throwing it in the fire."

Ripley barked.

I sat down with a sigh. She was instantly in my lap.

With my shoulders tensed and jaw clenched, I read the first page ... then the second and third, until I finished.

I immediately started it from the beginning to read again without being blurred by tears.

Then I read it again.

It was the final paragraph that broke me.

With Lily's natural talent in photography, it would be easy to envision a different path for the woman who touched so many. A lifetime of rewards and accolades, full magazine spreads, and a name of notoriety would certainly have been within her reach, but then she wouldn't be the woman who touched a town, she wouldn't be the mother and friend to many. Every person I spoke to couldn't mention Lily without also mentioning her apparent and fervent love for her son, her kindness, and her overarching aura of peace. She held on to a truth about life that so many of us realize too late. If success is measured by some standard that involves only accolades and money, then it might feel like Lily could have hoped for more, but Lily seemed to have an inherent wisdom that nothing would ever mean more to her than a present life with her son in a town that she loved. However, if legacy is measured by lasting memory and love, then the legacy of Lily Carmichael will far surpass most of ours.

She hadn't even mentioned Richard Stanley or the scandal. There wasn't even a hint of ugliness in the story because Claire hadn't needed to. That wasn't the point of this piece she wrote for me. Claire understood what I never could. Lily didn't *give up* her life for me; she lived a beautiful life *with* me. Claire wrote this to help me see what I was too stubborn to accept.

I was so loved by two amazing women, and I let one man I'd never met make me doubt it. I let a need for retribution hide what was right in front of me. Exactly what I accused Claire of doing.

I brought a balled fist to my mouth to push back a gasp of pain, to not let it happen, but it was too late. The sob had escaped, and after that, another one hiccuped out. The flood had been bursting through the dam, and it was finally freed.

My head dropped to my hands, and for the first time since my mother died, I sobbed. I let myself feel the loss of someone truly amazing.

CHAPTER 31

Levi

Pace handed me the sledgehammer. "It's all for you," he said, sliding his safety goggles down and gesturing to the wall.

In the two weeks since I pushed Claire away in the worst sort of way, I mourned, truly, finally deeply mourned, the loss of my mother.

Claire had been right. I needed to do it in my own time, but I also needed Claire to show me the truth about my beautiful life.

I swung the hammer and blasted a hole through the drywall of the storefront on Main Street.

I made an offer yesterday to Billy Mackenzie and would be opening by the new year.

I just had the holidays to do a ton of work. Thankfully, Pace and the town had been an incredible help.

For all my talk of having a good idea of who I was and what I wanted, it was never more clear to me that I had been hiding. The things that I thought made me strong were just a different version of fear. My stoicism was the fear.

I had Pace read the well-worn copy of the story, read dozens of times by now. Not only because I loved hearing the truth and admiring my mother's amazing life, but because I could hear Claire in every word. It helped me feel closer to her.

Pace sniffled, and I set down the sledgehammer. "Damn, I miss that woman."

"Me too," I said.

He stood, and we hugged. "I was referring to Lily," he said, releasing me to give my shoulder a final squeeze.

"I know." I swallowed. "I was referring to both of them."

"This is gonna be great," Pace said, looking around to admire our work so far in transforming the former store into the Lily Carmichael Memorial Art Gallery.

"It is," I agreed, feeling a frisson of hope.

"I'm glad you decided to take this place."

"Me too. I would be stupid not to." There was going to be an entire wall for Lily's art, not for sale, just for viewing. "I was so ashamed to show my face in town. So convinced that everybody thought I should have done more. That's why I got so mad at Claire." I leaned on the hammer. "I never really thought she would write a story without my permission. She did more justice to my mother's legacy than I ever had."

I owed it to Lily to stop hiding out. I owed it to this town not to forget Lily. I owed it to myself to no longer be the loser in her story.

"Have you talked to Claire since she left?" Pace asked.

I shook my head. "I'm too chickenshit. I accused her of some awful stuff. And for a woman whose ethics are one of the main things she values about herself, I can't imagine she'll forgive me anytime soon."

"Have you tried apologizing? Explained the shit about feeling ashamed for not being enough?"

"You think I should?"

Pace stared at me blankly. "Do I think you should apologize for being a huge asshole? Yes, Levi. Yes, I do."

"Maybe I should drive down and see her. Maybe I should surprise her and—"

Pace held up his hand. "Stop, stop. None of that. Just go to her. Talk to her. Apologize. Don't let it go any further than that. Don't make any demands of her. Don't put any pressure on it. Let her take the time she needs."

"Okay. Be chill. I can be chill."

But first I had some things to do.

After we finished for the day, I brought the boxes from the house and set them on the table. One by one, I sorted through the photos. I set a few aside for the memorial, but I thought about what my mother would have really wanted. And as much as it was going to suck, I had to do it.

I loaded the photos into the portfolio and took a deep breath. I made my way over to Ruth's first.

"Levi, what are you doing here? Not that I'm not thrilled to see you," she asked.

"Do you have a minute?" I asked.

A little while later, with a pot of coffee and a package of cookies between us, I pulled out the photo of the B&B when she opened it almost thirty years ago.

"Oh," she gasped softly, one hand covering her mouth, the other tentatively hovering over the image of her and Jerry, her husband who had passed a few years ago. "That's lovely. We look so young." She laughed wetly as her eyes welled.

I ground my jaw to keep my own emotions from swelling. "I thought you might like this. I found it when cleaning out Mom's place."

She took a deep breath in, focus moving between the photo and me. "Thank you," she said.

"I know she meant for these to be seen."

"I absolutely will cherish it. Thank you, Levi. Your mother was so proud of the man you grew up to be."

I squeezed her hand across the table.

After Ruth, I made it through several more stops, each one special and heartbreaking and hard. I cried over the memory of Lily time and time again. Watched as her photos lit up the eyes of the people she continued to provide joy for even now. It was hard and so outside of my comfort zone, but exactly what I needed. I was wrung out while simultaneously fuller than ever.

More than anything, I felt incredibly grateful to have these memories and connections, thanks to my mother.

I thought of Claire with each stop. I thought of the questions she might ask. How she would love these small moments that felt so large, these *humans being cute*. I thought of how the emptiness at my side almost felt tangible now. They asked about her too. The whole town wondered how she was doing and when she would be back. Time and time again, I had to explain that I wasn't sure. If they weren't so grateful for the photographs, I was sure I would have gotten far more snarky remarks.

In the workshop, I uncovered the sheet on the unfinished, unnamed project and stared at it for a long while. Then I got to work, lost in my art for hours.

I made it back to Big Cabin feeling that same satisfied exhaustion that came with a good workout but in my brain. With Ripley curled up in my lap for courage, I sent Claire several rapid-fire texts in her style.

"I'm so sorry."

"I was wrong."

"Cozy Creek misses you."

"I miss you more."

CHAPTER 32

Claire

I sat on the milk crate in the small unit, staring at all the stuff that needed to be loaded into the moving truck rental. It wasn't too much, my desk and favorite couch that Kevin thought "clashed" with his aesthetic, and a few other boxes of memories and a small bed. The storage place was mostly abandoned on a cold winter day this close to Christmas, though occasionally, a bit of conversation or a door slam would drift to me. I could start loading the stuff, but I felt sad and cold and lonely. I studied all the doors next to my storage unit, wondering what secrets they held.

Did they all contain broken hearts and fresh starts? Or maybe I was projecting just a little.

My heart was well and truly broken. Worse than I ever thought possible. I didn't believe I was capable of falling so fast, and there, love went and punched me in the face when I wasn't looking. I thought I was smarter than that. I could outthink it. But Levi had been right, knowing all the information didn't stop the pain. I just didn't think he'd be the one to hurt me. I guess that's how I should have known that it would be.

But I've been thinking a lot in the weeks since I left Levi and Cozy Creek, and I still couldn't wrap my mind around how it all happened. Heartbreak aside, my pride had taken a massive blow. I thought I was a person who had ethics and morals and that would eventually count for something or matter. I never thought that Levi would assume something so awful about me, and that alone kept me from reaching out to him, no matter how badly I wanted to. Even when he sent me messages apologizing.

If he could think me capable of that, then I wasn't the person he needed, and he certainly wasn't what I needed. But then I would think about how deeply we connected on every possible level, and I would wonder if I wasn't holding him to some unrealistic expectation. Shouldn't he know better? Shouldn't he do better?

What if he never even read the story and still had this awful version of me in his head?

I was stuck in limbo, and it sucked.

But as the days ticked by, and Kevin still had his cushy job, the paper continued to publish stories funded by evil corporate monsters, and people like Levi thought me capable of the most massive type of betrayal; I started to wonder if nothing actually mattered.

I had felt a glimmer of it. Hope. A moment of "it's okay, nothing really matters, but people do." And the time we have. That warmth from the night I danced with Levi as I watched the people of Cozy Creek celebrate another passing season, I had a little taste of humanity. The stories that I posted to my online journal. They were nothing but also somehow everything. There was good, humans were fun little silly things, and life was sweet.

But maybe life just sucked.

Maybe I needed a snack.

I sighed and wondered how much longer I could sit here in inactivity when my phone vibrated in my hand.

Normally, the sight of my dad calling wouldn't cause an instant lump of dread in my throat like a hot ball of iron. I slid to answer the video call.

"Nooooo," I whined by greeting.

"I know, Claire Bear, I'm sorry." If Dad was calling me, then he wasn't about to land, and if he wasn't about to land, that meant he wasn't coming. I ground my jaw to keep from whining anymore, but lately, I was like a brand-new little baby capable of crying for communication's sake.

"They made us disembark," he explained, looking haggard. People behind him were in similar states of distress and dishevelment. "We were all set and ready to go and deicing the wings, but the storm hit way bigger than they thought. They canceled all flights to and from Midway and O'Hare."

"Damn. Damn." My thighs were going numb from sitting on

this milk crate, but all I felt like doing was melting into the personified version of "wallow." Would I spend another desolate night in my storage unit? Would I be doomed to repeat the history I tried so hard to avoid?

What I really wanted to say was, "What the hell? Life was so unfair, and everything was dumb and stupid, and I hated everything."

"What should I do?" I asked pitifully.

I was tired of making the next plan. I had been making one choice after another since Thanksgiving. Since *college*. I was tired of stupid grown-up life and stupid hard decisions. I just wanted to rest.

The plan had been for Dad to fly to Colorado Springs where all my stuff was in storage still, thankfully(?) and then we would drive down to Chicago, where I would reluctantly move into my childhood home because my life was a mixed-up cluster and all my strong morals and careful planning got me nothing at all.

"I really need to eat something," I grumbled to myself.

"The earliest I can get out if the weather doesn't get too bad is tomorrow, but it's not lookin' good, kiddo. Most likely two more days."

"Okay," I said.

"Don't make the trembly looking face. It's breaking my heart."

"It's not your fault." I took a breath in and out. "I'm feeling sad and frustrated and unsure, but that's okay, and it will pass. I won't always feel this way." Even as I said it, my bottom lip got more trembly.

"Aw, I'm so glad you like your new therapist. She is right. I know it sucks, but I will be there soon," he said.

The therapist worked with me through some of the trauma of my mom's sudden death when I was in college and the impact it had on me. It was constant work reprogramming my traumatized brain, but it was helping.

I nodded; my chin now wobbled uncontrollably.

The storage unit was a two-story concrete block with the appealing aesthetic of a prison. Fitting for how trapped I felt at this moment. I heard shuffling and clicking steps of shoes coming up the metal staircase and stilled.

I stared back at the screen. Maybe Dad was tricking me? But no, I very clearly saw the all too familiar look of Midway behind him.

My heart hammered with hope. Maybe it was Levi. Maybe he was about to come and apologize, solve all my problems, and whisk me away, as he had done so many times before. I slowly came to stand and stared in the direction of the approaching footfalls.

But he couldn't. No man could. I had to figure this stupid adult stuff out on my own.

But the cadence wasn't right. The shoes sounded too shiny to be Levi.

A man rounded the corner whom I never wanted to see again.

"Kevin?" Just when I thought my heart couldn't sink any lower.

"Claire. Thank God, you're okay." He scooped me into his arms as though we were still a couple. As though it hadn't been months since he kicked me out.

"Dad, I'll call you back," I said as I pushed myself free from his spindly arms.

"Was that Kev?" he asked.

"Hi, Ralph," Kevin called as I ended the call.

The last thing I saw was my dad flipping him the bird, unbeknownst to my ex.

"What are you doing here?" I asked him.

"I wanted to see you before you left. I'm in town for a meeting and saw your car," he said. That's right, he had said that because, inexplicably, he continued to text me even though I never responded. I should have blocked him.

"Why? I have nothing to say to you?" I stood from the milk crate and pretended to look in my packed boxes.

"Don't be like that. I'm here to help you." He smiled, and I clenched my jaw.

"Come to New York. You can find work there. Now that all the stuff with the article is behind us, let's get engaged."

He got to his knee and pulled a black box from his pocket. My eyes widened, and I looked around for a hidden phone because surely this was the making of a viral video.

This was insane.

"This is insane," I said.

Then it occurred to me. I never did know how he knew about me being fired before I did. He shouldn't have known any of this ...

Unless ...

"You think your boss would be cool with you shacking up with the woman who almost brought down a different finance guy?" I asked tentatively.

He gave a small and condescending smile. "First of all, no, you didn't. There was never any chance that article was going to get published. His pockets are way too deep, and he has way too many supporters. Anyway, they didn't even care when I told them we were dating."

"We aren't dating."

"But we were, and if you come with me now, we will be again."

"Did you tell them about the article, Kevin?" I asked cooly, even as a fire raged up my esophagus.

"Like I said, it wasn't going to get published anyway. It's time to move past this and start fresh. You'll love New York."

My mind instantly thought of Cozy Creek and how comfortable I felt there. More so than I ever felt in the hustle and bustle of even Colorado Springs.

"Does every man think offering a place to live is some sort of golden ticket access to my heart?" I said.

"Has this happened more than just today?"

"You'd be surprised." I sighed. "Kevin, even if I was desperate, I wouldn't move in with you. Not now, not ever. We are not on the same page at all. I won't be made to feel bad for having a moral compass, and I'm so much more than arm candy for your blooming career in New York, so you can go now. Your offer is ridiculous, and so are you. Please never talk to me again."

"Come on, Claire, don't be like that! I'm on my knees here.

And this floor is really hard," he whined.

Had I ever really loved this man? Having felt what I did for Levi, it was not possible. I was comfortable because I had, at some point, made the decision to be with Kevin, but I never loved him. The thought of it made me feel ill. Whatever I felt for him was gone and now replaced with oily regret that made my skin crawl.

"Am I interrupting?" a new voice said.

I turned to see Levi, a deep furrow in his brow, and Ripley's head popping out of his sweatshirt.

"Levi?" I blinked.

I looked at where Kevin knelt in front of me. Then, back at the man who I absolutely loved. I studied the strong line of his jaw covered in a five o'clock shadow, his deep, emotional hazel eyes that instantly made my knees weak. A flutter exploded in my chest. I had missed him so keenly that it was a physical pain. Handsome as ever. My arms ached, desperate to reach for him before I remembered our last interaction.

"Who is this?" Kevin asked, getting off his knees and finally putting that absurd ring box away.

"How did you even find me here?" I blinked in shock, still focused on Levi.

"Pace. Your dad wasn't kidding when he said he knew people up in Cozy Creek." Levi scratched at his chin, studying Kevin. He didn't seem annoyed. If anything, he seemed slightly amused. I wondered how much he had heard. "I can come back if it's a bad time."

"What is happening right now? Can't you see we are having a

moment?" Kevin yammered.

Levi gave his most intimidating stare down his nose at Kevin. God, how could I have ever let Kevin touch me? Seeing them standing side by side wasn't even a competition. One made me feel physically ill, the other, well, damn, the other lit me up and made me ache for him.

"Is that a dog in his shirt?" Kevin guffawed.

"No. He's leaving," I said, unable to break my eyes away from Levi and ignoring Kevin.

"Can anybody hear me?" Kevin said.

I stepped closer to pet Ripley. She wiggled wildly, trying to break out of his shirt as she licked my hand. I missed her. I missed him.

"I just wanted to try to catch you before you left for Chicago," Levi said.

My shoulders slumped slightly. I couldn't show my disappointment. And also, wasn't I just saying that I didn't want him to save me? He had hurt me. I wished my heart would remember that. Now my head and my heart weren't even communicating. This was so frustrating. What was the correct balance to all this?

"Where's your dad?" Levi asked. We still hadn't broken eye contact, even as Ripley had moved into my arms. We were inches apart.

"His flight was canceled because of snow."

At that, a little frown formed on Levi's brow. "Are you okay?" he asked.

I felt my demeanor cracking. It was the dairy case all over

again. One soft question and I felt my insides wanting to burst out of me.

Kevin moved closer to us. "Who is this guy, Claire?"

"I fucked up so incredibly bad, Claire. I have known your honor and your worth since the moment I met you. I should have never doubted it for a second. I didn't. Not really. I messed up."

"I'm sorry, what's happening here? Are you groveling?"

"Why are you still here?" I asked Kevin, even as Levi's words started to settle in.

"I'm here to *grovel* and get my fiancée back," Kevin said.

"On what planet?" I scoffed.

"You should go," Levi spoke to Kevin for the first time.

"I don't know who you are—"

Levi stepped an inch closer to Kevin, hardly even moving, but it was enough. Kevin flinched back.

"Screw this. I'm glad you got fired. I hope you're happy together." He stomped away, mumbling about what sort of woman meets a new guy in a few weeks or something along those lines. I had stopped listening. I was glad to have him gone.

"Please, carry on," I said to Levi.

Ripley wiggled free from my arms, finding the blankets I brought to pack around the furniture for cushioning.

Levi waited until we couldn't hear Kevin anymore before he turned back to me and held my hands. "I've known from the second I met you that you would shake my life up. But I was a chickenshit. I didn't want my life shook up. I wanted to stay hiding and mourn, but not really. I wasn't mourning my mother, though. I was in this awful holding pattern between self-disgust and doing nothing. When I told you how I felt about you, I felt small and insecure and a failure when you didn't instantly return my feelings." I looked down at our hands, but before I could speak, he went on. "But that wasn't fair of me. If I know anything about you, it's that you take your time to understand things. I should have been patient and waited." He took a deep breath and prepared himself to speak. "Worse than that, though. When you brought the article to me, my pride took a deeper hit. I felt like an absolute failure. You had known the truth for weeks and saw it clearly when I couldn't in thirty years."

"You read the story?" I asked.

He nodded. "It was incredible, and you were right. That was how Lily should be remembered. Not whatever it was I was doing. You are brave and full of love. I was fucking stupid to let my own hurt get in the way."

"Th-thank you," I said.

A relief like I didn't know I could feel suffused me. It shouldn't matter what he thought about me, but it did. I cared about what he thought because I cared about him. "You are a good man, Levi. Don't be so hard on yourself. You were struggling with loss. I wasn't close to it like you are. These things take time."

"I wish I had your patience," he said.

"I wish I had your emotional intelligence." I shrugged a smile.

His thumb lifted to brush my dimple. "God, I missed those." I smiled wider. "I just wanted you to know that everything I said was because I was an arrogant man full of pride and embarrassment for my actions. I never believed for a minute that you would do anything like what I accused you of. I'm sorry."

"Thank you." I lifted on my toes to lean into his touch.

He cleared his throat and stepped back. "But I am here to help you pack. I'm not here to ask for anything. Just help."

I hid my disappointment and gestured to the area. "Well, it's going to be a few days before I can leave, but I appreciate you."

We talked all night as we worked, sometimes quiet, sometimes laughing. He told me what I'd missed in town. Apparently, there had been a lot of drama in the past few months, even outside of our little bubble at the cabin. We only stopped to eat the food he brought. It didn't need to take that long. There wasn't much stuff, but what should have taken an hour tops took half the night with our long, comfortable conversation. I had missed talking to him.

After the truck was loaded, all too soon, we sat side by side on the liftgate. Ripley snored loudly in the cabin.

"I miss you too," I said boldly, my finger brushing his, thinking of his last text.

He swallowed audibly in silent space. "I miss you so much." His jaw flexed before he added, "All the time."

We missed each other. What did that mean now? Chicago was so far from Cozy Creek.

"Did you mean it? That day when I ruined everything?" he asked.

I turned to meet his hopeful yet guarded gaze. He was here. He still cared, and it meant more than anything.

I knew what he was referring to. I nodded. "I did." It was my turn to swallow with effort. "I *do*."

He let out a shaking breath. "I love you too," he said.

We loved each other still.

Wasn't that supposed to be enough? Weren't we meant to have it all figured out now?

I slid my hand on top of his, and he stood abruptly.

"I meant when I said I didn't come to ask anything of you. I just wanted to help."

I felt his absence everywhere. The building felt cold and dark.

"Okay," I said softly.

"I should probably get going." He wouldn't look at me, keeping his fists balled at his sides.

I stood too. Shouldn't this part be easy? Why did it feel so hard and scary?

"I'm not asking for anything. I just wanted to tell you that your story changed me. It changed my life. I realized I was living in fear and labeling it as stoicism. You showed me courage and beauty and all that encompassed my mother and what she would want to have been remembered as." He reached into his pocket and handed me a brochure. "I wanted to invite you to this. I know it's last minute, but we are opening on New Year's Eve."

"Lily Carmichael Memorial Art Gallery. Levi, really?" I grinned up at him.

He blushed. "Pace had his friend Noah Cooper help make a website and all that stuff. I wanted to invite you."

I nodded.

"It'll feature some of my art." He took a bracing breath and shuddered. "And some other locals have already expressed interest. Do you remember Lu Billings? She paints watercolor landscapes?" I nodded a smile, having recalled the pretty blonde who often popped up around town. "Anyway, should be good. Lord knows we can get those tourists to pay just about anything if we price it high enough."

"This is amazing. Good for you," I said, meaning it.

"You think you'll make it?"

"I'm supposed to go back to Chicago. Dad said there was a temp job at the library where he volunteers."

He nodded and took another step backward. "Also, I have these."

He handed me several slips of paper with printed information. It took me a second to realize what I was looking at. "Rental agreements?" I asked, even more confused.

"If you need a place to stay. There's one from Ruth's place, though she will probably put you to work. There's one for the apartment above the Confectionery and a few others. I wanted you to have options. I wanted you to know that you are wanted and welcome but also have autonomy. You are missed all the time, everywhere. But you have options, no matter what you decide. These will stay open through the New Year." He held my gaze longer, something behind his eyes that made me want to reach for him.

"Oh. Wow, thank you." I stared at the options laid out before me. He understood the need to protect myself, he didn't try to control my future and I appreciated that more than he knew.

Yet there was one missing. A small hole in my heart pinched tight.

"Then there's Little Cabin." He handed me another sheet.

I bit back a small smile as I read the last sheet. "A list of rules?"

"You're always welcome at the Little Cabin, but I wanted to make some new rules. But it's there. You will always have a place to stay if you want it."

My eyes tried to read the new list, but he put his hand over it. "You can read it later."

"Thank you, Levi."

"Whatever you decide, just let the others know if you can, sooner than later with the holidays."

"Of course."

I kissed Ripley goodbye and hesitated before leaning forward to hug Levi.

He shuddered a breath before wrapping me in the safety of him. I felt him inhale a deep breath in the crook of my neck, a small tremor in his body as he held me tight. We both held on too long, neither ready to let go. How could one pair of arms feel so much like a home I never had?

And just like that, he was gone, and I wasn't ready for it to be the end. I wasn't sure where we would go from here. I didn't have a plan.

But I had a list of rules, and that was a start.

CHAPTER 33

The Listing – updated

Little Cabin - For Rent

› Single-bedroom guest home available in the Colorado Rockies. Ten miles north of downtown Cozy Creek, Colorado. **(My replies below in bold—Claire)**

› Serious inquiries only. **(I'm very serious.)**

› This is my land. If you can't follow these rules, don't bother applying. **(I'm already getting a little turned on.)**

› This guesthouse is on my property, but it is completely private and separate from my home. That being said, I will probably pass your window often to make sure you have fed yourself, that you have a fire going, and that you aren't working too hard. I will tell you that I'm checking the property, but in reality, I will be worrying about you. **(Perfect. I will pretend not to notice and secretly try to look cute. I might forget to do everything just so you'll be forced to come help me.)**

> One tenant only. This home has one full-size bed. One kitchen area. One bathroom. One extra photography room that can be converted to your office or whatever you need it to be. **(I bet two people could fit in that bed easily. This theory will need to be tested.)**

> The water heater is old and takes several minutes to warm up for showers. If you want to take a bath, you'll have to come up to the Big Cabin. **(As it happens, the shower has terrible water pressure anyway and I'm more inclined to take baths these days. Long baths.)**

> No heat or AC. I can fix that if you want but, in the meantime, if you are cold, I will build you a fire in the wood-burning stove. Or there is a fireplace and the perfect couch for reading up at the Big Cabin. **(I often forget to start the fire.)**

> You can have guests if you want, anytime you want. **(Dad is already planning his trip.)**

> I installed new internet so you have your own router and password. **(I never thought I'd see the day.)**

> Amenities include stove, refrigerator, coffee maker, microwave, washer/dryer. I will provide you with whatever else you need. Just ask and it's yours. **(The power is going to my head. What if I just want you?)**

- The last tenant left major shoes to fill. I hope you like long conversations about everything and anything, but somehow not *nothing* and late-night work sessions listening to my "sad college kid rock." **(I have missed it all so much.)**

- Be as loud as you need to be, take as long as you need to when working. When you come back to earth, I will be waiting for you. **(Whenever I leave, I will always come back to my home. And I can be very, very loud.)**

- There are no locked doors. Big and Little Cabin are both yours. You can lock doors if you need a break from me. **(But unlocked doors mean surprise visits in the bath ...)**

- If you take a walk, take me with you. Or at least proper supplies. **(You get lost one time ...)**

- This is wild land. There are wild animals and unpredictable weather. I will protect you and take care of you. **(I know you will.)**

- Ripley will still come and go as she likes. I have no control over that. **(As she should.)**

- You are welcome at Big Cabin anytime. **(Oh, be careful what you offer.)**

- You can book Little Cabin for as long or as short as you need. You will always have a home with me. **(Hmm, I'm thinking indefinitely.)**

- If ever anything changes, I will let you know. If we need to talk, I will talk. If you need time, I will wait. If you need clear rules and lists, we will make them. I promise to stay with you while you work through what you are feeling. **(Thank you. I am working on embracing my emotions, but I will be clear when I need time. I will help you talk about whatever is on your mind and make sure you don't get stuck in any feelings too long. Tell me what you are thinking, and I will listen. Rules be damned, just talk to me. Okay, actually, even typing that made me nervous. I'm not there yet; I still need lists and clear boundaries, and that might never change.)**

› You should know you are the only applicant for this rental. I will not be accepting any others at this time, but you can take as long as you need to decide. **(You should know that I am already here.)**

I love you. See you soon,

Claire

CHAPTER 34

Levi

I reread the last line of the email that I just received from Claire. And then read it all again.

You should know that I'm already here.

I scrubbed at my eyes as the growing realization hit me. I sat up in bed, only in boxers. When I left her last night, I drove throughout the night and slept most of the day. It hadn't even been twelve hours since I left her. And she was here?

I reread the email again.

As fast as I could, I pulled on pants and a jacket, tripping over a confused and cranky Ripley. She barked but followed me as I made my way to the front door, sensing the growing excitement in my clumsy rushing.

I bolted out of the house and flailed down the hill. Parked in front of Little Cabin was Claire, standing out in front of a rental truck. She wore the same clothes she had on last night and leaned against the truck, arms crossed, a soft smile on her face and tired but happy eyes. The sun was just coming over the trees behind her, glowing like a beacon in front of Little Cabin.

I skidded to a stop in front of her. "Claire." I said her name like a sigh.

"Hi," she said, gifting me with her dimples.

"You're here."

"I am."

It took everything in my power not to reach for her last night, not to hold her and beg her to come back with me. But it had to be her choice. She deserved to feel in control and choose the life she wanted. Only in my deepest, most secret wishes did I think she'd come straight here.

The same desire to hold her to my chest consumed me now.

"I decided to extend the lease. I assume you saw the email I sent?" she asked with a tilt of her head.

I swallowed. She'd said she loved me. She said she wanted to be here with me. "I did," I said with a throat that felt too dry.

"And that all works for you?" she asked.

I nodded. "I'm so glad you're here."

"Me too."

"And you're sure that's what you want?" There was part of me that worried this was all out of desperation. Her father couldn't make it to help her. Her crazy, delusional ex showed up. I wanted her with more certainty than anything I ever wanted, but I needed to make sure it was the same for her.

"It's what I want. I wanted to stay before when I realized I was falling in love with you." She shrugged.

"God, I'm so sorry about that. I was so wrong to push you away." I balled my fists at my side.

"I wasn't exactly easy myself. But as long as we stick to the rules, I think we will be okay."

I stepped closer. "And have room to change them as needed."

"Of course. What's the point of having strict guidelines if not to adjust them." She said it sarcastically but pulled me closer by the front of my jacket. "Can we kiss now?"

"God, yes." I pulled her into my arms, holding her as tight as I could, my mouth on hers. Her arms trembled slightly as she held me back, pouring so much into our kiss. She must be exhausted physically and mentally, but I couldn't let go of her, not yet. I was too relieved to have her back in my arms. I leaned back, breaking our kiss, to look at her. My jaw clenched as my gaze moved over her beautiful face. "I've missed you so much," I said.

I studied her dark slash of brows, the line of her cheeks, and the deep dimples on either side of her wide, luscious mouth. She licked her lips as I watched.

"I've missed you too."

I dropped my forehead to hers. "Let me help you unpack."

"Okay," she said.

"You need to sleep and eat. Maybe not in that order."

She closed her eyes and nodded against me. "You're probably right about that."

"I'll take care of the stuff I can while you rest."

She yawned, and I lifted her into my arms. "Eep! You don't need to do that." But she didn't fight me.

I carried her over the threshold to Little Cabin. There was no anxiety or hesitation as I stepped into the house. It only felt right bringing her in here, laying her back onto the bed, and sliding off her coat and shoes. With her tucked in, I kissed her forehead. She was asleep before I pulled the blankets over her. Ripley curled up into a ball in the throw blanket at her feet.

As those two slept, I unpacked the rest of the rental truck. It took some maneuvering to get the bed and desk, and I smashed my finger in the doorframe, but it was worth it.

"You did it all?" she asked, gobsmacked as she sat up in bed, rubbing her eyes, hours later.

"It wasn't so much," I said, still panting.

"You are amazing. And ridiculous. Ridiculously amazing. I was going to help." She yawned so hard that her jaw cracked. "What time is it?" Her hand drifted to scratch Ripley, who had rolled onto her back, paws straight up in the air, tongue hanging out, begging to be scratched.

"Now you don't have to do anything. It's time to eat." I helped her out of bed.

The sun was almost down as we made our way up to Big Cabin.

After we ate, we washed dishes and cleaned up. Claire slid the last plate onto the shelf as I wrapped her in a hug. Her head fell back onto me. Soft music played over the speakers as my hands drifted over her hips and stomach. I kissed her neck and lower.

She sighed, rocking to the slow tempo, as she lifted her sweater over and off her head. I pushed her bra strap off her shoulder to brush my lips over the soft skin there. She reached one arm up to run her hands through my hair, and I shuddered. Her other arm brought me closer as we continued to rock to the tempo. My hand reached into her bra and cupped her breast as she gasped out. She turned in my arms to meet my gaze. She held my face in her hands, and little did she know, she held my entire soul too.

"I'm so sorry I made you doubt my feelings. I'm sorry I doubted them at all." Her gaze moved over my face with a sadness that made my heart clench.

"I couldn't believe my feelings at first either. They felt so big, too big to be possible. But there is no doubt for me, Claire."

"There's no question for me either."

"It's a miracle that you found my listing and came into my life."

She nodded, stepping on her toes. Our mouths met and kissed until we were both panting.

I laid her out on the carpet in front of the fire and devoured her. I brought her to her peak and luxuriated in her taste. When I slid into her again, we were both unmoored and out of our minds. She held my face as I moved in her. This time, she never closed her eyes as we whispered our love for each other. We took our time, bared our souls, and lost ourselves.

A few hours later, stomachs and bodies satisfied, we lay on the floor half-naked in front of the fire. I meant to take her to the bedroom, but we didn't make it.

Her head was on my stomach as she watched the flames. My fingers gently brushed through her hair. Outside, the snow fell, and Ripley snored softly from under her pile of blankets. I lazily played with the strands of her hair, thinking about how beautiful she was. How much I loved her. How thankful I was that she was here. I told her so.

"I love you too. I love it here. It feels so right," she said.

"I'm glad you feel that way. You feel like home to me."

She rolled her head to kiss my chest, and I pulled her up to be shoulder to shoulder with me.

"No place has felt like home before I found you."

I kissed her gently but pulled away before my body wanted to start round three. Four?

We fell into silence for a while before she said, "I heard from my editor."

"Oh?"

"It sounds like the paper is close to folding. She said she might go elsewhere and will try to get me in. Maybe Denver."

"Yeah? Is that what you want?" A wave of panic threatened to ruin the moment, but I had to trust that no matter what happened, we would find our way through it.

"I don't know. I don't feel like I used to. I want to help people, but I am tired of throwing pebbles at barricades. I like telling individual stories. I feel like maybe that's the direction for me. There was this mom I met when I was writing that article. I thought that I needed to help her by getting justice for the money she lost to that evil man, but I think I could focus on these incredible ceramic beads she makes instead and her awe-inspiring life story. All that she has done for her kids."

"I think that sounds great."

"Are you happy about the shop?" she asked me.

"I am. I wasn't sure I wanted the store, but after I talked with people in town, I realized that it wasn't them I was afraid of. It was always my issues. I like being in town. I mean, not all the time. I'll still only be open a few hours a day during peak seasons. But it's a start."

"I love it. I can't wait to see it."

"I can't wait to show you." I sighed. "I think Mom would like that it's not about just her art either. I think, if anything, she'd want it to be an opportunity for others too."

"Amazing, Levi. I'm so happy for you."

"I reserve the right to change my mind about being in town that often."

She laughed softly. "I will help you too if you want."

"We'll figure it out together." I grabbed her knuckles and kissed them. "After all, it's a rule."

CHAPTER 35

A few weeks later

Claire

For a small town, Cozy Creek knew how to throw a New Year's Eve party. After Christmas and how the town had transformed, I shouldn't be surprised.

It felt like the whole town came out for the New Year's party on Main Street. The night was freezing cold, but almost all the storefronts were still lit up as the town milled from one building to the other, sharing champagne, looking at Lily's photos, and celebrating. I chatted with a miraculously healed Gigi, with Madi and Cole, who stared at each other like Levi and I stared at each other. Lu Billings whispered softly to Noah Cooper, a bright smile illuminating her face.

"Lu and the new Huber driver look awfully cozy," I whispered to Levi. I was secretly delighted in having many new friends and knowing the happenings about town.

"He doesn't drive for Jimmy anymore, and that"—he lifted his chin to the two who were locking eyes—"is a long story I'll tell you about later."

I raised my eyebrow, intrigued. Another local love story, perhaps?

It was perfect. I was buzzing with joy and happiness I never dreamed I could have. And Levi was there on my arm, making everything a million times better.

"And that's the thing about eels. Scientists really aren't sure how they reproduce. It's a mystery." I had been talking for a few minutes now. I wasn't really even sure how we got to the lifespan of an eel. Mrs. Kathy Wilson smiled and nodded, but her eyes pinged around the gallery behind me.

"Oh, yes. Excuse me, Claire. I see someone I need to talk to." She smiled and stepped away.

When she left, I shrugged and turned to Levi, still expecting on some level to see him wince or be embarrassed. Instead, I found him looking at me in that way that meant our plans were about to be overturned in exchange for getting naked.

"Don't look at me like that. We have hours until midnight." I bumped his shoulder with mine.

He leaned closer, his nose pushing my hair off my shoulder to better brush against my neck. "Nobody would even notice if we left."

"It's your gallery opening. Pretty sure they would notice."

He hummed, and it sent chills all over my body.

"I mean, maybe just five minutes," I gasped out.

He chuckled and grabbed my hand to tug me away just as Pace stepped up. "Hey, you two lovebirds."

Levi grumbled something not very nice.

"The place looks great. Cheers, man." Pace held up his glass, and the three of us clinked glasses.

"Thanks," Levi said. He cleared his throat. "And thanks for everything the last year. And not giving up on me." He held Pace's gaze as he spoke.

His best friend's eyes were wide, a goofy half-smile on his face as he listened. "Of course." He swallowed. "I know you'd do the same for me."

They clapped each other into a hug, neither of them speaking but clearing their throats and avoiding eye contact.

Pace's gaze shot behind us. "I gotta go. Happy New Year if I don't see you."

"You too."

"Happy New Year," I said as Pace moved away quickly, glancing over his shoulder.

"What was that about?" I asked Levi under my breath.

Levi watched his best friend disappear into the crowd, a look of consternation on his face. "I'm not sure. But I'll find out." He looked at me, and his features softened in a way that made me want to melt into a puddle just so he would have to scoop me back up. "I think I've been a little distracted lately."

"Is distracted better than being *bored*?" I asked innocently.

His eyes darkened. "Much. Much better,"

He grabbed my hand, and we toured the gallery as I admired the pieces. "There are so many here," I said, continuing to be in awe of Levi's talent.

"I've been inspired these past few months." Every time I looked at him, he gazed at me in a way that made me ready to get him home.

I stopped in front of one I recognized. It was the woman, encased in the trunk of a tree, mouth covered as she seemed to call out in pain. It was titled "Grief." My throat tightened. "I hope you didn't put this one out for me if you weren't ready."

"No. You were right. It should be seen," he said.

"It's beautiful."

"So are you."

The night went on. We made it until midnight and rang in the New Year. It was a fresh start, and being in town felt like symbolism.

After the ball dropped, we immediately closed the gallery to go home, change into comfy clothes, and be alone together. That also felt like symbolism.

This was my life with Levi now. The Little Cabin sat mostly unused these past few weeks, except when Dad visited or when I went to work for a few hours. My online journal had taken off, as well as the videos I was posting about them. I was getting paid for content that I enjoyed making and was helping other people in the process. The single mother with the ceramic beads told me my video got her so much business that she had to hire somebody to help her. It was more than I ever thought I could do, and it made a difference.

I was happy in this life.

"Next month, I'm driving down to New Mexico to write about this amazing little town I heard of. It's literally called Slippery Slopes, and you would not believe some of the crazy stories I've heard about it," I told Levi as we lay in bed well into the start of the new year.

"I can't wait to hear about it."

"As if you'll have a choice," I said. I shifted in his arms so I could study him closely as I spoke. "And you promise to tell me if I ever go too far or away too long? You'll bring me back to you?" I asked him. I still had the low-level hum of fear, even with the therapy, that if I relaxed too much and felt too happy, I would miss the signs of change around me and would lose everything.

"I promise," he said. He held my gaze as he spoke. "I will always find you and bring you back to me." I sighed. "Claire, some sort of magic drew us together, but it's the commitment that will grow us into something beautiful."

"Oh," I said.

"I promise to prioritize you the way we prioritize our souls' needs. I'll prioritize you in the way I prioritize art and you with your research, with a gentle determination and commitment to getting it right. I won't just stop if it becomes challenging because I know the best things are born of time and effort. You are the best thing. This life I want to make with you is as important to me as it was to my mom. All I want is to stretch these days into years and make memories with you."

I swallowed, throat too tight to say something as beautiful as he said. I kissed him deeply and slowly and held him until we fell asleep.

I would continue to show him how much I was committed to our life. Every day when we showed up for each other for all the years to come.

Want more Levi and Claire? Check out a bonus scene for Fall Shook Up *when you sign up for Piper's newsletter!*

Scan the QR code to get your bonus scene:

THE COZY CREEK COLLECTION

Fall I Want by Lyra Parish
Fall at Once by Nora Everly
Falling Slowly by Enni Amanda
Fall Too Well by Erin Branscom
Fall Shook Up by Piper Sheldon
Fall Me Maybe by Laney Hatcher

www.cozycreekbooks.com

ABOUT THE AUTHOR

Piper Sheldon writes Contemporary Romance and Paranormal Romance. Her books are a little funny, a lotta romantic, and with just a little twist of something more. She lives with her husband, daughter, and two elderly dogs at home in the desert Southwest. She finds writing about herself in the third person an extreme sport in awkwardness.

Sign up for her newsletter here!

ALSO BY PIPER SHELDON

UNLUCKY IN LOVE SERIES - CONTEMPORARY CELEBRITY ROMANCE

Stranger Than Fan Fiction, Book 1
Better Date Than Never, Book 2
Down For the Word Count, Book 3

THE UNSEEN SERIES - PARANORMAL ROMANCE

The Unseen, Book 1
The Untouched, Book 2
The Unspoken, Book 3 - Coming 2025

SMARTYPANTS ROMANCE

THE SCORNED WOMEN'S SOCIETY - SMALL TOWN ROMANCE

My Bare Lady, Book 1
The Treble With Men, Book 2
The One That I Want, Book 3
Hopelessly Devoted, Book 3.5 - A novella
It Takes a Woman, Book 4

THE TEACHER'S LOUNGE - SMALL TOWN ROMANCE

Band Together, Book 2 in a multiple-author series

You can find all of Piper's books and more info at her website: **pipersheldon.com**